Also by Susan McGeown:

A Well Behaved Woman's Life

Rosamund's Bower

A Garden Walled Around Trilogy:
Call Me Bear
Call Me Elle
Call Me Survivor

Rules for Survival
Recipe for Disaster

The Butler Did It

Published Faith Inspired Books
3 Kathleen Place, Bridgewater, New Jersey 08807
www.FaithInspiredBooks.com

Copyright Txu1-172-290, April 12, 2004
ISBN: 978-0-6151-4873-1

Footnote credits appear at the end of this work.

A Garden Walled Around Trilogy

Book I

Call Me Bear

By Susan McGeown

Faith Inspired Books

To My Husband, David

(My very own Bright Feather)
"Always with breathless anticipation…"

Hebrews 10:24

Table of Contents

Rattlesnake, bear, and owl show this man the center,

where their voices rise as smoke from blue mountain.[1]

~Gladys Cardiff

Captive

Bare feet in grass soggy with the earliest of spring rains can cause a chill in a body so fierce it can be hard even to move. As I peer into the first rays of the morning sun just breaking over the ridge, I do a silent battle with the morning shivers. Once I get busy with my chores I warm up a fair bit, but having risen from a warm spot in a corner of Old Woman's hut, gathering water from the stream first thing in the morning is always a sore trial for me. The trees look almost as cold as I do, me with steam coming out of my teeth-chattering mouth and them with steam rising off their rain soaked bark. I try not to think about having to step in the freezing cold river to fill my deerskin buckets, afraid that the shivers will just take me over completely. A vision of me, frozen solid just outside the hut's door, could have almost made me laugh out loud were it not for my *present circumstances.* I've been in this village a few weeks now. I'm many things.

I'm a white captive.

I'm a fourteen year old girl.

I'm alone.

I'm frightened.

I'm no better than a slave.

But I'm not a red savage.

My family lives on a homestead in the state of Virginia. There's my Pa, my little brother Eli, and my older brother Henry. Ma died when Eli was born. We settled there after the second Great War with Britain in the year of our Lord, 1817. I suspect the choice of where we settled was Pa's decision. I don't ever recall Ma saying a word about it one way or the other. Pa told me once that he was bound and determined to get as far away as possible once and for all from any body – Royalist, Colonist, British or French – who had war thoughts on his mind. Said he'd spent his whole life surrounded by war. He'd survived fighting in one, and he was damn certain he was not going to try his luck a second time. Furthermore, he didn't for one moment believe that any people who even had so many as ten rifles between them would be peaceful for long.

Our homestead is beautiful. Looking off the front porch, the sight of the mountains rising in their blue mist often causes a body to stop and stare at the wonder of it. But I suspect Pa chose it mostly cause it was the farthest piece of land he was able to get. Away from wars and hatred and killing and such. We were right happy there for a time. When I think of happy thoughts, I think of those early days building and planting and laughing. Then Ma died and much of the happiness went with her. I worry about Eli the most. I was the only Ma he knew and now I'm gone. It's a wonder to me how a life, as comfortable as an old shoe, can disappear in just the blink of an eye.

The red savages come one evening just before nightfall. They whoop and holler and sound terrible fierce. Pa grabs Eli and shouts to me, "Run, Elle!! RUN!!" I hear the great fear in his voice, and it's almost more frightening than the savages' screams. Then I see their black painted faces and I see their eyes that are so filled with hate and I change right quick what makes me scared. I try to run to the forest, but my skirts trip me and I fall. As I struggle to get up a savage grabs me by the back of my dress and hauls me across the front of him like I'm a sack of potatoes. I'm so frightened I wet myself. I'm so frightened that I can't move. I lie there across that horse certain my heart will beat right out of my chest and fall on the ground just like my pee does.

We ride and ride those first days and nights only taking time to rest the horses, I suspect. Riding face down on a horse is downright uncomfortable, but I'm not in a position to complain. My head and stomach ache something fierce. I look at a foot that's red, bare and filthy and my nose twitches at the smell of my captor. He's as close to naked as a body can be without showing the important parts.

By the start of the third day, I drag my feet some and struggle as I get hauled up once again onto the horse. I've had nothing to eat and only managed to drink some water from the stream. My stomach especially tells me enough is enough. My captors no longer have black painted faces, but red is just as terrifying as angry savage words are said, and I'm pulled roughly by my hair and dress back into place: face down, staring at that same dirty, red foot. I can't help it as my stomach empties in one great gush. *There*, I think, *at least I gave your foot a wash.*

I end up flat on my back trying to catch my breath. As I struggle to sit up Dirty Feet gives me a hard kick in the side, and I lie back down. I stare at the eyes of my captor as he ties a rope around my neck like a pet dog. I decide to keep my mouth shut and my head down. No need to court more trouble than I'm already in. As I walk alongside Dirty Feet it seems that my head and stomach will get a rest, but that might not make my bare feet so happy. Two times I end up face down in the dirt because I don't move fast enough. Dirty Feet holds my rope and watches as I haul myself up to standing. He doesn't even give me time to catch my breath or spit out the dirt in my mouth. I try real hard to pay a bit more attention to things so that I don't give Dirty Feet another chance to have fun with my rope.

The days that I travel with the savages are full of darkness and worry. We travel up into the misty blue mountains, up and over and then past some even bigger mountains still. Even in my fearful state there are times that I just have to catch my breath at the beauty of it all. I'm pretty sure we travel mostly south because I watch the sun. Maybe west a bit, too, I can't exactly say. I walk all that day and for the first time we rest for the night. Good thing my feet are tough and strong. Being barefoot is something I'm used to. I spend most of my time working to keep my mind as blank as the faces of the savages I travel with. Whoever would have thought that it's nigh onto impossible to think of nothing instead of something?

Those worry thoughts are like a jigger under my skin. I think about running away back home which will be a might difficult as I seem to have become Dirty Feet's newest pet. There's not one moment when my rope is free. Besides, how would I manage to get away? How can I out run the savages in their own woods when I couldn't manage it in my own yard? And which way would I go? I decide running is not something I should forget, but something I need to wait a bit on.

I wish I knew if Pa and Eli were safe. My heart says they must be safe while my head says, *Can Pa run faster than an angry red savage on a horse?* I make my head be quiet and let my heart sing its song. I'm fair certain that Henry is all right. He'd driven the wagon into town the day before the savages came to get seed for early spring planting and was not expected back for another day or so. Being almost eighteen, Pa said he could handle such a grown up chore, although I think he was a bit scared to be going off by himself like that for the first time.

I think and think about where they are taking me. And why me? Would they not have taken Eli, a strong boy of six, if they took me? Could they have killed a six-year-old boy? Could Pa have stopped them? Will someone come for me? Is there even a body that will miss me? When my head gets to aching from asking all these questions, I work hard on thinking of nothing again.

Three days of walking finds me limping something fierce and eating more dirt than I care to mention. Finally, even Dirty Feet looses interest in his rope game, and I find myself staring at his bare back, more than a might scared that I'm going to be dragged by my neck rope the rest of the way if I fall from the savage's horse. When we break into a gallop I'm forced to hold on to Dirty Feet, my face pressed to his body. Even with my eyes tight shut, my nose will not let me forget where I am and who I'm with. I'd rather eat dirt again.

The savage's village we finally arrive at is twelve full days from my homestead. There are more than thirty huts, some shaped round and squat and some shaped long and tall. Some are big enough to house large families and some seem to be for just one person. As we ride down into the clearing, I think the village looks a little like a wagon wheel with the biggest hut in the center and the others stretching out in all directions.

Dirty Feet brings me to a hut almost right in the middle of the village and dumps me at an old woman's feet, rope and all. There were so many sights and sounds that first day I can't remember them all. I remember seeing lots of naked children running around – boys and girls! – and thinking that maybe Eli would like it here. He always loved the summer because that was the only time Pa would let him run naked by the pond and go skinny-dipping. I remember lots and lots of barking dogs and was afraid I'd get bit. Dogs don't like strangers, do they? And I sure look strange compared to everyone else as far as the eye could see.

These are not the first red savages I've seen. I've seen pictures drawn in a newsprint once. Twice on the trail when we moved to our homestead we saw them watching us go by. Once at Cooper's General Store I saw one up close. And three times that I know of they passed through our homestead rather than go around as they should have, and Pa had to scare them off with the rifle. But each of those times it was always with my Pa close by, never by myself, lying in the dirt filled with too many feelings for one body to figure out in a lifetime. I look for something familiar to help me stop this spinning terror that's slowly pulling me under. But there's nothing I recognize. Not even the thoughts inside my head.

I'm not sure that anyone is happy with Dirty Feet's gift of me. There's not one smile or even a nod. No one gives him a pat on the back or shakes his hand. In fact, no one says much at all. Do savages even smile or laugh or sing or hug? I sure have never seen such. They all gather around and look silently at my sorry self sitting in a heap, lost and alone. I try hard not be rude and stare, even if they don't seem inclined to follow the same example. Finally, even the dogs stop barking.

    The old woman of the hut has a face more wrinkled then a winter's dried apple. She dresses entirely in deerskin, with decorated moccasins on her feet. At first I think she has paint on her face, like the savages did the day they took me. Old Woman has lines and dots between her eyes and up across her forehead. But after a week or so I'm sure it isn't paint; it doesn't wash off, and I never see her redraw it. Somehow it's on her face for good. She isn't mean to me, but she isn't what you'd call kind either. She shows me what chores I'm expected to do, and if I don't do them fast enough or the right way she gives me a fair slap or kick. I learn right quick I'm never to touch the herbs and things she has hanging and stored all around her hut. I think she might be a healer. She puts a funny smelling salve on my neck when the rope is finally taken off. But once I get the rhythm of the work, she almost pretends that I don't even exist. She feeds me funny gruel made with grains and a bit of meat. It fills my stomach, which always seems to be growling and unhappy. I sleep in the corner of her hut and even have a few furs to keep me warm on these cold early spring nights.

    Twelve days away from Pa, Henry, and Eli, I think over and over. Twelve days, and only three of them I walked. I can't get my head to figure how I'd manage to get back home. I'd get lost. I'd be hungry. I'd be frightened. I'd not be able to defend myself against dangerous animals or furious red savages coming after me ready to teach me a powerful lesson. I get angry at myself when I realize that the person I am is what makes me a prisoner more than the place where I stand. With that thought I feel like I've finally lost a big fight that I hadn't even realized I was in. Even though I'm no longer tied up, I'm a prisoner just the same, and there's nothing I can do about it. Running, I now know, is something I need to forget.

    I think I take to most things quick. I watch and learn. Pa always said I'd have been a fast learner at school had I ever gone. Ma taught me my letters, and I took to reading and writing right swift. I don't have so much a memory of how I did the learning; it seemed to just make sense and flow into my head like learning a song. I do remember Henry being angry at how I could keep up with him in most of the lessons. Pa made sure all of us practiced our reading from the big Bible each night even after Ma died. Already Eli at six can spell his name and do some easy figuring. I could keep house by the time I was eight, which was when my Ma died. I cooked and cleaned and sewed and cared for Pa, Henry, and Eli from the moment it was clear Ma never would again. *Who cares for them now?*

I struggle most with the quandary that I can't understand a word anyone says. It just sounds like foolishness to me. On the trail, traveling with the savages when they first took me, they made hand motions when they said something to me. Sometimes I understood, like when I was to sit against the tree and get tied at night or mount up on the horse to ride the next day. Sometimes I didn't though, and they'd give me a hard cuff to the head letting me know just how stupid they thought I was. I'm not stupid though, I just don't understand their talking, that's all.

If I were forced to choose, I'd have to say that I like days better than nights. Days I can keep so busy I scarce have time to think of Pa, Henry, and Eli. Each and every day is the same, filled with chores for Old Woman or any one else who might be inclined to take the trouble to get me to understand what they want done. I gather sticks for firewood, I grind corn, I fetch water, I stir the cooking pot. Old Woman only notices me if I'm too slow. I work very hard not to be slow.

Nights, lying in my corner, I try real hard to fall asleep quick. But it seems no matter how hard I try and no matter how tired I am, I can't get my head to shut down fast enough and just think of nothing. Sometimes the ache to see Pa, Henry, or Eli is so great I fear that I'll just shatter into a million sobbing pieces and mess up Old Woman's hut something fierce.

Even though Ma died more than six years ago, I remember some things. She told me that to pray was to talk to God personal like, just as if He was close enough to whisper to. One of my strongest memories of Ma was nighttime prayers and me whispering in God's ear about all manner of things. When she died, I wondered whether the whispering had done any good. I did not whisper in God's ear about Ma's dying or living; was it my fault she died? Those late nights as I sat up with Pa helping to care for screaming baby Eli, I found myself thinking did Ma take God's ear with her? Can He still hear me or has He moved on? Pa still does prayers each night, but there's a different feeling to them, almost like seeing the maple syrup jug but knowing it's finally empty. Not until the savages came to take me do I try to whisper in God's ear again. Lying in my corner trying to sleep, I make deals with God. "If You let Pa and Eli get away then I'll stay here in this village and not ask for one thing else, God." Or, how about, "I'll bide my time quiet like and wait until Pa comes to get me from here." I even try, "I'll never complain or ask for anything else if I can just go home, soon. Please."

But sometimes the strangeness of it all, the worry of who I am and the terror of where I am gets so big I can't catch a breath. There are some nights that nothing – not weariness or prayers - can make my head be quiet or get my heart to sing, and I'm bone weary when the sun comes up. For the truth is this: I'm a captive of the savages. I'm a white and they are red. It makes no matter how hard I work, how fast I move, how small I try to make myself; the difference will always be right there on the skin of my hands and face.

Another week passes and I find myself thinking more and more about skin and the colors it comes in. I remember when Pa caught me trying to get a look at myself one time in the water trough and teased me for a day or two. Told me about a poem he had read one time that said, '*And all the carnal beauty of my wife, is but skin-deep².*' But not until I was the only one with different color skin did I really start to think about what is *underneath* it all. Does the color on the outside make a body different on the inside? I always thought that was so. Black skin makes a nigger slave, red skin makes a savage, and white skin makes a person like a farmer or a soldier. Ain't that the way it is always so? Never once, until my sorry situation, did it occur to me that maybe, *just maybe*, skin color's got nothing to do with it.

Squatting outside Old Woman's hut, stirring the venison stew for dinner, I look at my white hands and realize I have to puzzle this through a bit more. For the only one with white skin in this village is a slave. And those with red skin are the farmers and the soldiers and the healers and the children. The only real savages I've met so far are Dirty Feet and his three companions. But something tells me it has nothing to do with red skin and everything to do with heart. *Maybe,* my head thinks, *it's what's underneath it all that's the only thing that counts.* I'll have to ponder this some more.

The little ones in the village are the only ones that make me smile sometimes. The babies don't care who I am or what color my skin is; they just want to see a friendly face and I'm happy to oblige. Mothers wrap their babies in blankets around a board that they either strap to their backs or hang from a tree branch. Each babyboard looks different, and I find I remember the babies more by how the carrier looks than the baby! Some are decorated with embroidery and porcupine quills, some have shades built over the top, and others have some of the funniest objects dangling in front for the baby to look at: bird skulls, feathers, and animal claws. Those babies go all over with their mothers, when they're tending the gardens, washing by the stream, foraging in the woods or preparing meals. There's something peaceful about watching the babies swinging in the branches fast asleep. Watching all this, I learn that savages do laugh, cry, and love. I find it mighty surprising.

The older boys, eleven or twelve or so, the ones that wear clothes, are the meanest. Scuttling down to the river to fetch the day's first water I look down at myself. They must have a good chuckle over my clothes, since the way they look now deserves a good laugh; torn, dirty, with all manner of smells and stains on them! They throw rocks and sticks at me like I'm a moving target. They try to trip me when I'm hauling wood and think nothing's more funny than seeing me sprawl in the dirt covered in sticks and dust. They spy on me when I'm trying to have a private moment in the woods. They make me tired. They make me mad. Were I to have the right words and were I to be in a different place, I'd tell them a thing or two. But I work to stay small. It's easier. It's safer.

The older girls, around my age I suspect, work almost as hard as me but stay away from me. I'm so different. I feel their stares all the time. Pa always taught us it was rude to stare. It made no matter how interesting the sight was you were wishing to see. There was red savage girl at Cooper's General Store one time. She was tied by the waist and roped to a trapper's belt, more dirty and worse for wear than I ever saw a body to be. Even at my worst time with the savages so far I don't think I've ever had the look she had in her eyes. She was a dead body that just hadn't laid down yet. But I did not stare. No sir. I waited to ask questions until we were in our wagon and on our way back home. That was when Pa explained the way of things to me before I even had a chance to open my mouth.

"Mind your own business, Elle. Worry about your own troubles. Keep your head down and your mouth shut. Most battles in this world come about when people stop following that rule."

I pondered that for a while and then felt obliged to ask. "Doesn't that mean that the strongest always get their way?"

Pa took so long to answer that Eli had time to crawl into the back of the wagon and fall asleep leaning against a sack of grain. But finally he said, "There are a pile of things in this life that are stronger than you, Elle. Always will be, too. War is stronger. Hatred is stronger. Death is stronger. Some you can avoid ... hide from." I remember the look on Pa's face that day and the shadow of sorrow that settled there like a dark cloud as he thought of Ma. "*And some things will find you no matter what you do to hide from them.*"

"So that savage girl ..." I'd tried to ask.

Pa interrupted me, hoping to end things quick like. "Is none of our business, Elle. The savages had their time. Their present circumstances are not our concern. Our homestead is on what used to be the red savage's land. Bought by the government with cash money and signed away by the savages free and clear. Made available to families like ours. Those savages have made choices how to live just like we have made choices. My choice was to live separate. Apart. Where no one could bother us or interfere or force us to fight a battle or choose a side." He'd looked at me. "I will not choose sides anymore, Elle. I just want to be left in peace! No more wars for me, no more debates. I have moved my whole family – everyone I care about - far, far away. I am an honest, law abiding, and God – fearing man. If I see something I don't agree with and it has nothing directly to do with me and mine then I just keep my head down, my mouth shut, and I mind my own business! It is the right path to take. The only path to take! You hear me?" He was fair shouting at me. Eli stirred at the sound of Pa's raised voice.

"I heard you, Pa," I say out loud to myself and my memories. But now I know something else that can be stronger than hatred or death or war: fear. I think about that savage girl tied to the trapper's belt, and I touch my neck that still has a healing rope burn. I suspect Pa never thought I'd be a captive in a red savage village. Would he have wanted someone who saw me tripping and stumbling and eating dirt with a rope tied 'round my neck to 'keep his head down and mind his own business'? It would appear to me that life tends to change a body's way of viewing the world, that's for darn sure.

It takes me almost two weeks in the savages' village before I notice that there are not too many men around. Young men I should say. There are lots of mothers and children and old ladies. There are many old men, too. But there seems to be only a few fathers. I think to myself that Pa would be disappointed in my slowness. He used to say to me, "*Elle Girl, you make a body more tired with your questions than a full day's plowing does!*" But I really just haven't been myself. It took a long time to notice the lack of men, but less time to figure out why. They must be raiding, attacking other places, just like the savages who took me. Or hunting, I guess. Even Dirty Feet and his companions were gone the very next day.

I sense a change in the village just a few days after I figure out the men are gone. Maybe it's just me seeing something new, like when you walk the same path in the woods everyday and then one day spot an owl's nest. Each time after that you always check to see if you can see the owl; the walk is just different. Old Woman works me close to death these days. I carry wood, grind grain, gather herbs and plants in the woods with her sometimes, work in the big garden doing all manner of things, and prepare fish the young boys catch. I just never seem to stop! By the second day,

I'm stumbling around stupid with tiredness. Old Woman slaps me three times that day. She didn't hit me that much even in the first days. When I spill an entire bowl of ground corn I'd just finished she looks mad enough to kill me. She does almost worse, she sends me to my bed corner without dinner.

I lay there in the dark with my stomach cursing me and my clumsiness. I think about Pa, Henry and Eli. I think about our dinners together, sitting inside if the weather's poor or outside on the porch if the weather's warm and the bugs are cooperative. I think about me making dumplings and venison stew. I can almost smell it cooking. I can see Eli grinning at me because he just loved my dumplings and venison stew. I see Henry hunched over his bowl shoveling it in almost faster than an eye can see. I hear Pa saying, "*Why don't you just swallow the whole thing, bowl and all, Henry?*" and us laughing and laughing at the thought. I feel myself finally drifting off to sleep just when the screams and whoops and shouts erupt. It could almost be funny; here I am in a red savage village being terrified by the same sounds that terrified me at home with Pa, Henry and Eli!

I creep to the opening of Old Woman's hut and see a sight that chills my blood almost to a stop. Red savage men, more than I can count, mounted on horses, painted and armed, galloping and whooping through camp. I hear a strange whimpering in the tent and look around surprised because I think I'm alone. It takes a moment to realize that *I am alone*; the sound's coming from my own throat. And then I see a sight still stranger, a savage woman, long dark hair loose and blowing out behind her, running fast as lightning, not *away* from the fierce savages but *towards* them. One savage separates himself out from the terrifying band and lets out a piercing yell, one that sends goose skin up my arms. I watch, unable to look away, knowing that the woman is seconds from death. In one quick move the savage leans low over to one side of his horse, reaches down, and hauls the woman up behind him. It's almost like a dance to watch the two of them; her yipping and screaming and laughing holding on to the back of him while he wheels his horse around and charges back into the chaotic mass. And then I know. The village men are home.

Celebrations go on all night: shouts and screams, laughter and shrieks. The smell of roasting meat makes me weak with hunger while the sounds make me weak with fear. The world outside, which had only begun to feel safe, is strange again. I look down at my torn and ragged clothes, filthy bare feet, and cracked and broken nails. I touch my hair, knotted and tangled and limp with dirt and grease. I know how horrible I look, yet I know I'm no longer as safe as I'd been yesterday. I'm unfamiliar with the ways of men and women but not stupid. The enemy is here now, right outside my door, and I'm all alone. *Keep your head down. Keep your mouth shut. Mind your own business. Worry about your own troubles. Prisoner, captive, slave. White … red … savage …* Somehow, Pa's advice doesn't seem to work so well anymore. Why does that make me feel even more alone?

Towards dawn, as the sounds quiet, I drift off to sleep only to be roughly kicked awake by Old Woman before the sun has even fully lit the sky. She makes a motion with her hand, *Get on with your chores as usual,* and stumbles to her pallet exhausted from a night of celebrating. Weakness from hunger and tiredness is not the only reason I hesitate leaving Old Woman's hut. I'll never be able to make myself small enough or red enough not to be seen.

Had Old Woman stayed awake I'd have received a hard kick for taking so long to get busy. But she's already snoring on her pallet, twitching in her dreams. Can I hide in the hut all day? At last, I finally ask myself just who do I fear more, the Old Woman or the unknown men outside? I step outside the hut and head to the creek to get water, shivering *this* morning with the cold, as well as fear, tiredness and hunger. You don't need to be a red savage with a painted black face to cause a body to tremble, just a face as wrinkled as a dry apple with a nasty temper to match.

My fears are without cause in these early morning hours. The entire village including many of the children is exhausted from a night of celebrating, and I go about my chores with less bother than usual. I even manage to eat a hearty bowl of leftover stew that I find from the night before. My stomach at last is happy … for the moment. During the later part of the day the village begins to stir to life, but it's slow and I'm able to go largely unnoticed until dinner.

By dinner, Old Woman has stirred and grunted her approval at me for having done all my chores without her watching. I'm fixing the evening meal when I hear footsteps coming. My head is down, but I'm able to recognize the visitor right quick: Dirty Feet. I hear his voice and his companions' laughter. He grabs me by the hair and roughly pulls me to my feet. I struggle to stay on my feet and not cry out with the pain. He points to the stain on the front of my skirt and the laughter gets louder. Part of me wants to curl up in a ball and disappear, but part of me wants to put them in their place. *Is it my fault that I'm in this state?* Angry thoughts growl in my head. *Have I done something to deserve all this?* My hatred boils up like a cook pot.

When he lets go of my hair, I find myself raising my head. I'm fair certain that there's nothing I can do that can keep this unwanted attention off me. I look into Dirty Feet's mocking eyes and let my eyes say what my slow tongue can't. I feel my fear alive and kicking, tightening my chest, stopping my breath. But then I feel something else. It's hatred. *I hate you, red savage, for who you are and what you've done to me and mine.* I understand now why Pa said hatred could be strong as I feel it fill me and push aside a bit of my fear, making room for me to draw a shaky breath. I work hard to hate Dirty Feet more than I fear him.

Even though I can't speak I'm fair certain that Dirty Feet gets my message loud and clear. Pa often used to say, *"Why waste your breath over something unworthy?"* After a moment or two one of his companions mutters something under his breath and shoves Dirty Feet who stumbles. Everyone laughs but the mood has changed. Old Woman chooses this time to make an appearance, and she speaks to the men in the same tone she uses with the big boys when their teasing of me gets in the way of her needs. As Dirty Feet and his companions leave, I'm still standing staring at their backs. I turn to look at Old Woman, and she looks at me for a long moment and seems to *see* me for the first time since I've been there. *You watch yourself, Old Woman,* I think to myself, *I suspect I can find enough hate for you, too, should I be so inclined.* She says something to me and then snorts with laughter and walks into her hut. It takes me a moment to realize that she's not cuffed me for standing still for such a long time.

There are more celebrations that night. This time, I'm expected to serve and fetch and carry and *work*. At least there's plenty to eat even if my bones ache with tiredness and lack of sleep. I fear I'll not last the night. Finally, late in the evening, I know that no one is paying me any mind and creep toward Old Woman's hut to collapse. The risk of a beating for leaving seems worth a bit of sleep. For once I believe that I'll fall asleep without thoughts of Pa, Henry and Eli.

In the darkness outside Old Woman's hut, I'm roughly grabbed from behind. Tiredness makes me slow and weak but I kick and struggle anyway. I'm slapped hard across the side of my mouth when I begin to scream, and I taste blood. Instructions are hissed in my ear. Meaningless as they are to me, I know what they mean, *Shut up.* I continue to struggle but feel the last of my strength seeping out of me. *Maybe,* a small voice says in my head quite clear like, *maybe you will die now.* I'm so terrible tired that the idea is no longer something to be scared of, it's a relief. I stop struggling and just go limp. My attacker is not prepared for this and we both end up tumbling to the ground. As he scrambles to stand and I lay in the dirt, my tired mind is not surprised to realize who my attacker is: Dirty Feet.

Grabbing my arm, Dirty Feet pulls with all his might to get me to stand, causing me to cry out. A white-hot pain burns through my shoulder and my arm falls useless to my side. Furious, he bends down, scoops me up, and throws me over his shoulder. A loud scream is ripped from my throat as my arm and shoulder are again moved; then everything goes black.

I awake in an unfamiliar hut. It's one of the larger huts that contains a large family group. Bigger than Old Woman's hut and shaped like a rectangle, its sides are open to let summer heat out and cool evening breezes in. I lay there for a moment and take stock of my hurts. My shoulder and arm are right painful and tightly wrapped against my body making it awkward to sit up, but I finally manage. The side of my face is swollen, and I still taste blood in my mouth. I can feel a tooth loose as my tongue wanders. My head aches. My stomach growls. I roll my eyes. It seems some things never change. I make my way out of the tent to find some privacy and deal with the awkwardness of being one armed when two are needed.

It's near night, and I assume I've slept the night and day away. Do I feel better for sleep? I shake my head "No" to myself and then groan at the pain of it. No, I don't feel better at all. I begin to make my way back to Old Woman's hut, worried to have missed a full day of chores. What will she do to me? I head toward the center of the camp knowing that I can get my bearings once I'm near the great main meeting area. My head aches as I try to concentrate on the layout of the village as I remember it. As I get close, I begin to have second thoughts. It seems the whole village is present. Murmurs run through the crowd as all eyes seem to notice me. I wish for a hole to hide in. Before I can disappear, hands roughly grab hold of me, and I'm brought to the center near the great fire. There stands Dirty Feet, Old Woman, and the man I have always thought to be the Chief. He wears necklaces of animal claws; bear and cougar are two I recognize. He's naked aside from his breechcloth as all men in camp are. Across his face and chest are patterns in stripes and dots. On his shoulders is a cape made of glorious feathers of every color a head can imagine. The first time I saw it, I wondered how it would feel to touch it, but he's terrifying to look at. Beside him, wearing the pieces of a bright red coat of a British officer, sits a woman. Strung around her neck are buttons of gold, more than one army coat could ever have. She, too, wears marks on her face that I suspect won't wash off. Tied in her hair is one dark feather that seems as much a part of her as her dark black eyes. She looks as peaceful and calm as a fully alert rattlesnake, and in many ways Red Coat is more frightening than the man I call Chief. I'm seated next to Red Coat.

The Chief is talking back and forth with Dirty Feet and Old Woman. Dirty Feet seems to be angry when he speaks. Old Woman seems to be put out. Both look often at me. There's no doubt that I'm the topic of discussion. I hear a sound often. Is that their name for me? At last the Chief speaks, and another young woman steps forward. Although she's a red savage, she's a slave I'm certain, but puzzle over how I know for a time. I finally decide it's because she has the same fearful look in her eyes as I know mine have. Her clothes are a mixture of savage and white; tattered cloth skirt and dirty buckskin top. The Chief speaks without emotion although he makes an effort to be persuasive and respectful I think. He motions to me and touches his right arm, the same arm that I've hurt. He runs his hand down his arm lightly touching his skin and touches the captive savage girl's skin. The meaning is obvious even to me. Why would Old Woman want a broken white girl when she can have a whole savage? No one would be so foolish as to turn down such an offer. Old Woman is no fool. With a brief comment and a nod of her head the red savage captive's ownership is transferred. Dirty Feet's look to me says, *You are mine!*

The Chief turns to address Dirty Feet. He speaks in the same tone he has addressed Old Woman, without emotion. I close my eyes and listen to the sound of his voice flow up and down in a calm, rhythmic flow. Dirty Feet's voice is angry and loud. I open my eyes to see him shouting and waving his hands, spittle flying from his mouth. The Chief does not respond to Dirty Feet's speech; clearly his decision had been made. He has spoken. Dirty Feet stalks away into the dark night. I take a deep breath. Now what?

The Chief turns and looks at me and seems to have the same thought. *Now what do I do with you?* It's an obvious question. I stare back at him, aching all over, inside and out. I'm tired. I'm hurting. At least I'm no longer afraid. That makes me sit up straight and think. *When did I stop being afraid*, I wonder? I try to think but my head hurts too much. And then I remember: it was the moment I thought that death would be a relief. That's when the fear left me.

At last the Chief speaks. A red savage man steps forward. His long dark hair is decorated to one side with bright feathers in the colors of yellow, red, and blue, and he too has permanent marks on his face. Beside the feathers in his hair, the marks on his face, and the knife at his waist, the savage wears no other decorations. The Chief speaks in short, clipped, phrases to the savage who stands tall and quiet before him. His face does not let you know any of his feelings. The savage never speaks to the Chief, but he does speak directly to me before turning and disappearing into the dark night. Although I don't understand a word he says, I know what he means. *Follow me.*

I scramble to stand and follow after this savage I'll call Bright Feather. He never once looks back to see if I follow; he never once slows his pace. When he finally stops outside a single hut like Old Woman's on the edge of the village, I'm winded from the pace and from all of my hurts. Bright Feather motions to the hut and speaks briefly to me and then turns and leaves me alone in the dark. What should I do? With no place else to go, I crawl into the hut, which is similar in many ways to Old Woman's without the herbs and the smells that go with them. There are furs neatly piled in the corner. I fall into an exhausted sleep in the same corner where I've always slept in Old Woman's hut. Still a captive. Still alone. Still lost. I sigh. But maybe not so much afraid anymore.

I wake before dawn at the time I usually start chores with Old Woman, and Bright Feather is nowhere to be seen. I get up and step outside to greet the morning. All my aches and pains sing hello, some more loudly than others. I've noticed most men are part of a larger family unit: being sons, husbands or fathers. From what I've seen few live alone, but those that do seem to receive a share of the crops and are cared for by neighboring women or distant relatives. A majority of the huts in the village are large enough to sleep mothers, fathers, children, grandparents, aunts, and even uncles as best as I can tell. Old Woman has received the same kind of care from one nearby hut, and I often did work for those people as well as for Old Woman. As I stand in the cold dawn a savage woman with a babyboard on her back appears out of the morning mists. I think she's very pretty with her hair loose and her deerskin dress decorated with small fringed edges at the sleeve and hem. The straps of the babyboard show detailed stitches of decoration, too.

She seems surprised to see me, although she makes great effort not to let me know. It's something about her kind eyes I think that give away her shock. She holds a basket in her hand; Bright Feather's breakfast? For a moment we stare at each other and then she motions to my arm. I touch it protectively. *No, you can't touch it, it hurts too much,* I will her to understand.

She places the basket down near the fire and then approaches me slowly. I back away just as slow. Then Bright Feather appears and a long talk starts. He looks at me without speaking. *Sit down*, his look says. *Let her look at your shoulder.* I sit. She unwraps the bandage and the ache makes me just about swoon. I look into the eyes of the baby peeking at me from the babyboard as it leans against a tree. She wraps my shoulder up again. There's a lot more talking between Bright Feather and Kind Eyes.

Bright Feather goes into his hut. He comes out with his weapons and other things I don't know about. He hands Kind Eyes a bundle of furs, beautiful in their shades of brown and gold. He unhobbles his horse, mounts and rides off without looking back. Kind Eyes touches my arm, motions and smiles. *Follow me.*

I'm clean! I've washed my body! Kind Eyes has given me a soft leather dress that reaches to below my knees and leggings that lace up to the top of my calves. I've washed my hair. It's clean and combed and bound with pieces of leather. *I'm clean!!* Kind Eyes helped me wash myself, she was gentle with my shoulder, but even still I fairly died whenever it was moved. I think, though, if I had to do it all over again – pain and all – I'd do it just to feel this good about being clean! The savage women wash near a bend in the river. It's a place not chosen so much for privacy but for ease and speed. *Never is there so much white skin for all to see as bathing at the river*, I think as I strip and scrub. The water runs swift but is not too deep, and there's plenty of fine sand for scrubbing. Kind Eyes has herbs that she rubs in my hair that smell clean and make a kind of suds. Oh, it's heaven to be clean!

From that day on a pattern happens. I sleep every night in Bright Feather's hut, although it's many, many nights before I see him again. That first night I go to prepare a meal for Bright Feather, but Kind Eyes stills my hand and shakes her head. *He will not be here to eat dinner.* Every morning I rise before the sun and make my way to Kind Eyes' hut and it's there that I start my chores, helping her do things that need to be done. Most of the chores are the same I did for Old Woman with one exception: I get to help care for Kind Eyes' baby. In my head I call him "Owl", always peeking out from his babyboard with those big, wide, dark eyes. I find out right quick he's a boy. I try to take all my loneliness and miss-you feelings for Eli and give it to Owl. Beside Kind Eyes and Owl there's also Kind Eyes' husband who I call 'Coon. He's quiet and fierce looking, and I give him his name for the raccoon tail that swings from his hair.

I'm taught how to plant the savage way, it being spring. A huge garden is prepared by all the women that's for the entire village. There's the turning of the earth, preparing the soil, planting the seeds: corn, beans (that they will have grow up the cornstalks), squash, sunflowers, pumpkins, and others I'm not sure of. The small children and old women mind the birds, shooing them away should they be mistaken and think there's an easy meal nearby. Hampered with my arm, I spend a lot of time amusing and caring for the many small children who are always present wherever the women go. I still do all my other chores as well, such as hauling water, collecting wood for fires, grinding corn (that was tricky, but I manage to hold the bowl 'tween my legs), and helping prepare meals. I'm clumsier seeing it's my right arm that's hurt, and it's my right arm that I'm more inclined to use.

Kind Eyes always works to include me in everything and makes sure I'm doing what needs to be done the way it needs to be done. I'm right pleased that the women trust me with their children. Pa used to say, *"Don't always listen for the words, Elle, watch for the actions."* In fact, as the weeks pass, I take it as a downright compliment that so many of the women allow me to care for their children while they work in the garden doing the heavy work of hoeing, digging, and planting.

As the days and weeks progress, it's with Kind Eyes that I finally begin to understand my first few savage words. They come very slowly. Pa may have thought I was quick with some things, but not with this. I begin to hear sounds that I put with things; words like "fire", "wood", "grain", "corn", "sit", "go", and "baby", although I'm not sure if the word I think is "baby" is just Kind Eyes' name for her child. I'll have to listen and see if the other mothers call their babies by the same sound. But mostly it all just sounds like a jumble of sounds to me, like a pile of mush on a plate. Every once in a while I recognize a sound that I hear and if I work real hard finally

I seem to piece it together with what I know. I've never once tried to speak it though! That's nigh on impossible.

I have to be shown how to prepare the meat and the skins as it's not something I know how to do. It's also powerful hard work, and with my arm the way it is, I'm little use. Although it's better, it still pains me, especially if I do heavy lifting or hauling (which is often) but I no longer keep it wrapped, and I'm happy to say that the tooth that was loose from being hit is solid again in my mouth. So I watch careful as Kind Eyes works the hides so that when I'm able I can do it on my own. From start to finish it can take a full week of hard, hard work to do a hide proper. I look around me in the village at all the moccasins and pants and dresses and I see weeks and weeks of hard break-your-back work. *No wonder so many go around just about naked.*

I travel daily with the women to collect herbs and learn about many new ones. Kind Eyes always takes the time to try to explain what each plant does – for stomach ills, lady cramps, tooth aches, and skin rashes. If we are not working in the garden we are gathering in the forest. The men may do the hunting, but it's the women who seem to do everything else. I suspect Bright Feather notices the strings of herbs hanging to dry from the roof of the hut when he is in the village, but he says nothing as usual. I enjoy a treat of maple syrup drops one day, and I look forward to that chore in the fall!

From Kind Eyes I learn the rhythm of the camp. Some ways are powerful familiar, like the way they tend their clothes by the river and the way they love their children. The children near to Eli's age seem to spend their days full of laughter and fun and play. Little ones are well loved by the grown-ups here, spoiled and teased and cared for with as much attention as I cared for Eli. I watch two old men sitting outside their huts give a group of troublesome boys a dressing down and I remember Old Mr. Hobson sitting at Cooper's General Store in the corner by the checkerboard frowning and giving me the evil eye for something Eli had done. I puzzle over that. Savage and white the same? Until my time here I'd not have even thought to ponder such a thing, let alone believe it to be so.

I see the way two savage girls giggle and laugh and whisper like they are friends, and I'm stunned to realize that I wish to be a part of that. I smile at 'Coon as he teases and tickles little Owl, and I think of Pa singing to Eli at night as we all drift off to sleep, and I long for that closeness with a body, too. My head stretches and creeks a bit like an old house as it shifts to make room for this new way of thinking and looking at the people I'm living with. For the first time I'm not so sure that 'savage' is a word that fits them all. For maybe they are all more like me than I care to admit.

But then there are many things that are so downright strange it would be like if you were to try to go through your day walking on your hands instead of your feet. I still struggle mightily with this savage language which I suspect I never will fit in my thick head. And it seems to me that no one thinks much of possessions or ownership or property much like Ma did about her fancy china dishes and Pa did about his gold pocket watch. Then there's the fact that everyone here lives together so close, and all Pa wanted to be was away from *everyone*.

As the spring flows into summer, my life with the savages takes on a pattern as regular as my life at home. I cook, I clean, I work in the garden, and I care for children. Sometimes I laugh at the antics of the children. Sometimes I share a smile with Kind Eyes. I'm not so sad, I'm not so fearful, but I still struggle with the fact that I'm a stranger, still a captive white girl in a borrowed buckskin dress that can't even manage the simplest of talk.

I still miss Pa, Henry, and Eli but the ache's like my arm that's slowly healing. Even the worst of injuries, if it doesn't kill, finally begins to heal. Nights are not so hard for me anymore. It isn't that I don't think of my family, but it's more like I've decided to carefully put them to rest in my mind like some treasured item in Ma's chest.

Ma had a big cedar box that Pa called her Hope Chest. Sometimes he'd let me and Eli look through it, and it was full with all manner of treasured things: clothes, letters, locks of hair (Pa said they were Henry's), a beautiful colored quilt, and even some pieces of jewelry. My memories of

Ma have been put away for a long time. There are so very few and they are shadowy like the way things look in the early morning mists that come down from the mountains. Pa told me I look like Ma with my long brown hair and green eyes. I suppose many of things I do around the house reminded him of her, but I can't remember what she looked like. It upset me at first that I could not remember her face clearly after a time, but I treasure the memories of her hands. They were good hands. I can see them more clearly in my memories than her face. I see them covered with flour kneading bread, and doing other chores that have to do with cooking. I feel her hands smoothing my back and stroking my face in comfort over something Henry has done to tease me. I remember her hands combing and braiding my hair each morning and teaching me how to lace up my shoes. I see her hands clasped in prayer at night by my bedside and listening to me whisper into God's ear. Looking through that chest and smelling the special smells, I can almost conjure up Ma's face in my head and almost hear her voice. Henry never wanted to look in the Hope Chest, I suspect for the same reason. Odd how that is, I think; I'd get comfort and Henry'd get upset from the same thing: memories. Eli couldn't remember Ma, of course, but I'd tell him what I remembered.

So my memories of Pa, and Henry and Eli and Ma I keep now neatly stored in a private place in my mind, 'cause I for certain have no Hope Chest. I take them out whenever I like, but they no longer tear at me like a festering wound. I let different things fill my head as I lay on my pallet at night waiting for sleep to come: new words I'm trying to remember, herbs I'm trying to recall, and the cute way Owl looks at me when I play peek-a-boo with him.

Bright Feather is often gone three or four weeks at a time. He never stays in the village for long, no more than four or five nights. He returns with meat (deer, turkey, rabbit, and once even a goose) and furs in many rich shades. Does he set traps? Pa used to do that. I wonder how it's different and how it's the same. He makes no move to talk with me. It's just like living with Old Woman 'cept he doesn't hit or kick me. Not even once. A few times Kind Eyes takes time to show me how to do things that I suspect Bright Feather told her I'm doing wrong. He speaks with her just now and then. I cook for him and he eats it, so I suspect that's a victory. Once I learn the way of using their birch bark containers I manage quite well. They are sturdy enough to boil water by dropping hot stones into them and can even be set directly on the fire, but once that's done I've discovered it's not much use to you after that! I don't fear him, I'm glad to say. Course I do my best to have everything just as I should, and even with my bad arm I try to be quick with my chores.

When Bright Feather is in the village, most evenings are spent at the main hut where the Chief and Red Coat can be found. Many of the men spend their evenings there, and some of the women, too. It's not a place for me, and I make every effort to avoid meeting times there. I'm happy to stay out of sight at Bright Feather's hut.

I continue to struggle mightily to learn the language and try to get more words each day. I make an effort to pick up two or three new words a day, but some days I can't even do that. Still, after nearly four months, I've yet to utter a single savage word fearful that I'll do it wrong. I now know the name for Kind Eyes and her baby, even the name for Bright Feather, but I don't understand the meaning so I continue to call them the names I know them by in my head. I know "fire" and "fish" and "stick" and "river" and "corn" and even "no", "yes", and what I imagine to be "Go! Get out of here!", which comes from spending so much time with the mothers and the young children. I know the word that you are supposed to yell at the birds when they try to steal the seed, like my "Shoo!" although they don't sound anything alike. Kind Eyes has taken to talking with me at night like we can really talk with each other. I concentrate so hard to understand and hear the different sounds that my head aches something fierce, and I've come to almost dread these times. I don't know if Kind Eyes ever gets fed up with me, but she's always patient and never gives up trying. I've no idea what 'Coon thinks about me.

I come to realize as I go about my days that the only thing that now keeps me apart from everyone in this village are just three things of my very own doing: my slow tongue, my white skin, and my thoughts of what is savage and what is not. For I'm almost always treated with kindness and respect, curiosity and teasing, and a regular dose of laughing wonder, none of which, as far as I can see, is that bad at all. Once again, being the only different one in a place has a powerful way of changing a body's thoughts about what is ... right and wrong ... *savage and not*. The more I ponder what truly makes a body a savage and what does not, the more tangled my thoughts become.

One hot summer day when we are all bathing at the river, I realize for the first time what everyone assumes about Bright Feather and me. As we wade into the wonderfully cool waters, splashing ourselves and rubbing our skin with the fine sand, one of the savage woman touches my flat, white stomach and the meaning is clear. *How come no baby?* I'm sure I blush right down to my ankles, and for long moments for once all of us are redskins. Kind Eyes looks at me for a moment then looks at the other women and shakes her head "no". There then begins a long conversation in which I hear Bright Feather's name mentioned many times. I would have done just about anything to understand what was being said. Even going back to being dirty.

When I say living with Bright Feather is just like living with Old Woman, I mean it. *That* aspect never even occurred to me, but it seems it has to others. Again, Pa, it seems I ain't so quick. For many nights after that day I worry about this new idea in my head. My sleep is filled with dreams in which I'm chasing something just beyond my sight and just when I'm too tired to go any further I realize that I must run because something terrible is chasing *me*. I wake with my heart pounding and my breath coming out in gasps. I lie there on my fur pallet and think about the savage woman's red hand on my bare white belly and think, is this what is expected of me? Of us? There are many young women in the village, some not much older than me I'm sure, that seem to ... be ... with a man in more ways than I'm with Bright Feather. Has he just been polite? Have I been just plain stupid again? Is he waiting for a sign from me that I'm so inclined? My gut clenches in a wave of panic that I've not felt in many months. Again I feel an anger with myself. If I could learn this language, I'd at least know what people say and think and expect of me. But no, not only am I a prisoner here because I can't help myself to escape, I'm also powerful stupid because I still can't speak, or even seem to learn the words I need to talk with my captors. I decide I'll try to watch Bright Feather more closely the next time he's in the village. *And,* my head says to me, *what will you do if you see what you are afraid is expected of you?* I've no answer for myself.

I'm going on a hunting trip with a group from the village, and Bright Feather is back and will go along, too. I suspect I was chosen to go because I've no child and they know I work hard. Some women are going along on the hunt who do have very small children, but most are young men and older boys and girls. Kind Eyes has tried mightily to explain, but she has finally just gone around and begun to make a pile of things that I should bring. She smiles a lot and nods her head. I think I'm supposed to be excited about going, but I'm frightened. Strange as it seems, I feel safe in the village now. Will I have to be with others I don't know? Will others take the time to be patient to show me what needs to be done like Kind Eyes does for me? Then other thoughts creep into my head: Will I be days closer to my home? What if Pa comes for me while I'm away? Kind Eyes smiles while I worry.

There are five men, ten women, and fifteen older boys and girls. Most of the men, including Bright Feather, are mounted on horses carrying supplies, while the rest of us carry light packs of supplies on our backs. Two of the men carry infants in babyboards hooked to their saddles. I delight in the cute faces staring solemnly out at the world flowing by. I know things'll be much heavier coming back. It being late summer, I know whatever we can kill will be important to feed us in the winter. Pa and Henry would be busy hunting whenever they weren't tending to the crops, too.

Bright Feather keeps to himself even within a group of his own people. He responds to questions or conversations when needed, but otherwise is a man apart. Even when we settle in the temporary hunting site, the lean-to we erect is farthest from the rest of the group. The other men seem respectful of him and keep their distance as well. As they laugh and joke amongst themselves, Bright Feather watches just like I do. He's a man apart and when he sees me watching him, he goes off into the woods.

The hunting party divides, leaving the women and girls to prepare and wait. Some go in pairs, but I'm not surprised that Bright Feather shows every sign of going off by himself. I'm stunned when he hands me my pack and motions to follow. We head out on foot. He seems familiar with these woods, and I'm not surprised when we stop at a ready-made lean-to where we set up our things. Bright Feather has been here before.

We sit almost all day silent and still in the forest. Even with me sitting just a small distance from Bright Feather, he blends in with the woods so well that I must concentrate to find him sometimes. It's the first opportunity in all these months for me to study him. The feathers I name him for belong to birds I'm familiar with: red for the cardinal, yellow for the goldfinch and blue for the bluejay. They are twined in his waist-length black hair that for this hunting trek is bound tightly with leather strips like a long tail down his back, just as I wear mine. I don't know how old he is nor can I even try to guess. His skin is smooth and unlined, but darkly tan from the sun like the polished wood of Pa's rifle. He wears permanent marks on his face like Old Woman, but of different designs, three lines across each check and down his chin. He's lean and muscular, but all savages seem to be. He never seems to smile, laugh, or show any feeling really. Maybe I should have called him Living Rock, I think, as I watch him sit unmoving hour after hour. Is this how he spends his days away from camp?

With a start I realize that Bright Feather is exactly like I expected all savages to be before being brought as a captive to this village. Unfeeling. Strong. Silent. Separate. Frightening. Not really a person. He fits the pictures I've seen in books, the glimpses I've seen with my own eyes. With Bright Feather I can still do what Pa told me to do: *keep my head down, keep my mouth shut, and mind my own business.* I study him in the dappled summer shade and ponder what would make a body wish to be so far removed from life. Bright Feather seems to want and need no one. Why, even 'Coon, for all his work to look and act fierce can make Kind Eyes blush with just a word and Owl giggle with a look.

The truth is I can no longer fit the people of the village to the picture of red savages I have in my head. They are mothers and fathers, grandmothers and toddlers. They laugh and cry, yell and sing, play games and give comfort when it's needed. Yes, they all have red skin, but I can't always fit together the words 'red' and 'savage' anymore. Those words must be kept separate and only joined if they're earned. Dirty Feet and those that traveled with him have earned them. And finally, I come to the conclusion as I sit and sit and sit that it's not Bright Feather's red skin that makes him savage. No, with great certainty I know that something else has made him this man who seems to enjoy no one's company ... not even his own.

A forest is a noisy place, but I never notice it until I sit that day with Bright Feather. First there's silence as every living creature with any sense scatters at your appearance. Then, if you sit still enough, long enough, gradually you are forgotten and the creatures with their noises return: birds and mice, rabbits and deer, squirrels and foxes. I sit and study the animal village we visit that day and wait and wonder just who Bright Feather is expecting. Just before dusk an elk of enormous size wanders into the clearing. I don't see him move, but all of a sudden Bright Feather has an arrow notched and ready and sits motionless again. I hold my breath as the elk moves closer, closer and closer still to us. ZING! The arrow flies through the air, the elk drops to the ground, and I hear Bright Feather say words quietly under his breath. We have just enough time before dark to quickly gut the animal and string the carcass up high to keep other interested predators away. We share a meal of fresh roasted meat in the light of the almost full moon.

A sound wakes us both late in the night. Bright Feather reaches out, and for the first time ever touches me, placing his hand on my bare arm. *Be silent. Be still*, the hand says. Soundlessly, knife drawn, Bright Feather creeps out from our sleeping spot. I can't resist and shift ever so slightly so that I can see who wants our elk. It's a bear! A large black bear, so intent on our elk hanging just out of reach that he pays no mind to the promise of death that's creeping up silently behind him. The bear is almost as big as Bright Feather, standing on its hind legs and grunting in frustration as he swipes at the dangling hoof of the elk. In one silent leap, Bright Feather jumps on the bear's back and reaches around and slits the bear's throat. The bear has only time to grunt in surprise and lower itself to all fours before it begins to stagger. I've time to think, *Can a bear be afraid?* as I hear Bright Feather again repeating words quietly under his breath.

If I could speak to Bright Feather, I might suggest we just sit here for a week or two and collect enough meat to feed the entire village for the whole winter! When I make motions to begin helping him deal with the bear he grunts and shakes his head no. So much meat, we can be careless it seems. The work can wait until morning. He goes and washes briefly at the stream down the slope and then returns to the lean-to. In moments we are both asleep. I dream of a great bear who comes and sits beside me. He talks in the savage language, and I tell him that I'm sorry but I can't understand him. "It's no matter," he says right conversationally, and gets up and lumbers away.

We work hard the next day; skinning, wrapping, and packaging the carcasses. It's hot, dirty, messy work. It seems funny to me that we spend all one whole day sitting doing nothing and then fair kill ourselves the next day doing enough work for five days. As we kneel exhausted at the stream at the end of the day and wash as best we can, I must chuckle out loud at the thought of it, for all of a sudden Bright Feather stops what he's doing to look at me. I look back, not sure what to do and certain with nothing to say. We are close enough to touch, and he reaches across to me. I'm motionless, not knowing what to expect, as he reaches up to my head, hands dripping water, and delicately takes something from my tangled mess of hair. I see it's a feather, a robin's I think, long and dark gray brown. He hands it to me as he stands to go back to the lean-to. I look at the feather resting in my clean, wet hand.

Thoughts of Eli, Henry and Pa no longer keep me awake at night, but sometimes, on nights when I'm tired to the bone, they invade my dreams. I never can remember the dreams, but they must be sad, for I almost always wake up knowing I've been crying. In the lean-to that night with Bright Feather I must be having one of those dreams and awaken him with my crying. I open my eyes to find him leaning over me and the bright moon shining behind his head. I know right away where I am, but can't understand what's wrong. He reaches out and touches my cheeks, and his fingertips glisten in the moonlight with wetness. *Oh*, I think, *a sad dream.* I sit up and scrub my face with the hem of my tunic. "It's no matter," I hear myself saying, startling us both with the sound of my voice. Nothing compares with the look of stunned surprise on Bright Feather's face. I've spoken to him in his own language.

We go back to the camp for strong backs to help carry out all the meat. The other hunters have been successful, too, but not as much as us. Great exclamations are said over the elk and the bear. Bright Feather stands stoic and silent; I stand dumb and stupid. What a pair we are.

Back in the village, Kind Eyes and I set to work to cure the bearskin and the elk hide. My arm reminds me how hard the work is and how much it still must heal. We spend days and days working, but I sense that Kind Eyes is glad for the help and the company even if I'm still as silent as a stone. Bright Feather has told Kind Eyes of my sad dream and my speaking to him, I can tell. I can see it in Kind Eyes' expressions when she talks to me and I concentrate hard to understand. I find that I feel more comfortable trying out some savage words and phrases with the little ones. "No." "Sit." "Stay." "Come here!" "Stop!" I know these words are clear because they work. I whisper endearing terms in the ears of the babies. Words that I hear the mothers' say with a tone of love and guess them to be "You'll be fine," "My sweet baby," "Don't cry," and "I'm here."

Fall is just beginning to add a smell to the air the morning I wake and make my way to Kind Eyes' hut as usual. Bright Feather has been gone for more than two weeks again, but not before giving me the bear pelt from the hunt for my own. Aside from the clothes on my back, the moccasins on my feet, and the robin's feather in my hair, it's the only thing I can call mine. I listen to the sounds of the forest and the village as I make my way - sounds of different families, dogs, horses, the sounds through the trees when the wind is rising up, and the sound of the summer bugs - some get louder with the heat and some get softer. The noise I hear as I walk to

Kind Eyes hut that morning is different, and at first I don't notice. But gradually, it's the silence of the forest that makes me turn and squint into the dim dawn light and the cool morning mists.

For those brief few moments I think that perhaps I'm really just asleep curled up on my furs in Bright Feather's hut having another funny bear dream. My eyes say, now can you really, truly be seeing a bear sitting on a horse? I stop in my tracks, bare toes curling in the cool wet grass and work hard to focus my eyes through the haze. And as I stand there, the bear and his horse move forward. It's the smell that makes me realize that it's no dream. I was very close to a bear a few weeks back, and a real one doesn't smell so bad. The vision grins at me then, a wide toothless grin through his tangled mass of dirty beard. It isn't a bear, my mind finally understands, but a man! Not a savage man, my head says to me, what's different about him? How long has it been since I've seen one? For he's a white man, wearing a filthy matted cape of an old bearskin and a fur cap stuck on his head. Two more white men slowly come out of the forest and rein in their horses.

My heart begins to pound as I squint closely through the mist at the three white faces before me. Could it be Pa or someone who has come looking for me at last?!

"It's a white woman," I hear one drawl in absolute wonder, and the words sound just as strange in my ears as the sights do to my eyes.

I take two steps back and the bear one starts to move his horse toward me with purpose. "Need some rescuing, girly?" he grins toothlessly at me.

Suddenly I hear Pa's voice in my head clear as if he was standing right next to me and we were still in Cooper's General Store more than three years back, "*That be Bear John, Elle. Don't look at him or talk to him. He's trouble wherever he turns up. As bad as he smells is as bad as he is.*" Then I remember the bite of Dirty Feet's rope around my neck and the red savage girl I last saw tied to Bear John's belt more dead than alive.

White skin. Red skin.

Savage. Man.

Fear. Safety.

Good. Bad.

Right. Wrong.

Home...

My world is tilting and changing, making no sense. Who am I? Where am I? What do I want? What do I do? Who do I ask for help? Who do I need? My feet don't move while my head sees one thing and my heart feels another. A prickling rush of fear starts in my belly and begins to travel through my body and finally reaches my stuck feet. I step backwards one step. Then two. Bear John is close enough to me that he begins to lean down out of his saddle and reach toward me. My mind, fair to bursting already, notices the bits of food stuck in his filthy matted beard as he smiles at me. The bulge of his belly peeks out from underneath his bearskin cape as he stretches out to grab me. "Ain't you just a pretty bit of a thing?" he says with absolute hunger in his voice.

I turn and run. I scream savage words I know that mean danger but don't necessarily fit the picture: DANGER! FIRE! STOP! BEAR! HORSE! NO! COME! FIRE!

It's natural for me to run towards Kind Eyes' hut, but too late I realize I've brought danger right to her. I turn towards the center of the camp, yelling my savage words. But Kind Eyes has already stepped from her hut at my noise. She has a puzzled expression as if to say, *What foolishness are you saying girl, the first time you decide to speak to us?* The change of her expression tells me how close the danger is. She starts to run toward the forest, stopping first to scoop up Owl in his babyboard resting against the hut.

Bear John's companions are laughing and shouting to each other, "Head west!"

"Don't go too far into the village!"

"Don't see no men! You were right, John!"

I can smell Bear John behind me. Kind Eyes begins to sob as Owl's babyboard sticks on a root. I turn to run to help and hear horse hooves slow and his raspy voice laugh, "Here, let me help you get that loosed." NO! Not Owl!

Kind Eyes screams as he leans down to grab the babyboard. My head doesn't think, I just grab a burning stick from the fire and swing. I miss, but the pass of the flame startles the horse, and it whinnies and screams and rears up. Bear John, leaning out of the saddle is unseated and falls hard on the ground winded and stunned. I step forward and hit him hard with the burning stick, once, twice, three times. His great bear cape and beard catch on fire, and he begins to scream.

The smell of burning hair and skin and fur mix with the stink Bear John has already brought with him. He rolls on the ground, screaming and swatting at the flames, but in his panic he rolls right into the fire that I've gotten the stick from. I turn and run after Kind Eyes and Owl who are almost to the woods now, with the screams of Bear John, the other white men, and the village rising up behind us. Owl's screams are the loudest of all. As soon as we stop, Kind Eyes puts Owl to her breast to hush his cries and keep him silent. Bear John and the other men are wrong; though a large party has gone out hunting just the day before there are men in the village. We can hear whoops and shouts and then silence.

I don't know how long we hide in the woods. My stomach knows the time better than me cause it starts complaining pretty loudly after a while. When we finally hear the sounds of hooves approaching, the sun is well in the sky. It's a savage pony that's for sure, as there's no sound of metal or creak of leather. Kind Eyes sobs with relief to see her husband 'Coon. He takes the sleeping Owl up before him and hoists her up on the horse behind him. I walk quiet beside as Kind Eyes talks and talks. Coon answers questions and asks some himself. Three times I can feel his eyes on me. Bear John is gone, but you can see which way he's been dragged, and his smell is still with us some when we get back.

There's much talking the rest of the day. Runners are sent out to find the hunting parties and Kind Eyes is questioned by the Chief. They talk to me, too, or try to. They show me Bear John's body and two of his men who've also been killed. All of their possessions are spread out on the ground, each having been touched and studied. Standing there looking at the bodies and smelling the awful smells my knees get to shaking so much that I finally just have to sit down in the dust.

Many in the village come to stare at me over the rest of the day while I try my best to act like nothing much has changed. The day is just the same as any other.

Except for the fact that I've killed a man.

A white man.

Men, women, boys, girls, and even a few curious dogs all troop by to have a look-see at the murderous captive white girl grinding corn and keeping watch over her birch bark bowl stewing over the fire calm as you please. I try my best to ignore the stares and whispers just like I always have. And it's impossible, just like always.

They give me Bear John's horse! What will Bright Feather think when he comes back and sees a white man's horse hobbled next to his hut? I hope Kind Eyes is nearby to explain, since all I can probably say is "Bear, John, fire, hot, no, run!" Too bad I can't say "stink." I'll just hold my nose. The poor horse appears to be better cared for than Bear John cared for himself, and certainly that savage girl I saw him with so long ago. *Life is sure strange me being in this savage village now and so far away from Pa, Henry and Eli,* I think to myself more than once.

Many of the men are back, and more than a few have come by to stare at me and Bear Johns' horse. Maybe I'll get used to all this attention after all, I think. I decide to call the horse Willow because her dark brown mane and tail flow like the willow tree's branches near the stream. I like the bright white socks on her legs. She seems like a gentle mare, although I haven't ridden her yet. I don't have much practice riding astride a saddle, let alone bareback. They didn't give me the saddle. I've brushed and fed her, and she seems happy with all the care.

Kind Eyes is in a state, brushing my hair and checking my clothes. I keep trying to do the usual chores that need to be done, and she keeps shooing me back and looking impatient. She finally takes my face in her hands and says words real slow like, willing them to seep into my thick skull. I concentrate hard and repeat the ones I understand: "Night", "Fire", "Chief", and the word that means me.

We eat no evening meal at the hut, but as night falls make our way to the center of the village. I'm not happy to be seated next to the Chief where all eyes are able to see me. Kind Eyes does not have kind eyes when I make a move to go someplace else. Her look is plain. *You sit right there and don't you move.* I sigh. I sit.

My head aches with the strain of trying to listen and understand. The Chief, Red Coat, and even Old Woman speak for a time. *When will I understand this speaking?* I think to myself, angry like. Most of the men and all of the women and children from the village are gathered. I don't see Bright Feather, but that's not a surprise. He has only been gone two weeks. We eat dinner, and my stomach is happy. Sweet venison, corn, squash, late strawberries and blackberries; my lips and fingers are shiny and bright with my eating. No wonder the men meet here each night when they are home, I think!

Someone begins to play a drum, and there's dancing and shouting and singing. Someone acts out a bear hunt, another acts out a battle with an enemy. I see a flash of color, and I recognize Bright Feather's red, yellow and blue colors in the dark on the edge of the circle. Had a log not slipped and exploded into a short bright flame I'd never have known he was there. I feel eyes on me as the drums play, but no one else steps forward, and then from the shadows I can see a shape emerging, a bear. I gasp in fear and the Chief reaches and touches my arm. He looks at me and back at the shape, then back at me and out to the crowd. *Tell your story,* his look says, *They want to hear your story.* How do I tell him that telling my story in front of all these faces is almost more terrifying than facing the real Bear John? How do I tell him that I can still smell him in my nose and hear his screams in my head?

I stand up and smooth my tunic; I'm barefoot and my hair is tied back like it was that morning. I realize I look just like I did on my way to Kind Eyes' hut: just like I'm supposed to. I try to ignore the fire and the crowd, shut my eyes and let the drums creep into my head and my heart and through my blood. It's calming because the drumbeat is slower than my scared heart is pounding, and I feel things inside me start to slow, start to quiet. I open my eyes and imagine walking to Kind Eyes' hut. I turn my head; what's that change in the forest's sounds?

I feel the terror and a sob of sheer remembry rips through me. I make them laugh shouting the savage words I know in warning. They slap their thighs, hold their sides, and wipe away tears from laughing so hard. Kind Eyes joins me in front of the fire and we do a dance almost remembering how things went. We even have Owl's babyboard – with a cornhusk doll inside instead. At the end, I break the tension again by holding my nose; remembering the stink of the burning bear man. Then with Owl's babyboard, Kind Eyes and I run off into the dark edges of the firelight.

They like my show. I want to wander off to Bright Feather's hut and curl up on my pallet and go to sleep, but that isn't how it's to be. Kind Eyes fair drags me back to the light and then, instead of letting me sit down and do my best to disappear, the Chief stands and begins to talk to me and the village. I hear Bright Feather's name, and Kind Eyes, even Owl's and Old Woman's. I hear "bear", "fire", and I'm fair certain I hear the name they call me which I don't know what it means. Then the Chief speaks just to me. He places his two big, warm hands on my shoulders and speaks like he talked to Dirty Feet, Old Woman, and Bright Feather that night so long ago - respectful and without emotion. He takes a necklace strung with bear claws and shells from around his neck and places it around mine. Old Woman stands and speaks quick like. She does not look at me once but speaks only to the Chief. I see others look at me though, as she speaks and I think, *Now what?*, but I don't know the answer for I can't understand her words. Red Coat steps forward, her gold button necklace flashing in the firelight, and ties a belt with a knife sheath around my waist. I'm handed Bear John's knife, and even I knew its value, for it's real metal and not flint. Then the Chief turns me to face the village and says one last thing. He calls me 'Bear'. And the village cheers.

As the cheering quiets, the crowd parts and makes room for a man I immediately recognize to be Bright Feather. He leads Willow, who whinnies nervously from all the unfamiliar sights, smells and sounds. She's no longer bareback but has a beautiful thick woven savage blanket thrown over her back and a savage rope harness around her head. I recognize my very few possessions: moccasins, bear skin, plus some splendid pelts I know

Bright Feather has kept carefully aside from all the others he has used and traded. He walks through the firelight to stand in front of me and reaches for my hand, in which he places Willow's reins. He bows his head every so slightly and says simply, "Bear," and turns and walks away.

I'm not sure of anything. But I think I'm a member of this tribe now, no longer a slave. I think I'm called Bear. And I think I'm without a place to sleep.

I know who I am, what I am, and what I can do or cannot do.

I am a Cherokee and I am proud of it.

There is no one who can take that away from me.[3]

Charlie Soap

Bear

Autumn is heading quick to winter and there are many surprises and just as many discoveries for me. Right quick after I'm given my name Bear and begin to sleep in Kind Eyes and Coon's hut, I begin to dream in the Indian language of the village. It's powerful strange not to understand what's said around me day *and* night. Then POP! one day it seems that regular small talk I hear walking past huts or over the fire at dinner makes sense in my head. I hear Raccoon call Kind Eyes by the name he has always used for her, and I know that her true name is Otter. I hear Otter call Owl "Little Bird" and I understand. One day as we hike through the forest collecting pine cones and firewood, almost knee deep sometimes in fallen autumn leaves, I ask Otter in her language, "Is Bright Feather your brother?"

She stops in front of me, Little Bird's piercing stare and drooling mouth swings out of my line of vision and I see a pair of surprised, kind eyes instead. She takes one step, then two towards me and asks me, "Who is Bright Feather?" But she knows. She just wants to hear me talk.

"The one who wears three colored feathers in his hair. The one who's hut I kept. The one who is never here."

She stares at me for a moment and then grins a great wide grin. "At *last*," she says and turns to continue walking, nodding as she says, "Yes, he is."

I feel her excitement and her desire to talk and talk and talk. But she waits, letting me take things at my own pace. "What does his name mean?" I ask, and I say the confusing long string of sounds.

"His name means 'One Who Is Always Alone', but I like 'Bright Feather' better. Long ago he was called Hawk because he was such a great hunter."

At the evening meal, seated around our small fire, Raccoon is eating. I'm shy around him and hesitant to speak. He thinks nothing of my silence. Otter is like a little child with a surprise she has trouble keeping. He notices her mood and teases her. "Impatient to get to our furs tonight?" She blushes furious and so do I, but Raccoon does not see. She looks at me finally with a stare, *Either you say something or I will!*

I stir up my little bit of courage and ask, "Raccoon, will you teach me to ride my horse, Willow?" Raccoon chokes on the bit of meat he's eating and coughs and sputters while Otter laughs and laughs, pounding him on his back. I wait hopefully for his answer yes.

He looks at me real fierce. The permanent marks on his face, across his forehead and down his nose make him look even more frightening. But I know what a good man he is, I've seen him with Otter and Little Bird. I'm not afraid of him even a small bit. I look back at him and finally have to smile. His look softens at last and with a slow smile he nods, "Yes, I will teach you how to ride your horse." Then he looks at Otter and says, "You said you thought the words would come soon." She looks smug because she was right.

Otter and I spend days and days talking. It's like we're best friends who have been apart for months trying to tell each other all the things that have happened over our whole lives. Raccoon puts bits of fur in his ears to drown out our voices that never seem to rest. I've never had a real friend, I realize. It was always just Pa, Henry and Eli when I lived in Virginia. Our homestead was the farthest west of any that I knew of from the nearest town known as Ward's Mill. The closest families to us had no children my age and were more than a day and a half ride by horse. The few times we went to town, excited as I was, what time was there for me to make acquaintance, first with a baby, then a toddler, and finally a spirited boy in tow?

I learn that they call themselves The Real People and they believe the center of the world rests right here where we live and walk and breathe. They believe that as long as the world is in balance that life is good; good crops, good health, good weather. It's The Real People's job to make sure the world is always good. This particular area of The Real People's land is called The Maple Forest.

The Center of the World. A mighty far cry from the red savage village you once thought it to be, my head says to itself.

"Even within our lives," Otter explains, "we try for balance: women farm, men hunt. At the Green Corn Ceremony late each summer we clean out our homes and council circle, we throw away broken pottery and baskets, start new fires, end unhappy marriages, and forgive old wrongs. We celebrate by eating newly grown foods we pick from our gardens. We start fresh each year to make the world a better place than it was the year before."

One day as we speak more about this idea of balance and harmony and the center of the world, I feel I must make a point or two. Little Bird is sitting happily in Otter's lap chewing on her finger. A big puddle of drool is collecting in the dirt in front of them. Now I can see that Otter's, and Raccoon's, and Little Bird's lives seem mighty happy and balanced. They are together and strong and healthy. I look across the fire out into the village and, I suppose, the center of the world moving quite smoothly as far as the eye can see as it goes about its evening chores and prepares to bed down for the night. Things seem calm and peaceful if always a bit busy.

"I don't suspect," I feel compelled to say with a careful tone, "that my Pa would agree that The Real People have made his world particularly good. Or balanced. Or filled with harmony."

It's a measure of our friendship that I feel comfortable enough to say such a thing and that Otter stays calm enough to hear it. Even more so, that she takes the time to try and say a bit more to help me understand. "Bear, a wrong must always be made right, a bad deed must always be punished and a slight must always be revenged." She pauses for a moment and then says in a rush, "Even your presence here in this village was an attempt to right a wrong and restore balance."

That's mighty surprising to me, and I say so. "What could have happened that would cause me to be brought here?!" I sputter with confusion. "What did my Pa or Eli or Henry or I do?!" But Otter purses her lips and suddenly will not answer my question.

I feel compelled to say one more thing as Raccoon joins us, scooping up a squealing Little Bird. "Perhaps," I say with just as much care as I did before, "the problem is deciding who has the say who is right and who is wrong, what is in balance and what is not ..."

Raccoon looks at Otter's tense face and then at my careful one. "There has always been a sacred trust between The Real People and the world," he explains quietly. "We honor the animals, and it is with great respect that a hunter apologizes to the spirit of each animal he kills." I think of Bright Feather and the words he said as he killed the elk and the bear, and I realize he was talking to their spirits. "We are careful with the land, and it is with great thanksgiving that we harvest the gifts that the earth gives us each fall." He takes the time to tickle a giggle out of Little Bird and then looks at me directly, "Does that sound right or wrong to you?"

I open my mouth and then I close it, gathering my thoughts.

"We have learned," he continues, "that the words the white men say are not to be trusted, that they honor the things they own or wish to have more than harmony, and that they can be vengeful without a wrong being done to them. They have taken our land through trickery. They have brought sickness to our people that has made entire villages disappear. The desire for white man's guns and metal have made some of our people greedy; at one time there was no such thing. There are some Real People who say that the white men will destroy us, that there will be a time when The Real People are no more. Tell me, who will keep the world in balance then?" he asks me. This time it's me who purses my lips with no answer to give.

Otter encourages me to go and sit in the evenings at the council fire where much of the village gathers to talk. When I say I wish to stay behind she says, "You have earned the trust of The Real People, Bear. Learn what you are now a part of. You are no longer the captive, scurrying from one place to another hoping not to be seen or caught. You are now Bear, of The Real People of The Maple Forest."

Am I? my ever confused head says in a quiet voice that only I can hear. I smile and nod and follow along behind Raccoon, Otter and Little Bird. To look at me you would see that I travel with the women and no longer need to be shown the right and wrong ways to do things. I can laugh and visit and talk with anyone I wish. The children still seek me out because, I suspect, no matter how I dress or sound I'm still an oddity in this village with my white skin and my ability to kill bad white trapper men with flaming sticks. I sigh. In some ways I feel more lost and alone then ever now that the village has claimed me as one of their own. *Shouldn't I feel happy?* I think to myself. *Peaceful at last?* But I feel none of these things.

I think about Pa, Henry, and Eli and I look at Raccoon, Otter, and Little Bird. I still don't feel like I fit in this village and suspect I never will. But the more terrifying thought is that I don't know if I'd fit any better at my homestead anymore. I'm a white girl who has lived with the *red savages*. Even worse, I've killed a white man to protect those *red savages*. I'm for sure not the same girl I was many months ago making Pa's favorite cornbread and wiping Eli's runny nose.

The Chief in this village is called Great Elk, and I learn there are many villages throughout the land of The Real People like this one in The Maple Forest. They trade with, support, and defend each other. It's not uncommon for different villages to socialize at times and to become connected through the joining of a man and a woman.

On the nights I sit at the council fire and listen to the conversations back and forth, I study the faces that I've come to know and listen to the words I've come to understand. There's talk about weather and crops, debates about hunting and fishing techniques and stories about the antics of old and young alike. I never speak, just watch and listen. Different nights bring different people and different moods. I sit and learn about The Real People of The Maple Forest and this center of the world.

The woman I called Red Coat is really called War Woman. She's almost as silent as me at the Council Fire, but I begin to find it mighty disturbing that her favorite thing to watch each evening seems to be me. She's the head of the women in this village and has great influence even in the surrounding villages. Even though Otter continues to try to set my mind at ease, War Woman's stare still reminds me of that rattlesnake waiting for me to make a wrong move.

"Why does War Woman stare at me so much?" I grumble one night as we make our way back to our hut.

Otter looks thoughtful. "Have you spoken with her?" she finally asks.

I shake my head. Why would I think to talk to her? Getting stared at by her all the time is bad enough.

"She does not think too much of whites," Raccoon seems inclined to mention as he carries a sleeping Little Bird over to his spot in the hut.

Otter gives Raccoon a look and then turns back to me. "Perhaps you should make an effort to speak with her, Bear," she tells me and I wish I'd had the smarts to keep my mouth shut in the first place.

"The feather she wears in her hair distinguishes her as a *warrior*, victorious in battle," Raccoon makes a point to tell me. He turns to Otter and asks casual like, "How many redcoat soldiers did she kill when she was just a young girl? I think it was fifteen?"

Otter rolls her eyes at Raccoon and walks over to me and takes my hands. "You are Bear, of The Real People, of The Maple Forest," she says softly to me. "You are a part of this hearth now. This worry and uncertainty you carry with you *is all your own*. No one can help you set it aside but yourself."

Otter turns to glare at Raccoon, who is busy making himself comfortable on their pallet, working hard to look like he's already dozing off to sleep. "War Woman is wise and kind," she says. "One of the many things she does in this village is to offer support, encouragement and advice to any who seek it. *You have no reason to fear her.*"

"I think she slit the soldiers' throats as they slept," Raccoon says out loud without bothering to open his eyes. "It is a painless way to die, I am told."

I look at Otter's face by the flickering bear-fat lamp. She looks me right in the eye and says, "You need to decide who you trust, Bear. No one can do that for you but yourself."

As I do the hard work of curing a hide the next day, I hear someone say my name and turn. I try hard to keep my face casual like as I look into War Woman's stern, unsmiling eyes and say, "Welcome. Shall I find Otter for you?"

She folds herself into a sitting position and says, "I am here for you. Otter says you wish to speak with me."

I take the time to set my tools down and wash my hands in a container of water we keep for such purposes. My thoughts are whirling around in my head like a pile of angry bees. I join War Woman, keeping myself busy stirring up the cook fire and adding some sticks. "I don't know why Otter sent you to me."

War Woman just looks at me like she has done so many nights before. I puzzle over the idea that she never seems to blink.

Finally, I feel compelled to say, "You watch me nights at the council fire." When that gets me nothing, I add with a shrug, "Raccoon says you do not like whites."

"Are you white?" she asks me.

I frown at her and hold out my hand. "You can't tell?"

At last, War Woman blinks. I know because I see her do it. She says patient like to me, "We have welcomed you at the Council Fire. You speak the language of The Real People. You wear the clothes of The Real

People. You answer to a name given to you by The Real People. Maybe you need to answer that question for yourself."

I shake my head and look down at my hands now clasped tightly in my lap and feel a strong need to speak the truth, even though I suspect it will not stop her from staring at me any time soon. "I don't know what I am anymore. I will never be red. But I don't feel so white anymore."

War Woman sighs. "I watch you because I try to see how you are coping with the blood on your hands. It is not an easy thing to become accustomed to."

White hands that can never be washed clean. *Oh.* Now I see why I'm so all fire interesting to watch. Bear John. The man I've killed. I hear his screams in my head and can almost still smell the smell of him burning. My stomach roils at the memory. I close my eyes and try to take a deep breath.

"I killed six men before I turned sixteen summers," she says quietly, and I look up at her with stunned eyes, hearing all the things that Raccoon said last night again in my head. "They were white men," she says matter of fact, "soldiers who fought for the British army. Did you know that some of our people fought in your wars - The Great War with the British and others, too?"

I shake my head 'no' because I'm not so sure my voice will cooperate.

War Woman nods slightly. "We supported the people we had made treaties with, even though they did not keep all of the promises that they made. When they came and told us of this great battle that was to come and the need for our people to help, it was decided that it was the right thing to support their cause. We had given our word to support and defend the people called The British, and so we were obligated to do so. But, once again, they did not stay true to their words. Those we fought with did not treat us as equals. They did not provide us with the same food and supplies as the white soldiers were given. When the white enemies of The British attacked our villages because our braves had fought alongside The British, no one came forward to protect our women and children." She spoke quietly and with great sorrow. "Many of The Real People died in

The Great War whether they were warriors in battle or just women and children waiting home in their villages. In the end, it seemed as if we fought alongside no one, and all white men were our enemy.

"I was just a young girl traveling with the braves who fought with the British during The Great War." She shrugs. "It was not a very important job. I was to provide them with food and care for them as they needed. I thought it would be a great adventure when I was told that I could go…" She looks at me then, and I let her see in my eyes exactly what she's showing me in hers: my despair, my confusion, and my horror.

War Woman sighs a deep, weary sound and nods in understanding. "I saw when a Real People's village was attacked by the white enemy. The white soldiers we were with did nothing to defend the village and would not allow our braves to do anything that would reveal our position. Some of the soldiers even laughed as they watched women and children being killed." War Woman is quiet for long moments. "It was then that I realized that all of those men in their bright red coats with their shiny brass buttons were just as much the enemy, if not more so. So, in the night, when they all were asleep, I killed the soldier who would not defend those innocent women and children and his comrades who laughed at the slaughter." She fingers the buttons that hang around her neck, enough for six coats I now know. "I restored the harmony that had been unbalanced and was honored for my deed by being given the name War Woman."

War Woman extends both her hands out in front of her. They are red, strong, capable hands. "Even though those men deserved to die, I struggled with what I had done." She shakes her head. "In the heat of the moment, I did not take the time to think it all through, but afterwards…" A long silence stretches out between us, both of us lost in our own thoughts.

"I am not sorry for killing Bear John," I say at last. "Otter and Little Bird's lives are worth the trade." I swallow. "I have trouble with the differences it is making inside of me, though. I … do not think that I fit … home, with my Pa … anymore."

She nods, seeming to understand exactly what I'm fighting to say, and stands in one graceful, fluid movement. She surprises me when she says, "I never went back to my village after I became War Woman. My life has always pulled me forward faster than I feel ready for. Only much later in my life did I realize what was happening to me." War Woman turns and begins to stride away.

"What was it that was happening to you?" I call to her back, mighty curious to know.

Her long bound hair, filled with much gray but still some black, swings as she turns and looks at me over her shoulder. "I was becoming a wise and powerful woman instead of a girl," she says. "It is the same journey that you are on."

I make sure to tell Raccoon as soon as he returns to the hearth that night that War Woman killed *six* white soldiers, not fifteen. And he doesn't seem happy to hear that I've told War Woman what he said her thoughts about whites were. I promise Raccoon that the next time War Woman and I talk I'll make sure to find out how she killed the soldiers, and I want to know is there anything else he wishes me to ask her? He says no, that I've certainly done enough already.

Otter has spoken before about this 'powerful woman' business. I like the sound of it I must admit, for I for certain am not one. *A wise and powerful woman.* I roll the phrase around in my mouth and test it out. *Not a girl.* Now that sounds even better.

"War Woman is not the only one of power in this village. Each and every woman you see has much power about all that she does: her life, her family, the village." Otter gives Raccoon a sweet smile as we sit around our hearth eating the evening meal. "Even who she chooses to join with."

"Who you marry – *join with* - is the woman's choice?" I ask in a surprised voice.

Otter nods. "When a man joins with a woman, he goes to live with her people, he becomes part of her clan, and the children they have trace their history through their mother's people. Should they cease to live together as a couple it is the woman who keeps the children and all the possessions."

Within a Real People village, families are divided by clans, like our families at home, I imagine. There's the wolf clan, the turkey clan, the otter clan and so on. Otter says with great pride, "I am Otter, of the Wolf clan, of The Real People of The Maple Forest, and through our joining so is Raccoon, and because he is my son, so is Little Bird."

"My white name is Elle Graves," I tell her. "My Pa's name is Andrew Graves and my Ma's name was Elizabeth Graves." I explain how it's just the opposite with white names and all. I tell them a bit about Henry and Eli. Otter and I laugh about what a struggle it can be to have brothers.

But Otter saves the best part for last. Perhaps the most amazing thing is that she tells me that all this now applies to *me*. I'm Bear, of this village. *You are a woman who has great power, too,* Otters tells me.

Me? Powerful? Twice in one day two women have used that word to describe me and not meant to be funny.

I ponder this new way of thinking. It's like peering into a looking glass and learning to do things opposite. I feel like a flower bud opening up to the warm spring sunshine. The wonder of it all… All of a sudden *I* can make choices about my life instead of everyone else doing it for me? Where, who, what, how… all those questions are just up to me?!

"I can learn to ride Willow?"

"I can learn to shoot a bow and arrow?"

"I can learn to hunt?" I ask.

Each time Otter smiles and nods her head, *Yes*. "And you can choose who you wish to join with, too," she's inclined to add. Otter looks down at the basket of dried apples and pretends to look hard for the perfect one. She picks up one and makes a face and tosses it aside. She picks up another, looks closely at it, sniffs it, makes another face, and tosses it aside. She picks up a third apple, turns it all around carefully, sniffs it, smiles, and hands it to me with a nod.

But she's stunned by my next question. "Can I choose not to marry?"

"Why would you do that?" she sputters. "You, who love children more than anyone! What would you wish to do instead?"

I think about my whole life. All fifteen years, for a birthday has happened for me sometime in the late part of autumn. I think about not so much the bad parts or the good parts but about the wonderment of having the chance to make a choice. I think about my time with Pa, Henry, and Eli and my caring for them and all that I did. I can't remember a time that I was able to get out of my bed and not have a list of things that I knew had to be done, and no one to do them but me. I think about Dirty Feet and Old Woman and Bright Feather and how I came to be here. I think about my days being filled with the weight of listening and watching and learning and doing.

There has been no real time that I can remember since I was a young child that I had a choice in what I wanted to do or be. I think about this center of the world, this Maple Forest where I sit. Being able to pick and choose and do something all because that's the direction *I* choose to put my foot, now *that's* an amazing thing to ponder. How can I explain this to Otter so that she will understand? I pick my words extra careful. "I would wish to do it because I *can*. I would wish to do ... *just a little bit of everything.*"

As the fall is just beginning to fade away and winter begins to blow its cold breath, Raccoon at last finds time to teach me how to ride Willow. It's a new experience for both my horse and me. Willow is a white man's horse that is to learn to be an Indian pony. I'm a white girl who has to learn to ride like an Indian. White people's horses are taught to listen to their riders with their mouths. Indian ponies are taught to listen to their rider's knees. I think if I were a horse, I'd prefer the Indian way.

First, Raccoon teaches Willow. She's a very smart horse, I decide. She's cautious with strange men, which Raccoon certainly is. I talk to Willow and try to explain that the marks on Raccoon's face and the raccoon tail in his hair are just a special way of making him stand out like her beautiful brown tail and mane and the bright white socks on her legs. "Isn't that so?" I ask Raccoon. He gives me one of his fierce looks which I point out will only make him stranger to Willow.

"Do you have special words that you say to a horse before you ride one," I ask, "words that will help the horse understand the balance and harmony of being ridden?"

He stares at me while I stroke Willow's nose and let her taste my tunic as I wait patiently for him to answer. He finally tells me that no, there are no special words. "Is there a special ceremony that makes a white horse officially an Indian pony, then?" I ask.

He stares at me again for long moments and finally tells me no there's no special ceremony.

"I think that until Willow feels comfortable with all these changes, that you are going to have a difficult time," I feel inclined to caution Raccoon.

He tells me what a good rider and horseman he is, and that he was training horses since before I was able to stand up on my own two legs. With a sudden leap he's on Willow's bare back, and with a sudden hop and back kick Willow has him on the leaf-covered ground staring up at the almost bare trees. I look down at Raccoon and say, "I think Willow is unwilling to change her mind about things until she's shown that the new way is better." Willow and Raccoon don't want any company for a couple of weeks until they work out all their problems.

Finally, it's time for Raccoon to teach me. Raccoon mounts Willow and shows me how to talk with my legs and body so that Willow will listen. Willow is a very good listener. I ask, "What special things have you said and done so that Willow is now happy to have you as a rider? I want to make sure that I can do as good a job as you are doing."

Raccoon sighs and says, "As long as you have done the riding ceremony, any Indian horse will accept you."

"I have not done the riding ceremony," I say with a bit of worry in my voice.

He looks mighty surprised. "How can that be?" Raccoon shakes his head. "I cannot teach you to ride until you have completed the riding ceremony," he says with regret as he slips down off Willow's back. "Come," he says leading Willow by her halter and walking deeper into the woods. "First, we will do the riding ceremony. *Then*, I will teach you how to ride."

The riding ceremony takes us all afternoon. I must be silent and not say one word or Raccoon says it will not take. I must do everything he tells me to do, which means I stand silent beside my horse watching the sun move across the sky for a very, *very* long time. I can't move. I can't ask even one question. Finally, Raccoon says that we can go back to the village now that the ceremony is over.

When we get back to our hearth, Otter asks me how my first riding lesson went, and I tell her about the riding ceremony. "Bear," Otter says after she glares at her husband as he's playing with Little Bird, "there is no such thing as a riding ceremony."

Raccoon looks up at me and gives me a slow wink, although he does manage not to smile. *So that's how it will be*, I think to myself suddenly much wiser. I look at my friend Otter and say, "Actually, then, the first riding lesson has taught me much more than I ever thought it would."

My riding lessons continue, with me much the wiser. Most every day if I can find time outside my chores, Willow and I practice the new things we have been taught by Raccoon. It's as I'm riding through the woods one of these days that a thought comes into my head that stops me still. I look down at Willow and out into the woods and I think, clear as day, *twelve days - twelve days ride from home and Pa, Henry, and Eli.*

For moments I can't catch a breath. My heart pounds and I wait for someone, *anyone* from the village to come rushing toward me to grab and hold me back from leaving. Then Willow knickers and stomps her feet to ask what she should do next, and a bluejay reminds me to move on and leave him be.

Not only have I been given a name by The Real People of The Maple Forest, but I have been given a horse. *And a knife*, my head reminds me. I'm the powerful woman, Bear, who has many choices. I realize that I've everything I need to go back home - *should I choose to.*

Suddenly, everything's different.

The only thing that keeps me here is myself. I've a horse I've only just learned how to ride. I've a knife that's as much decoration as the robin's feather in my hair and, I'm forced to admit, just as dangerous since I've no skills to use it. I'd get lost. I'd be hungry. I'd be frightened all on my own. I'm as trapped as ever.

Actually, nothing's different.

I sigh. I'm stuck, I realize. I live as a member of this village but still feel separate. Otter says I'm now a powerful woman, but I still act like a confused girl. There are many wonderful choices to be made, but I stand still with the confusion of it all. *So?* my head says. *Now what will you do?*

Maybe, my head thinks, it's time you make some choices and see how it will feel. Maybe, making just one choice will help you make another.

At home, Eli and I never liked winter as much as the other seasons. I suspect Pa and Henry felt the same, having to do so many outdoor chores in the bitter cold, but I don't recall them saying. For me and Eli, it was too cold, it got dark too quick, we were stuck inside too much. We had a puzzle that Pa said was a gift to him and Ma when they were married. It was a map of countries far across the ocean. Pa called it *Europe*. Eli and I did that puzzle more times than I could count. We would hide a piece and play a game: who would be the first to figure out what piece was missing? It was always fascinating to me to watch all those little bits slowly join together. Separate, each piece was alone and seemed useless, but once the entire puzzle was joined a whole picture could be seen. The loss of one piece could ruin the whole puzzle by making the picture incomplete. Pa said a puzzle was a lot like life.

But winter in an Indian village, to me, means freedom. No garden to tend, no herbs to gather, no fish to prepare, no meat or hides to cure. There are still meals to cook and firewood to find, and a whole passel of other things to do, but there's time to ride Willow, too. I take to riding at noontime after morning chores and before the evening meal is to be prepared. I ride Willow out into the forest and gather firewood and listen to the world around me full of harmony. In the privacy of the woods, me and Willow get to know each other, and we discover that we like one another quite a bit. Once Raccoon is satisfied with my skill, sometimes I ride out with Little Bird on my back to show him the sights of the winter forest.

"You know," I say one night at the dinner fire with Otter and Raccoon, "I was thinking that if I knew how to shoot a bow and arrow when I went out riding on Willow, maybe I could do some hunting." Little Bird crawls and plays in the furs and snow falls quietly outside.

Sometimes I think Raccoon can't wait until Little Bird is Big Bird and he does not have to be alone in a hut full of powerful women. "I am not so sure I have my strength back from teaching you how to ride," Raccoon says in a tired voice. Otter told me that Raccoon said he never met a person who asked as many questions as me. But how's a body to learn something they don't already know? I'm not discouraged by Raccoon.

"Who do you think would be strong enough, then?" I ask respectfully and Otter claps her hand over her mouth so not to laugh out loud.

Raccoon is in a spot because whoever he says, he knows I'll seek out, and whoever I seek out, he knows they will know that he sent them. He thinks and thinks and then sits up straight. "Cloud!" he says with certainty. "Cloud is the one to teach you!" Otter's look is not so certain.

Cloud must be one hundred years old, I think, when I go to see him for the first time. He's the oldest person I've ever seen, let alone talked to. He has hair as white as snow, and it flows loose down his back like a frozen waterfall. He's blind and he's almost deaf and his joints ache him so that he usually stays wrapped in furs by his fire. His hands, though wrinkled with age and crippled with pain, still move and dance as he speaks for Cloud loves to talk. He seems to enjoy answering my questions that he can hear and says he would be delighted to teach me how to shoot.

Bows I learn are best made in the spring when the sap is running new and the trees are coming alive for the summer. Hickory, ash, white oak, or cedar are the best wood. I fear I'm out of luck until Cloud lends me his bow on the promise that I'll return it when I've made my own. It's beautiful and smooth and shiny in my hand and heavier than I thought it would be. Unstrung, it rises almost to my waist from the ground. I must learn how to care for the bow, for even though he's no longer able to travel and to hunt, Cloud cares for his bow each and every day. When not in use it's unstrung, the deer sinew unnotched from one end and carefully wrapped around the other. I learn that nettle woven into a strong fiber or, best of all, snapping turtle skin are used for the bowstring. He shows me how to oil and rub the bow to protect it from moisture and keep it in best working order. It's always stored and carried in its bow sack which is strapped across the back underneath a quiver of arrows. Boys, he explains, are taught to make bows from the time they are young. He looks at me with sightless eyes that twinkle just the same, "And sometimes young curious women, too, it seems." For a time, after he was no longer able to hunt, he was the one to whom everyone came to make and repair their bows if they wanted the best work possible. "But now," he says sadly holding up his hands that look like carved wooden bear claws, "these old hands can no longer even do that."

He spends a full day explaining the shape and size and texture of the branches I need to make arrows and then sends me off. There's a tree that's perfect for arrow shafts, and it's called arrowwood! Dogwood, too, is good he says. "A fine piece of wood can be straightened if necessary," he tells me but he's hopeful that I'll be able to find a collection in the woods that's workable without that extra effort. Willow and I search for three days until I've a good assortment. Cloud examines, sniffs, and even tastes each one. Of the thirty I've brought him, he rejects seven, and I add them to the fire. By the end of two weeks I've twenty-three arrows with various tips. Some are sharpened to a point, some are blunt on one end (Cloud says to shoot small birds with). Each has feathers split in half and trimmed and tied to the shaft with deer sinew. "Animal glue or spruce gum will hold the feathers on, too," he tells me, and I file it away in my head carefully. The feathers are important, I learn, because they make the arrow fly true. "A good arrow wants to do its job but does not understand that each end has a different job. Feathers at one end remind a good arrow which end does the killing and which end does the guiding."

We examine his arrows, and I learn that there are still more kinds to make and use but not for me yet. He has arrows in his quiver that are tipped with sharpened flint stone, with bone, horn, shell, and even copper. "Learn to shoot with these first," he says touching my precious collection of twenty three, "and then you can move on to these," he says motioning to his various tipped ones. To hold them, we make a quiver out of buckskin with a piece of wood inside to keep it stiff. "Some braves like to decorate these," he says in a tone that says he does not think much of the idea. "Let your shooting speak for you not the designs on your quiver." His quiver is well cared for but plain. It takes more than two weeks, but finally, I stand with one bow in its bow sack strapped to my back and twenty-three arrows – some blunt and some sharpened to a point – in my plain quiver. The bow is only borrowed, but Cloud says to call it mine for now. The bow and quiver lie across my back peeking over my left shoulder and down past my right hip.

He has who I believe to be his great, great grandson, Red Fox, show me how to hold and shoot the arrows – under his supervision. I think Red Fox must be my age or maybe a bit older. Red Fox is shy but patient with my fumbling first attempts as Cloud shouts out instructions to both of us: where to put my feet, how to hold my bow and arrow, where to look with my eyes, the angle my head should be tilted. I think Red Fox is very kind in not laughing at my shots, and I make sure that Raccoon hears of his patience. We practice two full weeks out in the cold, with Cloud wrapped in all his furs making comments, and our noses growing red, and our fingers becoming numb. I try not to get discouraged, but it seems like I'll never master all the things I need to know and still hit the target. Finally, a day comes when I'm able to hit the target not once but seven times. Cloud tells me to go into the woods away from laughing eyes and practice. My lessons seem to be done.

Riding Willow becomes a time to go off on my own, learn the forest, gather firewood, find more sticks for arrows, and practice my shooting. With no one else to give comments, except Willow who tends to keep all of her opinions to herself, I learn the feel of the bow and arrow with my fingers. Some days Red Fox offers to come along, and I find I like his company. He has good suggestions and never laughs at my shooting as I know Raccoon would. We tramp through the cold snowy wood, often on foot, for he does not have a horse as I do, and find good places where we set up targets to shoot at. He shimmies up a tree just like a squirrel to put a target up high and blushes when I tell him that he should be called Quick Squirrel instead of Red Fox. I think he's happy to help me learn to shoot better because he shares in the teaching of it.

Red Fox can shoot from a horse for he often borrows Cloud's. I'm happy to return some of the many kindnesses he has shown me and offer to let him ride Willow so that we can both practice riding and shooting. Willow is patient and willing to help out, too. Maybe she hopes Red Fox will do better at this bow and arrow business than me, which isn't saying much. Even though Red Fox does not have a horse of his own, he's a better rider than me and there's nothing for me to teach him. We have a lot of laughter running and riding around in the cold winter woods taking turns being the hunter or the hunted. We use the bird arrows that have no sharp tips, but there's no reason to worry since we never seem to hit anything anyway.

I do discover one thing right quick: learning to shoot an arrow from a *moving horse* is just like learning to shoot an arrow standing still for the very first time. There are so many things to think of; steer your horse, find your arrow, load the bow, sight your target, aim your shot … *Watch for low branches! Watch for uneven ground! Watch for rocks! Watch for streams!* It seems to me that just when I think I've got everything in order a new piece gets thrown in that I must remember. After a time, even Willow starts making snorts of disgust about my mistakes and failures. I realize that I may be able to hit a target while everything is stock still, but I don't expect much otherwise. I begin to think as the weeks go by first, that I'll never get this and second, that I'm glad Raccoon is nowhere near to see me and make fun.

Red Fox is full of good advice. "Cloud says always to remember one thing; it wasn't the loss of his sight that caused him to lose his ability to shoot his bow and arrow true. It was the loss of his feel because of his joint aches. Even sightless, he would listen and smell the wind, notch his bow and the moment a deer would start to run it would find an arrow in its throat. I saw."

He tells me wonderful stories of hunting trips he has been on. Tales of black bears larger than a man sitting on a horse, and of elk antlers too large to be carried by one person. But the story I find most interesting is of the 'lord of the forest', a large cat that hides up in trees and is bigger than a full grown man. Red Fox has traveled far into the forest surrounding the village and beyond, and I hear stories of places and adventures that fill my head with excitement.

"Are these real stories?" I finally need to ask him, and at Red Fox's hurt expression I take some time to explain the riding ceremony Raccoon made me do.

"Ahhh," he nods in understanding. He takes the time to look at me serious like for a moment and then says, "I promise, Bear, I will *always* tell you the truth. You can always count on my words."

As we stand there in the cold and the snow with our steamy breath making clouds around our faces, I make the same promise back to Red Fox. I smile at him, for it seems I've another friend to add to my list.

I tell him about my one trip helping Bright Feather and about the elk and the bear. I even tell him about my bear dream. My story is not as exciting as Red Fox's, and yet he seems happy enough to walk beside me and listen.

He tells me with sadness how there are fewer and fewer animals in the forest, and that there are some winters when The Real People of The Maple Forest are hungry. "The Real People believe that everything is equal and that all are kin to one another. No one is better than the next. No one is more important." We are sitting quiet on a hill in the forest in the shelter of a big rock overhang that protects us from the winter winds. "I am no better than the earthworm, the bear is no more important then the tiny goldfinch. Our only reason for being here is to help Mother Earth care for the rest of creation. We are all part of the Great Circle. Respect for life is so important that one would rather starve than take another life without permission, without asking the spirit of the animal for food and fur for warmth. This balance and harmony in our life has been kept for many, many years." He's quiet for a while.

"But things have been different lately. The balance and harmony in our life has been disrupted. The white men do not think as we do. The need for balance in Mother Earth is not something they seem to care about. They hunt and trap and prepare the earth for farming without a thought of others. They wish to take things from the forest for others besides themselves without respect or thoughts for those who remain. Too many animals are hunted and trapped, too much land is taken for farming, and those of us who live by these things become hungry, lose our homes, grow weak," Red Fox looks at me with eyes that seem all of a sudden older, "and frightened. The way is changing, and there is nothing The Real People can do about it."

He talks to me as if I'm not white, I realize. I wonder, *What does he see when he looks at me?* I'm wear fur - lined moccasins and pants underneath my tunic and wear my bearskin as a cape. My hair is wrapped and tucked inside my tunic and my robin's feather whips about my head in the brisk winter wind. Aside from the tips of my nose and fingers I'm toasty warm. I still have white skin. And green eyes. *Does he see all these things or just some of them?*

I think about the way of things with my life and how until just recently there was nothing I could do about it. *Is that what life is?* I think to myself. *Do we all just hang on as we drift down the river like a dry autumn leaf?* I've no answer for myself and no words to comfort Red Fox.

Raccoon tells me that he thinks my name should be Dog because once I grab onto something I won't let go like a starving dog with a juicy bone. That's because I want him to take me winter hunting with him, and he says no. Each time I ask him in another way, polite and kind, he says no. After he makes the Dog comment I tie three dog bones to his horse, but I do stop asking. He comes in holding the bones and looks at Otter and me who have innocent eyes. "Bear," he says finally to me, "would you like to come hunting with me today?" I'm ready to go before Raccoon is.

I try real hard to stay quiet on that first hunting trip with Raccoon. I ask no questions – not one; just watch and try to remember everything we see and do. Perhaps Raccoon thought I *couldn't* be quiet or *couldn't* be still. He hadn't gone with me when Bright Feather and I'd hunted so he didn't truly know. We sit in a spot for most of that winter's day, me never more thankful for my furs. I remember that summer day with Bright Feather and go through my mind about all the things that have changed since then besides the temperature. I conclude that aside from the robin's feather still stuck in my hair there's not one thing that's the same.

I think about what Otter has told me about Bright Feather (she calls him that now, too, in the private walls of the hut). He's always gone all winter. He leaves during the first sign of frost and returns at the first thaw. He hunts and traps the whole mountainside and brings back many furs that he then takes to trade. I now know that he had a mate and they had a son. Otter said that it was a time five summers ago that Hawk became known as One Who Is Always Alone. I want the missing pieces to this puzzle something fierce, I realize. But I learn right quick that Indians don't like to talk of the dead, and so since no one will speak of them, that leads me to obvious conclusions. It wouldn't be right to say that I miss Bright Feather, but I think I'd like to be able to show him how I can ride Willow now and how I can shoot my bow and arrow, and perhaps thank him proper for my bearskin.

I think all these things sitting with Raccoon that afternoon. Twice I catch him looking at me in wonder at my silence, I suspect. The second time I show my teeth and growl like a camp dog. He can't help but chuckle and shake his head at that. Finally, into the clearing comes a buck. Raccoon said later that he was very, very old, lame, half starved, and probably deaf *and* blind, but I shoot it! I'm so proud I nearly burst. Raccoon teaches me the right words to thank the spirit of the deer for the gift of his life and in the quiet of the forest I repeat them with great respect. I've learned working side-by-side from Bright Feather how to gut and skin and prepare the carcass. Raccoon and I are quickly ready to go back to the village. Raccoon has me ride right to the council circle and Great Elk's hut. I give Great Elk the buck's heart and War Woman the liver (Raccoon said such would be expected), but to Cloud I give the antlers and he whoops and laughs with pride like he'd done the kill himself. I'll make something special with the hide.

Sometimes the men allow me to come along on their short day hunting trips after that first hunting time with Raccoon. I never get to shoot much, and so I never kill anything, and I suspect that I'm only allowed because of Raccoon, but I'm happy just the same. I study how the other men hold their bows and ride their horses. If I forget myself and start asking too many questions on these trips, Raccoon tends very casual like to stuff anything he can find in his ears – leaves, sticks, even pieces of dried venison one time - to muffle the sound of my voice. It's another thing I learn: watch others to see how your acting makes them act.

On these occasional trips, one brave named Beaver is always most patient with me and takes the time to point out things in the forest that I don't notice. I learn to tell the scat from a deer from the scat from an elk from the scat from a fox. I learn the shape of footprints in the snow and what animals they go to and to watch certain kinds of rough tree bark for bits of fur. Beaver is always most serious, and even Raccoon behaves when I'm with him. Often he takes so much time to teach me what I need to know that the others we are traveling with wander off and leave us all on our own.

Beaver is older than Red Fox, not because he looks it so much, but mostly because he acts it. Always serious no matter how many summers he is, he's inside an old soul as Pa would have said. Being taught by Beaver leaves no time for teasing like with Raccoon and no time for laughter like with Red Fox. Learning with Beaver is all business, and I best pay attention to not miss a thing.

When Beaver finds out that I can't start a fire on my own, he takes the time to show me how to start one from a fire kit he carries with him *at all times.* Right there in the cold winter woods, in the shelter of a fallen tree with nothing around us but the snow and the wind and the two of us and our horses, Beaver sets out to make a fire. The others once again ride off without a backward glance, I suspect glad to be rid of the one who doesn't know enough and perhaps the one who knows too much.

I watch Beaver's face, solemn and sure, as he reaches down and clears a spot and scans the area for things he needs. His voice is deep and mellow, smooth a little like slow moving molasses. "The ceremony of life begins with the origin of the first fire," Beaver says, and I look forward to the magic he weaves with his words. He's full of stories of The Real People and is always happy to tell one. His hands, red and strong and sure, snap the kindling sticks he has found around us and make a careful pile. "In the beginning there is darkness and no fire. The Great One sent the Thunder Beings to bring life to Mother Earth. The new Earth is cold, and Sun had just started to heat the land during what we now know as day. Still, the nights are cold, as Moon's task is to protect us and to slowly start the germination of seeds for trees and plants on this new island called Mother Earth. One of the sacred trees to come to this new land is Sycamore; many others, such as Oak and Pine will come later. Some of the trees, such as Redbud and Cherry Tree, are eager to come to this new land, but they have to wait because they need much light to bloom and to create fruit for the animals.

"The Thunder Beings send their lightning to put fire at the bottom of a sycamore tree that is on a small island in the water by itself. All the animals see the smoke, but they are not sure how to bring the fire back to their tribal council. The animals meet in council and decide that all the animals that can swim or fly will go and bring the fire back to council. First to make the trip is Raven. He is a beautiful large bird with white feathers until he flies over the sycamore tree where fire and smoke rise high in the sky. Raven cannot land on the tree, and his feathers become scorched and black. He returns without the fire. The same thing happens to Owl, who gets his eyes blackened with the hot smoke as he looks into a hollow part of the tree. To this day, members of the Owl tribe have rings around their eyes, and they have trouble seeing except at night."

Beaver has made a small pile of sticks, as dry as can be found, and from his fire kit he takes out more bits of kindling and what looks like cat tail down. He stops his story and takes time to explain all this down to the placement of the sticks, the amount of kindling that is just right, and the need for there to be air space for the new fire to catch a breath. When he is certain I've all this information stored away in my very empty head, he continues with his story.

"It is decided that the Snake tribe would swim to the island. First is little Racer Snake who got close to the burning fire. He is blinded by the hot ashes, and his body is scorched black. Ever since, the racer snake darts back and forth as if trying to get away from the fires. The same thing happens to Blacksnake.

"Finally, little Water Spider says that she will quickly move across the water and weave a bowl to carry a hot coal on her back. The council agrees. Thus, Water Spider brought the fire to the First Council on Mother Earth, and she is always honored in ceremonies that recall that first fire. Fire is held sacred by The Real People, and it is always in the center of the Sacred Circle in ceremonies."

He takes his fire rocks and strikes once, twice, and sparks fly. Leaning over he blows carefully into the small, smoking bits, and like magic small orange flames spring to life. Carefully, slowly, he feeds in more bits of his precious kindling, explaining all the time exactly what he's doing. Finally, the fire is dancing brightly before us, and I put out my hands to enjoy the warmth. He makes it all look easy, but I make sure to be on my own the first time I try to do this and be sure Raccoon isn't around to watch. It's another thing I must practice *on my own away from laughing eyes.*

Beaver looks at me with his stern face and says, "Fire is the reminder that we must always go back to the center and celebrate life as our main focus in our thoughts and actions. *Fire is life.*"

"Can a person loose her center?" I ask watching the firelight cast dancing light across Beaver's face.

He nods his head. "Yes, that happens when there is nothing in your center strong enough to draw you back."

"What if it is not so much that there is nothing in your center but *too much?*" I think about my red and white self dancing and crowding each other in my center making it impossible for me to be still and peaceful.

Beaver takes out a piece of dried venison from his pack and hands me a piece. I take out a dried corn cake and share a bit with him. We munch in silence. "You struggle with the two worlds you have walked in," he says after a time. "It is a struggle that The Real People have been fighting for many more years than you have."

"How is that so?!" I ask with surprise.

He shrugs, and his long black hair slips forward and shadows part of his face. "The Real People struggle with the life that the white man wishes us to lead. In many ways, just as *you* have been forced to lead the life of *the savage Indian,*" and I wince as the words sound foul and wrong coming from his mouth, "we, for many, many years have been forced to change to the life of the white man. No more hunting, learn to be farmers and raise cows and chickens. No more migrating to suit the seasons and the land, learn to set down roots in one spot, and never move like an old oak tree. No more honor and trust, instead sign papers and take *things* to prove a trade. Learn to want instead of give and learn to force instead of allow."

His serious face is full of sorrow as he looks at me across the crackling fire. "You say, 'yes' and you say, 'no'. You must decide who you wish to trust, and honor, and ... love ... most of all and put them in the center of your life. Then you must be forceful with what you allow in and what you keep out. Maintaining your center is a job that only you can do, Bear. For it is *your center,* and no one else's."

"So I must decide if I have a white center or if I have a red center," I say with a voice filled with defeat, for I'm right back where I have always been.

"No," Beaver says, "that is not what I have said. "I do not believe that you, Bear, can ever be only white or red. Why should that be? What I *said* was you have to decide who you will trust, and honor, and love." He begins the process of putting out the fire, pushing snow across the embers, and I listen to the hiss and steam of it all. "If you choose the right things from both parts of your life, then you will have the best and brightest center of us all."

"The best of my red and white self ..." I say quietly and I get goose skin up my arms.

It's late winter and I've traveled with the men quite a few times when a herd of winter elk is spotted not more than a half-day's distance from the village. It's hoped that two or three animals may be brought down, and I'm invited to go! It's the largest hunting party I've ever been with - eight braves and me. Red Fox is along, too, riding on Cloud's horse. I think he's as excited as me, but he tries very hard not to let it show. So do I. I'm excited because maybe, *just maybe*, I'll be able to do some real hunting.

I think that I see some signs that spring will be coming soon. My favorite places show very small signs that the earth may be waking up from its long winter's sleep. Following behind the men on this day, I see bare patches of ground where snow has been. The brown, bare trees look like they are ready to pop with color. I see some robins hunting like we are. Everywhere I look, squirrels are chasing each other across the forest floor and up the tallest trees.

At the top of a ridge we spot the herd of maybe fifty animals. The men discuss the wind and the land and who goes where and who does what. I'm paired with Raccoon, a curse he regularly bears with silence. As we head toward the spot we are to take charge of he says casual like over his shoulder, "How's your shooting coming along on a moving horse?" I realize that he has seen my practicing with Willow. I'm embarrassed and a little mad.

"Better than my hearing is for strange people in the woods," I say with what Pa would have called a smart lip.

He laughs out loud. He doesn't turn around so I can't see, but I hear a smile in his voice. "You learn quick, Dog," he says. Sometimes he calls me that when he's trying to be funny, although I never laugh as I feel it's best not to encourage him.

"Woof," I say.

I've never hunted in a large group like this. Raccoon for once must do more talking than me to explain how things must be done. Some of the men travel all the way down to the farthest part of the herd. The rest of us are in spots along the way where we know the herd will run once they are startled. Each of us, hidden along the way, will have a few brief moments to shoot at the passing herd as it runs terrified past us trying to escape.

"So," says Raccoon, "you let off your first arrows seated still on your horse as the herd comes towards you. Once the herd gets alongside you, you begin to ride and shoot more as it passes. If you see a wounded one, try to kill it with your knife - if you can get close enough." He grins at me. "So you can have practice with being still and moving. Maybe there will be a very, very old, lame, deaf, blind *elk* you can kill this time." For once I choose just to be quiet and say not a word.

We wait. I practice over in my head all the things I need to remember when I'm moving, the horse is moving and my prey is moving. I think of the times that I've practiced on my own and with Red Fox. Of course Raccoon has added a new piece I've now got to consider, the jumping off your horse and using your knife part. Will there ever be a time when I've got all the pieces in one place, I wonder?

We hear the whoops and shouts and the pounding elk's hooves before we see anything. But what a sight when it all comes into view! The largest animals can easy look me square in the eye, and the bucks with their antlers are taller than Willow. I see Beaver and Red Fox whooping and shouting and following behind the herd. I realize it's hard to keep yourself still, let alone your horse, when you see a sight like that pounding toward you stampeding wild with fear. I fix my sights on the biggest, tallest animal, because my thinking is it's the easiest to hit. I see it's eyes wild with fear, and I let one arrow fly and am pleased that I've time to let a second arrow fly before it's time for me to start practicing my shooting while on a moving horse. I don't know where Raccoon or any of the other men are, but I can hear shouts and whoops as Willow and I take off at a run towards the edge of the herd. I load my arrow and take aim, watching the trees and watching the ground and watching the herd. I pick the closest animal and let an arrow fly. My arrow goes wild as Willow jumps over a fallen tree trunk. I load another arrow and aim at another animal. I shoot and am amazed to watch the creature stumble and fall to the ground my arrow piercing the lower side of its stomach. It's a young male with small antler stubs just peeking through his skull. His eyes are wild as he jumps and bucks and tries to rise and run away from me. Willow is trained well and stands still behind me where I get off, and I find myself talking softly to the animal that's dying right in front of me. I know the terror it's feeling, and I pull out my knife and cut it's throat so it will stop its struggling and escape from its fear. I say the words of thanks I know are right to say that Red Fox has told me, and whisper with great respect, "Thank you, spirit of this elk, for the food and hide you will provide us." Then I stand and look. The herd is no longer to be seen, but there's still a distant rumble like thunder as they continue to stampede away.

I'm standing proudly by my buck with my knife still in my hand and Willow munching grass behind me as Raccoon rides his horse over to me. I grin a huge grin, "WOOF!" I say, "He does not look very, very old, or lame, or deaf or blind. And we were both *moving*," I feel that that's important to add.

Raccoon dismounts and looks very intently at the buck. He examines where my arrow hit and how I cut the animal's throat and then looks at me and says very serious like, "But he looks very, very dumb I am thinking."

All in all we take down five elk. Beaver and Red Fox have taken down a large buck whose antlers alone I can't lift! We take the major portions of meat and leave the carcass for the wolves and other scavengers. On the way back, we see Bright Feather coming through the trees. Just as Otter has said, he returns with the first thaw. Greetings are exchanged and information is shared. I can see from the back of the group where I'm mounted, that not only does he have his own horse but a pack horse as well, loaded high with beautiful pelts. I see fox, beaver, and otter. I never knew that brown can be such a rich and glorious color. All the pelts glint in the fading sunlight. I know that winter trapping rarely gets you more than the meat you need to eat, the furs are the treasure you hope for.

Bright Feather asks polite questions about the success of the hunt. It's Raccoon who seems happy to point out that one of the five elk was brought down by *Bear*. I watch Bright Feather's face and enjoy seeing him look through the group of nine before his eyes settle on me. I sit straight and tall on Willow, who moves not a muscle just like I've taught her. I think how I must look to all of them with my white skin and red cheeks, my bear cape and bow and arrows peeking over my shoulder. Bright Feather does not speak to me but looks at Raccoon and says, "Can she understand our spoken word yet?"

Raccoon has his back to me, and I can just imagine the face he must make to this question, and all of a sudden I'm not happy about being talked about like I'm a deaf and dumb piece of rock. "Welcome back, One Who Is Always Alone. It would seem that your trapping has been successful this winter," I say loud and clear in the silence of the forest.

He turns to me and studies my face for a long time, it feels. "So it has been, Bear," he says.

We return together as a group to the village in high spirits. I try not to gloat too much over my elk and speak only when spoken to. Otter has saved us all portions from the evening meal and Bright Feather, Otter, and Raccoon talk about the success of the hunt and his winter trapping. Bright Feather talks of his travels, and reports on animal as well as people movement he has seen or not seen. There's a discussion as to when he will travel to trade his furs and what the village can use in the way of supplies, but I fall into an exhausted sleep on my pallet to the murmur of voices still speaking over the nearby fire and don't hear the answers.

I dream of my bear again, but this time I'm home with Pa, Henry, and Eli. I'm busy in the barn milking our cow, Two-Bit, and my bear peeks in to wave at me.

"Come inside, to the warmth of the barn," I say all friendly like.

But he shakes his head sadly and will not come in.

"Why not? Two-Bit will not mind."

"I cannot," he says, "for I am not dressed proper."

"What?!" I say with a laugh. "You look just fine with your thick, dark coat and shiny black eyes. You look more smartly dressed than I do for this weather." I look down at myself and stick my foot out to prove a point. Underneath my skirt and all my petticoats are my fur lined leggings and moccasins.

"That's what I came to tell you," he says, just as sad. "You should not be in here either. Your Pa just came and told me that you have got to go, too."

In the morning, I prepare breakfast for Bright Feather like I've always done although now the silence between us is strange, I think. I'm shy now with my talking, worried that Raccoon has told Bright Feather all of my bad points. He has teased me that while *he* thinks I'd better be named Dog, there are many in the village who think an even better name for me would be Never Stops Asking Questions. So I work hard to stay quiet.

It's Bright Feather who makes the first effort to speak as I prepare his breakfast over the fire. "What is your horse like?" he finally asks.

And so I tell him how I call her Willow because of the way her mane and tail look like the willow branches to me. I tell him how smart she is and how Raccoon helped me train her and what a good Indian pony she is now. I tell him she's fast and obedient. I tell him she's gentle but brave.

He asks if I've trained her to sounds, and I don't know what he means and say so. He explains, "You can teach a horse to listen to special sounds that come just from you like a whistle or a hoot that works in a time when your knees are not close enough to talk," he explains.

Questions boil up in my head. *Oh no*, I think. "Has Raccoon told you that I ask more questions than any person he knows, and that I make him more tired with my talking than a full day's ride does?" I ask Bright Feather.

He stares at me for a moment or two and then finally nods his head. "Yes."

I look at him right in the eye and say, "I don't want to tire you out either," and go back to fixing the food.

He chews on his stew, thinking about what I've just told him. I feel him watching me closely, and I hope he realizes I've given him an honest warning from a powerful woman. "Ask your questions," he finally says. "I will go away when I get tired."

So I do. I take a deep breath, and out they pour: "Is it difficult to train a horse to sounds? How long does it take? Are there special sounds or can they be any old sounds? Are some sounds easier to teach than others? Can all horses learn or only extra smart ones? What kind of things can you train your horse to do?" I pause to take a breath and he has stopped chewing to sit and stare and listen. He blinks but says nothing, so I add in a rush, fearful that he's already tired and planning on going away, "Could you help me see if we could train Willow? And, if yes, how soon can we start?"

Bright Feather finishes the last bite of stew, sets his bowl down and rubs the side of his smooth, brown cheek. I wait, certain he's going to stand up and run to his horse to get away. I should have only asked one question, I think. Or maybe two.

He takes a deep breath and begins to tell me how he trained his horse and says, if my horse is as smart as I say, that he can certainly teach me how to train Willow. He answers each and every question, patient and slow, and then promises to help me during the time I tell him I usually practice riding and shooting. I rush off to get my chores done.

Otter teases me as I hurry through my chores to get them finished. "Are you off to play with Red Fox in the wood," she grins at me over her shoulder as she wrestles with Little Bird, trying dress him in some warm furs, "or has Beaver thought of something new he needs to teach you besides hunting tips and starting fires?"

I shake my head. "I am going to teach Willow some new things, and Bright Feather said he would help me."

She stops and turns to stare at me. "One Who Is Always Alone wishes to help you train Willow?" she asks her voice filled with surprise.

I nod. "Even though he says Raccoon warned him about how tired I can make a person, he still says he will help me." I feel compelled to add, "He said that when he gets tired he will just go away again."

"Is that so," she says in a very thoughtful tone. She studies me as I bustle around, frowning in thought. "Did you ask him to help you?"

I stop and look at her and nod. "He asked me about Willow when I brought him his breakfast this morning, and we got to talking."

"*You 'got to talking'?*" she asks me now with more wonder than surprise.

"Yes," I say slow like for she seems to have trouble understanding my talking today. "It is the first time we have really spoken; when he was here last I was as talkative as a stone. At first I was a bit shy, but you should make sure that Raccoon knows that *Bright Feather asked me the first question.*"

"He asked the first question...," she repeats to me still sitting, looking at me while Little Bird has managed to escape her and is now digging through one of our storage baskets with great delight.

"Are you all right, my friend?" I feel compelled to ask.

She suddenly notices Little Bird and snatches him back to finish the job of dressing him. "Yes, I am fine," she says. After a moment or two, Otter says, "Training a horse to sound is not as easy as you think. Bright Feather's horse is the only one in the village that I know of that has learned the skill. It takes a lot of patience ... and time to succeed."

"Willow is as smart as Bright Feather's horse," I say with certainty.

Otter nods her head. "No doubt," she says.

Later that day, Bright Feather and I ride out to a spot not too far from the village. I tell Bright Feather about how I've learned and practiced all winter to be able to ride and shoot. I tell him all about learning about the forest and describe to him some of my favorite places that I'm sure he knows about already. He nods his head a lot. I do most of the talking. "Am I making you tired?" I finally ask him.

He's ahead of me on the trail. He shakes his head "no." "Not yet," he says. I'm relieved.

Bright Feather calls his horse Companion. At first I think it's a mighty odd name for a horse. But then I think, for a man who is on his own all the time, it makes perfect sense.

We come to a clearing we both know of and dismount. Bright Feather says to me, "Otter says you have a name that you call me. I would like to know it."

I swallow. Names are special things, much more so than white man's names like Henry, Eli, or Elle. I was told in no uncertain terms that I was *never* to call Old Woman "Old Woman" to her face. Her name is One Who Knows, and she holds a position in the village of great honor, almost as great as War Woman. She's the village healer and wise in the way of sickness, births, and wounds. Otter speaks of her with great respect and even some fear, I think. "She can explain your dreams, and sometimes she knows the future. When you have a question or a concern, she's the one to seek out," Otter tells me with great seriousness. Nor am I to call Dirty Feet "Dirty Feet", for his name is Weasel. I commented to Otter that I didn't think that 'Weasel' was much better than 'Dirty Feet', but Otter didn't laugh. In fact, the subject of Weasel seems to make her uncomfortable, and it's soon changed. When I try to ask more questions, she ends up silent, just looking at me. Her silence speaks of death, I think. At last I say to Bright Feather as he stands silent and patient in the winter woods, "I call you Bright Feather because of the feathers in your hair," and watch his face real close to see if I see anything at all.

"Do you know the birds they are from?" he asks me after a brief moment.

"Yes," I say. "Red for cardinal, yellow for goldfinch, blue for bluejay."

He nods his head and scratches Companion's ear. I'm correct. "The cardinal," he begins to explain as he looks into the forest, "is a beautiful but hearty bird that stays put even during the harshest weather of the winter and survives. The bluejay is distant and unfriendly to strangers of all kinds and often to its own breed as well. The goldfinch is hard to see even in the best of seasons. You can search all summer and hardly catch a glimpse of him." He looks at me then and I think, *All of those birds are a little bit like you.*

He hesitates a moment and then says, "I had a name for you, too, but it does not fit anymore."

I'm powerful curious. "What name was that?" I ask.

"Mouse," he says, "for the way you scuttled around all the time doing your chores, trying not to be noticed and moving so quick you did not notice much yourself."

I think for a moment, and I remember my early time in the village with One Who Knows and Bright Feather. I think about how all I wanted to do was get my chores done, get back in the hut to safety and stay small. I was just like a mouse.

"Raccoon sometimes calls me 'Dog' and people in the village say that I could also have the name 'Never Stops Asking Questions'."

"Names are windows to the heart, Bear. What people call you are what they see and think of you. A wise person watches and listens and learns more about himself through watching how others behave when they are with him." He turns and strokes Companion's neck. "That way, if a person feels inclined to change, he knows where to start." He shrugs and says, "You may call me Bright Feather if you wish."

I think about the window of my heart that I show people. I can be a bear, a mouse, a dog, and always asking more questions than most people want to hear. Even my window shows how mixed up inside I still am, I realize.

"It is a good thing that you became Bear," he says quietly interrupting my thoughts. "Now why don't you show me how smart this horse of yours is?"

Companion comes when Bright Feather whistles, trotting right up to Bright Feather's outstretched hand. He stops when Bright Feather clicks his tongue and does about five other things just by sounds alone. "Can you whistle?" Bright Feather asks me. I nod my head "yes." He motions towards Companion. *Try and call him.*

I whistle and whistle. Companion never even raises his head from cropping the grass he's eating. *"That's* the hard part," he says to me finally.

I decide that the first sound I want Willow to learn is to come when I call. Bright Feather stands with Willow at one side of the clearing, and I hold in my hand some sweet clover that Willow loves. I whistle and she keeps eating the grass right in front of her. I take two steps closer and whistle again. This time she looks up but still does not move. I take two steps closer and whistle again. Two more. Finally I'm close enough that when she lifts her head when I whistle if she stretches her neck as far as she can she can just grab the clover with her lips. Who would say she's not smart? This is going to take a long time I think.

We practice until it's close to dark and until Willow couldn't care less what I feed her because her belly is full. "Show me how you shoot," Bright Feather says to me when it's clear that Willow's lesson is over for the day.

I take out my bow and arrows and quiver, and I tell him all about Cloud and Red Fox and my practicing when I *thought* I was on my own. He listens as I talk about Red Fox and how helpful he has been teaching and helping me learn to shoot even better and better. He nods when I speak of Raccoon and how I pestered him to take me hunting. Bright Feather grunts when I get to the part about the very old, very lame, deaf and blind first deer I killed. I explain all I know about tracking an animal from what Beaver has taught me, and I'm proud to be able to tell Bright Feather that I can start a fire on my own from my fire kit.

He examines every arrow and my quiver. I tell him how my bow is really Cloud's but he said I can call it mine until I make my own. "This is good work," he finally says, looking at my arrows and quiver closely. I show him how I shoot. He watches and tells me to change my footing just a little and lift my elbow just a bit higher. He watches me until I've emptied my entire quiver. As I go to retrieve my arrows he says, "Keep practicing." I guess he's more impressed with my arrows than my shooting which I must admit is not a surprise.

As we ride back to the village I ask him about his traps and the woods farther from here than I've ever been. He tells me just a little bit about his travels, and says traps are easier to explain when they are in front of you to see.

As we get to the village and dismount and are walking our horses, I say, "Do you ever go into Virginia?" That's all I ask, but we both know that there's a lot more hanging in the air. He stops, so I stop and he looks down at me.

"No, I always go west, Bear. I never cross over the mountains unless it is to trade, and then there is only one place I know that is safe to go to," he says. He looks around at the village with all the activity around us. "No one in this village ever goes east."

"Except Weasel," I can't keep myself from saying it, and get quiet. I've talked very little with Otter about Dirty Feet, who is called Weasel, and that time almost a full year ago. Mostly it's because she seems to not want to speak of it, but also because it's still a part of me that causes the most pain and sorrow. Why all of a sudden do I feel comfortable bringing this up to Bright Feather?

Because he carries a sadness and a loss around him just like you, my head says as soon as I ask the question. Because there's no one in the village that seems as lost and as confused as you but him.

"I think I will say that I am tired now, Bear," he says quietly, but he stops and waits, and I must tilt my head up to look at him. It's very small, but I think I see a sadness in his face he works hard to push back inside. "But that doesn't mean you can not ask me that question again another time. When Willow learns to come when you whistle, let me know, and we will work on a new sound." With that, he and Companion begin to walk away. I think of something and call to Bright Feather. He stops and turns and waits for me and Willow to catch up with him.

"I never thanked you proper for the bear skin," I say, looking back at it thrown across Willow's back. "I could not have done half of the things this winter had I not had it to keep out the cold."

Nodding, he says, "That makes me happy to hear," and turns and walks away toward his hut.

Otter says that spring is well and truly here, and much to her delight it seems that there are some with mating on their minds. Raccoon, working on a new set of arrows, says, "Good thing you are becoming such a wise and powerful woman, Bear. It seems as if you will have to do some choosing soon." He looks like a camp dog that has stolen a choice piece of meat from the fire.

I've learned always to take what Raccoon says with a great bit of care. I look to Otter and her grinning face and ask, "What do you know that I do not?" Raccoon snorts and shakes his head.

"Red Fox came looking for you a while back," Otter grins at me. "Says he wishes to have a word with you."

"Or perhaps an entire, *long* conversation somewhere *far away* out in the forest where it will be *just the two of you alone*," Raccoon says without looking up because he's busy tying feathers carefully on the end of his arrow shafts.

"It seems that Red Fox enjoys your company very much, Bear," Otter says carefully. "More than any other young woman in this village."

Otter seems to think that Red Fox has begun to think of me in ways other than *I* thought possible. Raccoon seems to think that this is just what he needs as a new and interesting way to tease me. I sigh and think, *Just what I need: more confusing thoughts to muddle up my head.*

With Red Fox, we have spent enough time hunting with each other that an easy friendship has happened. I enjoy our times together and have greatly improved my shooting, too. The fact that I have Willow to share makes me feel that for once I can give back some of the kindnesses someone else has given me. When I'm in the woods hunting and shooting and laughing with Red Fox, it seems to be the only time I'm peaceful with myself and who I've become so far. We joke and talk and share and things are just *easy*.

But I tell Otter she has ruined all that for me now that she has pointed out how Red Fox seems *always* to be around, even when we are not hunting together. Raccoon suspects Red Fox never sleeps. Since he spends all of the daylight time following me around, he must be doing all of his chores throughout the night. It's like finding out that the horse you have been riding for many weeks is really a bird; once someone points it out to you, you can't miss it, but until then you were just busy enjoying the ride. Red Fox is there when I'm gathering firewood, he's there when I'm working on the early chores of the garden, he's there, just by accident, when I'm going out to ride or practice shooting whether I go right after my chores are done or just before the evening meal is set to be eaten. I think, *What do you do with your day Red Fox, except keep track of me and where I am?*

That same evening, just after I realize the truth of Otter's words about Red Fox, as Raccoon and Otter and Little Bird and I sit and enjoy each other's company by the fire finishing our meal, who should join us but Beaver. He sits down at the fire and talks and visits with us like he has done this every evening since I've been in this village. He talks about the weather and asks how my shooting is going. He and Raccoon discuss the techniques of fire starting, and I'm glad that that's something I've finally mastered. He talks with Raccoon about different concerns regarding boundaries being violated by white settlers to the east. He talks and plays with Little Bird. Otter looks like she's fair ready to burst making the effort to behave like everything is just like it always is. Her look to me says, *Spring is well and truly here now, Bear.*

Raccoon seems just delighted with Beaver's visit and invites him to come and share our hearth with us whenever we are not at the council fire. His eyes twinkle with positive joy as he finds it important to mention all the times that I've gone hunting with Red Fox over the winter, causing Beaver to offer to take me out and give me lessons on how to shoot while riding Willow. Raccoon then finds it important to mention to me how much better Beaver would be at teaching me to hunt from horseback *since Beaver owns a horse* while Red Fox does not. Raccoon grins at me across the fire while I glare at him to make him shut his mouth.

Raccoon mentions what an important skill knife fighting is, and Otter smiles and points out what a quick learner I am. Beaver wants to know if I've learned to handle my knife for anything other than gutting a deer or skinning an elk? When I say no, I've not, he says he will teach me that, too, and he offers to take me out tomorrow to begin the lessons.

"That sounds like a good idea, does it not, Bear?" Otter says with delight.

"Yes," I say looking right at Raccoon. "I would very much like to become deadly with a knife."

As we sit around the fire that night, I answer the questions and talk polite like but I'm thinking how I can make Raccoon as powerful uncomfortable as I am at this moment and enjoy it just as much as he seems to? I think of stinger ants and scratch ivy and places I can put them. Raccoon says he thinks that Red Fox and I are planning to go hunting tomorrow, and perhaps Beaver can go along and give us both tips on hunting and such. Perhaps Red Fox needs some tips on knife throwing, too? Beaver says he thinks that would be a fine idea. I decide where I'll put the scratch ivy.

So my knife lessons begin with Beaver. It's like a deadly dance, I think, slipping and sliding, whirling and turning. It may be hard to understand, but Beaver is beautiful to watch as he works to show me what to do. Always serious, he teaches me how to stand, how to move and how to hold and throw my knife. If I want to be good at this, he says the knife must be as comfortable at the end of my arm as my hand is. That's mighty comfortable. Many times we practice, sometimes just us two and sometimes with Red Fox. Occasionally, even Raccoon makes an appearance and feels compelled to add a comment or two. I suspect he just wants to see how springtime is coming along.

As the last few signs of winter slip away and spring wins the final battle, I'm one busy powerful woman between my knife practicing with Beaver, my bow and arrow practicing with Red Fox, and my horse training on my own with Willow. Of them all, I enjoy the quiet time with Willow most, although in order for it to be truly *private and alone* I often have to sneak out of the village without Red Fox seeing me.

One day as Willow and I are walking back from a quiet time in the woods, I think how deadly I'm becoming thanks to the attentions of all these kind men. I think about all the things that have kept me here in this Indian village and all the changes in me. I have a horse for the twelve days ride, I can shoot a bow and arrow so I can hunt, I can start a fire from nothing, and now, should you rile me enough, I can stick a knife in your throat from at least fifteen paces. *Sometimes.* When the wind is right. When you're standing stock still. When my hand is steady and I'm not shaking with fright.

I ponder this change in me. Over the course of one years' time, I for certain don't feel like a terrified young girl anymore. *At least on the outside*, my annoying head seems inclined to whisper. *Inside, you still seem mighty cowardly to anyone who'd care to take a second glance.* I sigh for it's true. I'm still afraid, still too uncertain to choose what I'm going to allow in my center of who I really am.

Am I Bear? Am I Elle? How white am I still? How red have I become?

I think about Pa, Henry and Eli and how much I still miss them. I open up my Hope Chest and let the thoughts swirl around me like a wind storm. The feel of Eli's arms as he hugs me around the waist, the sound of Henry's laughter over the silliness of life, the look of Pa's sad but loving eyes as he stares at me in the kitchen doing chores.

But then I add to those memories the joy of having a real, true friend such as Otter, the delight of Little Bird crawling into my furs with me in the morning and the teasing fun of living with a man such as Raccoon. I think of Cloud's whoop of pride when I brought him the elk antler's and War Woman telling me about being on the path to becoming a wise and powerful woman. I can't forget the blushing grins on Red Fox's face when we race through the forest playing hunter and hunted, the strong emotions Beaver shows when he speaks about The Real People of The Maple Forest, or even the quiet loneliness that Bright Feather has in his walk through life.

Swirling into the mix comes my joy of learning to ride Willow, the satisfaction of learning to shoot and hunt, the triumph of going from a scared, lonely, captive white girl to this … person I now am.

I stand in the cool spring shower, for it has begun to rain as I'm making my way back to the village with Willow and an armload of firewood. Cold wet raindrops fall down on me from the sky and from the brand new leaves just opening up on the trees. Like a whirlwind, my thoughts swirl round and round me and suddenly – just like that! - I know what is in my center.

"I have been thinking the wrong way all along," I say in wonder out loud to myself, Willow, and the raindrops. In being Elle and in being Bear, I realize, I've not been *two people*. I've been *one changing one*. Elle Graves was a white fourteen year old girl. But Bear is not, and never will, be a red savage; she's a mix of all I *was* and all I'm *becoming*. And even though looks may be confusing, I'm still the same person deep down inside.

What did War Woman say? Life has always pulled me forward faster than I felt ready for.

And then I know. I can't ever, ever go back. Life won't let me. It'd be like trying to put a small sapling tree back into the seed pod it started out from. "Bear," I shout out loud to myself and the woods, "is Elle Graves made into a wise and powerful woman!"

For the truth is, I'd miss someone else far more than Pa or Otter or even Willow were I to loose it.

I'd miss the person I've become.

I'd miss, Bear, of The Real People of The Maple Forest.

I sigh.

I smile.

Welcome to the center of my world.

Powerful Woman

My name is Bear. I've a beautiful brown horse named Willow. I sleep in the hut of Otter and her husband, Raccoon, and their son, Little Bird. I'm happy here in this Indian village even though to look at me you would see that I've white skin. If I've a chance to go back to my old home in Virginia, it would be just to say, "Hello" and see how Pa, Henry, and Eli are and give them a hug and kiss, for I still miss them fiercely. And maybe to take a remembry back with me from Ma's Hope Chest. But this place in The Maple Forest is where I call home now.

It's very early spring and those who knew me when I lived my life with Pa, Henry and Eli would scarce recognize me. Even I can hardly keep up with all the changes sometimes, but that's the way of life I'm told. A body might even have trouble seeing me were they to come across me in the forest. My long brown hair is tied back with leather strips and has my brown robin's feather tied to the side. I wear a heavy black bear skin as a cloak and long fur lined leggings and fur lined moccasin boots under my tunic. They are the warmest things I've ever had in my life. Around my waist I wear a knife that's from a white man I killed named Bear John. On my back are my bow and arrows I've made myself. Sitting positively still on Willow in the forest that's just waking up from its winter sleep, where the only color but brown is the occasional evergreen tree, do you think you could find me? *I don't think so.*

But as the business of spring begins for certain, days spent on my own with just Willow for company fade into my memory. Practicing my skills of riding, shooting, and knife throwing must now take second place to more important chores. The earth is waking up from its winter sleep, and the job of preparing the village garden is the job of every woman and child in the village. It's a group effort filled with laughter and sharing and a powerful dose of hard work.

At the council fire on the night of the new moon, we celebrate the ceremony of life. It's a time when The Real People try to make a fresh start, setting things right that may be wrong, and celebrate friendships and life itself. I've sat through this ceremony quite a number of times now, but with my new peacefulness over who I am and what I'm doing and where I'm planning to be, I let it's meaning seep into my bones and it makes my toes curl. *I'm a part of all this now*, my head thinks, *this is where life has pulled me.*

If we are not at the council fire, in keeping up with these rules of spring that Otter and Raccoon find so amusing, Beaver joins us at our hearth after meals almost every night. Raccoon teases me and says that it's the only time Red Fox is not busy watching me, when he's busy eating his evening meal.

Beaver is more serious and adult than Red Fox. I can't imagine running around in the woods laughing and taking turns being hunter and hunted. I don't know how old Beaver is; his ways make him seem old, but I think he's younger than he behaves. Sometimes he tells us stories that I'm sure Otter and Raccoon have heard many times, but for me they are new and exciting. His love of his people and their way of life is a powerful draw for me, and I find I enjoy Beaver's company quite a lot.

On the evening after the new moon Beaver says to all of us around the hearth fire, but I suppose to me in particular, "When we share warmth and energy with others, we establish and maintain the right relationships in the Great Circle of Life." He looks at only me and says, "That is why I have begun these visits to this hearth. I enjoy sharing this time with all of you and *establishing* and *maintaining* these *new* relationships."

After Beaver leaves, I put my head in my hands and moan. Otter is like a proud mother, though she's barely much older than me, and says I should be pleased, because both Red Fox and Beaver are from good families and are well respected in the village. Otter says that I should make sure to look real close at these apples before I toss them away because maybe the basket is not as full as I think. For the first time ever, I think I know how Raccoon feels and want to stuff something in my own ears.

"Why must I even be considering these things?" I ask Otter in frustration, hands on my hips. "What's the rush? Did you not tell me that it's the woman who makes the choice?"

Raccoon must add his words. "A woman pursued by a man has some space to make choices. A *man* pursued by a *woman* has no hope at all." He shakes his head in mock defeat. "Just ask any one of us."

Otter laughs at Raccoon, but then frowns at my mood. "But Bear, is it not good to know who you have to choose from? Red Fox has never shown an interest in any young woman in the village until you. Do you realize how special that makes you? And no one is more serious than Beaver in regard to what is right and best for The Real People. It is *such an honor* that he would choose to let you know that he is interested in you as well. Why don't you spend some *more* time with them and get to know them a bit *better,"* she says with a twinkle in her eye.

I look blank at her for a moment because she's giving me that look that says whatever she's saying is meaning something else. Then it dawns on me, and I blush as red as a dangerous red summer sun. Otter's words make Raccoon laugh out loud as he sets down the knife he's sharpening and watches me close for my answer. "*No,*" I say firmly to both of them, "my choice is *no.*"

I've done all my chores including helping prepare the garden for planting. I've gathered wood. I've done all the things needed to make dinner. I've fetched water. I've finished sewing a new tunic I've made for myself from the skin of a deer I've killed. I've worked on Bright Feather's pelts from his winter's trapping. Then I see Red Fox heading purposely towards our hut. Suddenly, I'm so tired! "I am going to ride Willow, I have not had a chance in two days," I say to Otter and jump on Willow's back and off we ride before she has a chance to say anything. I escape to my quiet place high up on the hill.

Already I'm tired of this mating business, and Otter tells me it has only just begun. Maybe there are not so many choices here as I think. Maybe when you scratch down past the surface of things, there really is no difference at all. If that's true it would make me mighty sad I realize. I think and think and think. There's no woman in the village who is not with a man, unless she's old and done with that. There's no woman who has an interest in traveling with the hunting parties. (I go only sometimes, but I think that it's just so they have someone to put up with their teasing.) I'm a good cook and quite like all the chores that are part of a woman's life in the village. Some of my best times in the village, besides being with Willow and learning how to shoot and hunt, have been with the children and the women. I ask myself real serious like, "What do you really want?"

My head flashes a million different pictures. I think about becoming a wiser and more powerful woman. I like that the women speak up just as much as the men at the council circle. What would that be like, I wonder, to have wise enough words that others would want to hear them? I think about the joy and freedom that I have here choosing to change the person I am. Now I'm a hunter, a fighter, and a tracker. What other things have I yet to learn? Fishing? Bow making? Trapping? The ways of healing and herbs? All of these seem exciting and interesting. There's a part of me who wants to see things I've not seen, places of wild beauty that Red Fox has told me of and that I suspect Bright Feather is already right familiar with. I can't begin to tell them all.

So I ask myself, "What don't you really want?" The only thing I know is that I just don't want to have to make any choice yet that will take away any other choices I can still have. My head knows one day I will, but right now I just don't want to. I say out loud, "A powerful woman makes her own choices and decides when, too." And I'm determined to become a more powerful woman with each and every day.

All of a sudden I know that I'm not alone. I hear the snap of a twig and the quieting of the birds, and two squirrels that were playful nearby me are now nowhere to be seen. I imagine my ears pricking up like Willow's do when she hears a sound and I look over very slowly to her and she's no longer cropping grass but has her head up, her ears perked and is chewing slowly. She's looking in the direction of the snapping twig. I've just a moment to feel proud at myself for finally knowing when I'm not alone when I'm expecting to be when my world goes black.

It's not the kind of blackness when I hurt my arm. It's the kind of blackness when your head is covered, and the sun is blocked from view. I fight like a wild thing this time for I'm not hurt, I'm not tired, I'm not weak, and I'm no longer a white girl. I'm Bear. Without even thinking I grab my knife, and I hear one of my captors grunt in pain when it finds a place to bite.

"She has a knife!" someone yells in Indian, although the sounds are a tiny bit different. My wrist is caught and twisted painfully and my knife drops to the ground. My arms are roped to my side but my legs are still free, and I kick and scream and fight with all my might. For a moment the bright sunlight blinds me and then a rag is stuffed in my mouth and darkness returns. When my legs are finally tied I'm hauled across a horse.

I think, *this shouldn't happen one time in my life, let alone two!* I hear Willow whinny, and I know they have taken my horse, too. Maybe that's good and maybe that's bad. I try to concentrate on directions and don't struggle anymore. I need to save my strength. I concentrate this time. *This time* I push my fear all the way down to my toes and I listen and I remember. I ride all day across the front of the horse tied, gagged and in blackness. I concentrate on the warmth from the sun, and I know that we travel south and west a bit, too. *I'm different,* I keep telling myself over and over, *so this time things'll be different.* It becomes a song I sing in my head over and over.

When we stop for the night I'm given one brief sip of water, one small piece of dried meat to chew, one brief very unprivate moment, and then I'm tied, gagged, and blindfolded just as before. We leave before the sun is up and ride south again all day.

It's not until the third night that my gag is removed for good, and I'm allowed to see the sky. The meaning is obvious; we are too far away for anyone to hear my shouts. There are four braves, none that I know. They are all Indian and dress in a similar style to what I know, although I see some white things that I've not seen in a long time: rifles, a cloth button shirt, a felt brimmed hat. I'm glad to see Willow. She seems all right.

We ride southwest for nine whole days before we get to a village. We are so far south that the snow that has just about disappeared by our village is gone completely here, and the trees are in full bloom. My hands are never untied, although by the third day they allow me to ride astride with one of the men. The rawhide strips make sores around my wrists which hurt something fierce. Willow is here, but they don't let me ride her.

By the time we arrive, I've made some plans. I eat whenever they feed me to keep up my strength, and I no longer fight or show any sign of anger. I've never spoken again after my first shouts so they are unsure of what I understand. I try real hard to keep my face still so that it doesn't do any talking like my mouth. The Indian braves talk little between themselves; just basic discussions about when and where to camp and comments on the weather and, aside from a few odd phrases, I understand all they say. I ask myself so many questions that I tire myself out. Why me? Why have they taken me? Where are they taking me? Have they chosen me special or would they have taken anyone? What will our village think? Will they look for me? How will I get free? The scariest questions I choose not to ask more than once. Will they hurt me? Will I ever get back? *Is this life pulling me faster, once again, than I'm ready for?*

The village is larger than ours and looks nothing like I'd have expected. We pass through enormous cultivated fields larger than the ones in our village, and more like some of the great plantations I remember from long, long ago in my travels out west to settle in Virginia.. But it isn't the size of the village or even the odd feelings I get as we ride in that are the most frightening. No, most frightening is the white men I see, some dressed in buckskins and furs and some dressed in clothes Pa would wear. They walk casual like among the Indians and that makes me truly become scared. The Indians of the village wear a mixture of Indian clothing and white clothing in any number of ways. Everywhere I look I see things that remind me of my time living with Pa, Henry, and Eli. These are people accustomed to each other's company.

The Indian homes are different here than at ours. Not so many are squat and round. Now they are all long. Some must have at least six families living in them. It's warmer here, so they have already shifted into the summer style of huts with sides open and just a straw roof across the top to protect a body from rains. I'm stunned to see two white-men style homes off to one side of the village surrounded by traditional Indian ones. As we ride slowly into camp, I see another building far too big to be a home, and evidence of still another building being built. I push the fear that has begun to creep up my legs into the pit of my stomach back down to my toes and say to myself, proud like Otter says her name, "I am Bear of Great Elk's village of The Real People of The Maple Forest" over and over. I sit straight and tall as we ride in. I look directly ahead and look in no one's eyes, but make an effort to remember everything I see. *Pay attention, Elle, you never know what you can learn from just looking,* I hear Pa tell me.

I'm taken to the large structure and finally my hands are untied. It feels good to move them. The sores are raw, and I try not to touch them much for they hurt. We sit on sturdy chairs and there are tables, too. There's a group of men who make attempts to speak to me, but I choose not to talk. *No need to rush,* I think to myself. There's another white language here that I don't know. It can almost be funny that I understand the Indians better than I understand some of the white men. I've had enough trouble learning the Indian language let alone a new white one! While some of the words are different that the Indians speak here, most are familiar. I'm happy to keep them guessing, and in front of me they discuss if I can understand the languages. *Maybe I'll learn something*, I think further. Even more reason to keep my mouth shut.

The white men speak the Indian language almost as comfortably as the Indians speak the English. Even the children respond to both. Beside the man I think to be chief there are two others of Indian blood and two whites who sit around the table in chairs that first day. One white man, all in buckskins, reminds me greatly of Bear John in his dress. He tries to talk to me in a white language I don't know. The other white man wears a black Sunday suit, although it has seen better days - I can tell by the careful mending I see in many places. He speaks to me in English. They ask me questions in voices that I'm to think are friendly. What's my name? Where am I from? Who is my family? How old am I? How long have I been in the Indian village of Great Elk's in The Maple Forest? I do my best to look like I used to before I understood everything at Great Elk's village.

I learn that the chief is called Dark Cloud and the white man in the buckskins is called Martin. I study Dark Cloud and I think, do I know him? I look at his face and his mannerisms and the sound of his voice and a part of my head says yes, and a part of my head says no. It's a puzzle. I study Martin careful like, too, and decide one thing right quick about him; he may not smell like Bear John, but he has the same look in his eye when he looks at me as Bear John did, and I'll not trust him, not one single bit. I watch as he speaks to Dark Cloud, and even though I can't understand some of his white words I know he lies because I can see it in his eyes. He's small, just a bit taller than me with dark hair and eyes that are shifty like a rat. I know what his Indian name would be.

"Perhaps the young woman has been so severely traumatized by her time with the savages that she has lost the ability to speak and think on her own," says the white man in the old suit. "God only knows just what she has gone through over the course of the past months or years." He studies me close like, and it's very hard to keep my face like a dumb piece of rock. I feel him try to probe deep into my head and see if there's anything worth rescuing. After a bit he looks away, I hope he does not see much.

"Your concerns are without merit, Reverend Wilder," Dark Cloud says, also studying me intently as I look back at him and struggle to keep my look blank. *Reverend? What would a preacher be doing here?* "I understand she fought like a wild thing when she was first taken and even used a knife to defend herself. She was alone, unescorted in the woods when she was found. She also spoke extensively in Indian." The look he gives me says, *I'm not fooled one bit.* I think, *Why do I think I know you?*

"Would not anyone defend herself in the face of such a brutal abduction?" Reverend Wilder counters with great emotion. "It is conceivable that this young woman has now been abducted not once, *but twice* by Indians! How did your braves come upon her? Where exactly was she taken from? Why was she taken and brought here by force? Look at her wrists! She has been forcibly tied for days!"

I'm desperate to hear the answers but Dark Cloud is still watching me like a hungry hawk. I try not to think mouse thoughts. "I will be happy to discuss these things later with you, Reverend. In the meantime, let us get this poor young woman settled and offer her some of our hospitality."

"I insist that she stay with Rebecca and me. I will not have her subject to further brutalities at the hands of strangers," Reverend Wilder says.

Dark Cloud looks at me, and I struggle to keep my dumb rock look. "I speak to you in the language of The Real People, for that is what I understand you spoke clearly. I also suspect that you understand English." He looks at Martin and then back at me and he puzzles for a moment, "But maybe not the *Francois.*"

"You have two choices while you are here in this village. You can be treated like a prisoner, or you can be treated like a guest. In either capacity, *you may not leave.* You will have noticed that there is extensive presence in this area by Indian and white. This is the center point of The Nation of The Real People, with heavy traffic at all times by both whites and natives. I can assure you of your safety within the walls of this village but outside it I offer no such promise. I will let you stay with the Reverend Wilder and his wife, Rebecca, as a *guest.* Should you try to escape, you will be then treated as a prisoner. Do you understand my meaning?" He gives me a look of great menace, and it takes all my thinking power not to respond or change my face. I think of the last time I rode Willow and the smell of the forest as it wakes up in the early spring…

"Two Killers," Dark Cloud says without moving his eyes from me. He speaks to the brave sitting at the table with us still, and who I recognize as one who took me from Great Elk's village. "Maybe the Reverend Wilder and Miss Rebecca will offer you their hospitality as well." As the Reverend Wilder helps me to my feet, exclaiming in concern over my pitiful state, Two Killers follows the Reverend and me out into the bright sunshine.

The Reverend's a short, squat man, balding, and with a constant flush like he has been running for a while. He walks as if he's always late, and I follow at a quick pace alongside of him. He chatters to me, "We must have Rebecca see to those wrists of yours. I cannot believe they would keep you tied for such a long period of time - if at all! What were they thinking? What were they afraid of in such a young slip of a girl?"

He points to the building being constructed that we hurry past, "*That* will be the mission school that will complement the church. Right now, we use the church as a place of worship, schooling, and council meetings. The United States Government and The American Missionary Board have been very generous in their efforts to civilize the red savages. Dark Cloud has been very willing to have us come and educate the youth and the adults who show interest. He recognizes the positive potential for a solid education built on a Christian foundation. I have been provided with implements of husbandry, stock animals for farming, five plows, ten hoes, ten axes, as well as money and materials to establish this church and eventually the mission school here. The men have shown great enthusiasm over the merits of farming, and we have had excellent crops these past few years. I have spinning and weaving equipment for the women so they may be industrious and productive as well, and the products that they make show great promise. I've already, of course, begun to preach out in the open air, and Rebecca has been schooling the children, but we have grander hopes! Eventually, I would like to build a large dormitory to house a hundred Indian youth that we would then educate and send out to save others from all over this territory! It has been a Calling From God since I was a small boy, and the Good Lord has sent Rebecca to help me fulfill this dream."

He stops abruptly and looks at me, and I recognize the expression as one that Otter used to have with me before she was certain I understood her yet desperate for it to be so. "These savage people," he sweeps his hand out in a wide arch and I glance at Two Killers standing silent and blank a few steps back, "must be civilized. Christianity and civilization always go hand in hand. These sons of the forest must understand that they must be moralized or they will be exterminated." We resume the fast pace and I roll the words 'moralized' and 'exterminated' around in my head. I'm not sure what they mean, but something tells me that they aren't good.

The Wilders live in one of the white homes, and I'm surprised to learn that Dark Cloud and his family live in the other. Miss Rebecca falls upon me as I enter the cabin like I'm her long lost daughter. She's almost a full head shorter than me, as round as she's wide, and speaks with the same breathless speed that the Reverend does. She sheds real tears as she exclaims over my wrists and my general savage appearance. Like her husband, she keeps up a running commentary, and she seems to care not whether I understand or answer. Within a very short period of time my wrists are washed and dressed with clean bandages, and my hands and face and feet are washed with strong, harsh smelling soap. When she makes a move to take my clothes I take a step back and without speaking give her a look that says, *That's far enough, thank you.* We stand there for a moment in the silence of the cabin with Two Killers sitting silent and still in the corner on a straight back chair watching. "Well, dear," she reaches up and gentle like touches my hair in an effort to calm me, I suspect, and says, "I don't suppose that I have anything that would fit you, anyway. We must work on getting it clean though…"

It's funny to sit on chairs again, eat off tables with spoons and plates, and sleep in a straw and feather tick bed, but I manage to do all of them. My sleep that first night is filled with busy dreams that keep startling me awake, although I can't remember them. I'm tired in the morning. I miss my own place.

Unlike my early time at Great Elk's village, I'm allowed no time when I'm unwatched. They expect me to run away the first chance I get, and I have to understand that they are not stupid. Someone is always with me, if it's not Reverend Wilder or Miss Rebecca then it's Two Killers or another Indian brave. Someone is always awake, for even in the middle of the night as I make my way to the necessary house out back I hear footsteps not far away, and I know I'm watched. I'm eager to run, but I understand I must choose the time careful like. I don't need a whole village of red and white men running after me, especially if I'm on foot. I've not seen Willow since I arrived.

I realize, with a start, that I'm already learning new things here. I'm learning to bide my time and working hard at becoming wiser by the moment. I say a quick whisper prayer to God and ask if that might be all I have to learn so that I can get back to The Maple Forest and home.

I spend much of my time those first days in Dark Cloud's village thinking and watching. Every day I'm brought to the church council building and asked the same questions over and over about who I am and how I came to be in Great Elk's village. Sometimes there are a few people present – white and red – and sometimes there are many. It suits me to keep them guessing and to keep them annoyed, and I speak to absolutely no one. They might as well have as many unanswered questions as me. Why do they care who I am? Why bring me nine days south to find out my name when they could have heard the story with a lot less time and trouble in Great Elk's village? I know there are pieces missing. I listen to Reverend Wilder and Miss Rebecca talk, and I know that they puzzle over why I'm here also.

As the days go by, I study what directions people come and go. I know where the white men camp and live and where the horses are kept. I remember what braves seem to spend the most time with Dark Cloud in the church council building and have decided who are the leaders. I know where the women go to bathe and gather wood. I know where the small village garden is as well as the massive gardens that the men are in charge of farming. I know the hut in which the women do their "industrious and productive" weaving. I even learn the sounds that they make to the dogs of the village to tell them to hush. I try not to miss anything that can help me when I run.

On the sixth day of my time at Dark Cloud's village as I enter the council church building to hear more of the same questions, there's a face sitting at the table I know, and all things make more sense. Seated to Dark Cloud's right is Weasel. As they both sit looking at me waiting for my reaction, I see what I've missed; Dark Cloud is Weasel's father. The same look that struggles not to say anything but says a lot. The same dark mean eyes and the same thin, tall body. I feel an anger that wipes away all my fear, and I think two times in my life I've been taken away from places I felt safe and from people I cared about, and both times he's the cause. There's no doubt in my mind that even though he was not part of the group that brought me here, he was the one who caused it. The anger grows white hot in my belly and grows and grows. It feeds on the fear I keep in my toes and the tears I've packed behind my eyes and the aches I keep in my heart, and it explodes in a blinding flash. I'm not held or tied, and I dive across the space between me and Weasel and I think, *I'll kill you before they will kill me.*

There are screams and shouts and an "Oh My Dear Lord!" from the Reverend Wilder, and by the time three braves have me held a distance away from Weasel all eyes are on me as I spit out of my mouth clearly for all to hear, "Weasel! I called you Dirty Feet! But I should call you Bear John because your insides stink now more than his ever did, even now! You watch your back and all you hold dear because the first chance I get I will cause you sorrow you cannot begin to imagine." I've nothing to throw, nothing to kick, nothing to hit, so I spit at him, and he must move his leg quick to make sure I miss him.

All around me are different kinds of faces. The Reverend Wilder looks like he's just about ready to explode with shock. Weasel has a look of such intense hatred it flows out of his eyes like smoke from a fire. And Dark Cloud looks triumphant. *I knew it*, his eyes say to me with something that almost seems like pleasure.

The brave holding my hair lets go, but the two holding my arms make me sit in a chair in front of Dark Cloud and Weasel and Martin and the still shocked Reverend Wilder and some others I don't know. The braves sit close to me on either side, tense and ready, but let go of my arms. I see women in the background who are often present serving and caring for the needs of the men, scurrying around cleaning up cups and pitchers and baskets with food in them that have been spilled and glancing scared eyes at me. The children who often peer into the windows when they question me make every effort to get as good a viewing spot as possible to see what I'll do next. It's almost funny to see one by one new black heads appearing in the windows. Dark Cloud asks me questions again and I refuse to answer any question he will already have the answer to from Weasel. At last he asks me, "Why do you not talk to us?"

"You have not asked me a question that you truly need the answer for yet," I say.

"I knew that after the length of time you were in Great Elk's village that you must understand the language by now," he says in a satisfied voice, and I realize, of course, the last time I saw Weasel was a very long while ago. He wouldn't have been able to assure them that I could speak the language, and that would have been one of their problems. I think about the last time I saw Weasel, and I know that he has not been in the village since the night I was given to Bright Feather, and I realize that there are many things he does not know about me *white* or *red*.

"Do you know that there are those who are looking for you?" *Who does he mean*, I think? *White or Indian?*

"Have them talk to *Dirty Feet*," and it makes me happy to see him bothered by the name I call him. "All who seek me, *red and white*, can get the answers from him," I spit out with much hate. I don't talk or look at Weasel, only to Dark Cloud. "Why have you brought me here?" I ask. Now it's my turn to ask a question.

Dark Cloud looks angered that a woman, a captive, should ask him a question. The women in the background look my way, tense and frightened. I don't think there are so many powerful women in this village, and they are surprised, too, it seems. Why are there no women sitting in the church council building, I wonder? Weasel leans over and he and Dark Cloud speak in quiet voices.

At last Dark Cloud says, "You were brought here at the request of your village. There is a danger for them in having you there since there are white people who search for you. It is dangerous for any village to have you present."

I think about this for a moment. I think about Great Elk and Otter and Raccoon and Cloud and Red Fox and Beaver and all the others who have welcomed me and made me a part of their village. As far as I know I'm the only white captive Great Elk's village has ever had, and aside from Bear John and his two companions, there has never been mentioned any other white faces within their boundaries. Would they have made this decision without speaking with me? Would they have caused me this great terror once again? Would they have left this in the hands of Weasel? *No, they wouldn't.*

I say very quietly, "And what will you do in *this village* with the danger you have with me *here*?" Both Dark Cloud and Weasel are shocked by my threat. The white man called Martin is surprised, too. The look he gives me says, *You are much more than I thought at first.* The look of hate I give him says, *Maybe you should also watch your back for you are in danger from me, too.*

"Why is Weasel here in this village?" I ask although I think I know some of the reasons.

"Weasel is a son of this village," Dark Cloud answers after a moment. "He became a son of the hut of One Who Knows in Great Elk's village of The Maple Forest for a time. He has come back to live with us now."

I realize the words not said speak of those that are dead and never mentioned - One Who Knows' daughter. Things about my first capture make more sense. Why I was taken, why I was brought to One Who Knows' tent, why Weasel thought his attentions towards me would have been allowed, and even, my mind thinks, why One Who Knows was happy to see me put Weasel in his place that one night when I was still a slave.

"What village will you try to get to take him next?" I ask slow and polite like although my eyes say different. Martin laughs out loud at this.

Weasel tenses and gives us both dark looks. *Watch your back*, I think again as I look at him.

"My dear," says Reverend Wilder. "Tell us please what your name is. Tell us who you are so that we may return you to your family; those that love and miss you and must surely be still searching for you after all this time." I know he speaks of Pa, Henry, and Eli but I look at Martin and Dark Cloud and Weasel. Their faces don't show the same concern that Reverend Wilder's does. With a flash I know that what Reverend Wilder believes to be so is not the truth or the way things ever will be. *They* know of my hatred for them, *they* know of the dangers from Pa should I tell him who these Indians are that are returning me. They will never trust me or risk their lives to *return* me when it's because of them *I'm here now*. I'll never be returned to Pa, Henry, or Eli by the same Indians that took me in the first place. Never. *They* know that, and *I* know that now, too.

"I am Bear, of the village of Great Elk, of The Real People of The Maple Forest," I say loud and clear and strong.

"But my dear...!" Reverend Wilder begins, but he's silenced by Dark Cloud.

"Perhaps you are right, Reverend. Perhaps her time in The Maple Forest has damaged her in ways we cannot understand. We are not equipped for something of this nature here in our village. Martin will take you back to his people, the *Francois*. They will have connections with people who know of those poor unfortunate children who have been tragically taken from their homes. From there it can be determined who you are in the white world and then you will be taken back to your own people to heal and become whole again. We are happy to aid in the return of you to your true family," Dark Cloud tells me kind like although his eyes tell a different story I can't quite understand.

"I will bring my horse with me," I say like it's already decided. "If you plan to do this *kindness*," I say with eyes and tone that mean different than the word, "then you must be certain that all of my things are returned to me." Dark Cloud hesitates, unhappy to be called almost a thief. He glances at a puzzled - looking Reverend Wilder and at last he nods that it will be so.

I say nothing else but I know pieces are still missing. I think I'll be patient and wait until I'm free of this too big village with its too many whites and Indians and wait until I'm with this little white man called Martin. And I've one more wish, I realize, as Reverend Wilder helps me to stand and guides me out into the bright spring sunshine.

I hope Weasel comes along on the trip so that I've a chance to put my knife in his back. Balance and harmony. Righting wrongs. It's the way of The Real People here at the center of the world.

I've been at Dark Cloud's village for more than four weeks, and I feel like a bow that has been strung too long without a chance to rest. I'm told there are many reasons for the wait. First, they say it's the weather. I tell them I'm not afraid of snow or rain and that they shouldn't worry; I don't melt. Then I'm told that there's the need to find two braves beside Martin and Weasel to travel with us. I'm just one small girl, I say sweetly, why do you need any others? After the first week, they will not answer my questions about the wait, and I just keep to myself.

They would like me to be more afraid I think. I'm happy to disappoint them. I don't talk to anyone, man or woman, white or red unless it suits me. I help the women in the huts when they will let me for it makes the day go quicker, but in most cases they seem happier to stay away from me. I play with the children who are brave enough to come close; once again they are the ones I find the most joy in. I help Miss Rebecca with her chores as well, and there are many days that I sit with her while she teaches and translate her words or needs to her students into the Real People's words. She seems to struggle with the Indian language even more than I did although the Reverend seems to know it well enough.

After watching the Reverend Wilder and Miss Rebecca over these weeks, I decide after much thought that they mean no harm. They seem to have a true love of the Indians and a sincere desire to help them, although I'm not so sure that I agree with their way.

I struggle with their great efforts to change The Real People from "savage" to "civilized". I remember my way of thinking when I first came to The Maple Forest and how I thought that black skin meant slave, red skin meant savage, and white skin meant all the rest. It was spending time with those in The Maple Forest that I came to see that it's the inside of a person that makes them what they are. Skin has nothing to do with it all.

But while the Wilders are quick to use the word "savage" whenever they speak of The Real People, they seem to already know what I spent the last year learning. And that's what bothers me. For, as far as I can figure, the Wilders seem to think that it's the *inside* that needs the changing. It's just as Beaver tried to explain to me so many weeks ago, *The Real People struggle with the life that the white man wishes us to lead. In many ways, just as you have been forced to lead the life of the savage Indian we, for many, many years have been forced to change to a life of the white man.*

Women don't need to be powerful and wise, they need to be "industrious and productive". They need to learn skills not like hunting and knife fighting, but weaving and raising children "proper" with school and church and such. Housekeeping should no longer be in deer-skin huts with birch-bark containers to cook in, but be more like a home where I grew up in with Pa that has wood floors and metal pots.

Men need not hunt but should instead farm cows and chickens. Farm enough to sell to others to earn money so that things can be bought. There's no need to train to be warriors, instead they should learn "diplomacy" and "forbearance". I think about my time as Mouse in The Maple Forest and realize I already know a lot about diplomacy and forbearance.

I realize that what upsets me something fierce about the Wilders is they seem to want to change The Real People's centers.

I think about myself in my now clean Indian tunic and hear Miss Rebecca call me *Bear*, and I wonder what they must think about me in particular. Have I gone from civilized to *savage*? At one time I'd have thought that to be true, but now I know I'm more wise than before. *Forget about my outsides*, I think, *I'm wiser than I've ever been in my life.*

Living with Miss Rebecca causes flashes in my mind of Ma: a certain way she sounds swooshing around in her great skirts, the smell of the baking bread in the oven and the way she comes by at night when she thinks I'm already asleep to adjust my covers and smooth my hair. I've many dreams, sleeping on my straw and feather tick bed, of times at home in Virginia that are mixed up with birch bark containers and War Woman sitting in my Pa's rocking chair.

The Wilders don't press me to find out any more about my white family. They make it clear they are powerful concerned about my welfare and especially my soul but have no desire to upset me by making me talk about things I choose not to. They are loving and kind to me and seem glad for my company. I find myself explaining to them my understanding of the ways of The Real People, and more than once Miss Rebecca takes me along into the women's places of gathering and asks me to translate while she struggles to sit in the dirt with them while they weave or grind or cook or just talk. She seems to have an honest wish to really know them. I'm amazed that these two white people seem to really *love* The Real People without understanding them at all. When I say something about that they both look surprised.

Rebecca says, "Our Dear Lord Jesus did not just stay with those He called family or those He thought acceptable, nor did He go to places that were always safe or always clean or always what He knew. He did all of this, knowing what unappreciative, violent, hateful, *awful* people we were simply because He had such a Great Love for us He could not abandon us." She grabs my hand and holds it tight to make her point. "*He loved us so much that He chose to die to save us rather than to live without us.* We are guaranteed to live forever if we just make the choice to believe that we are all sinners, that Jesus is the Son of God, and accept Him as the center point of our life. *The Real People* as you call them do not know of this Great Love, of this Great Savior, of this Great Promise, and James and I cannot sleep with the burden that we feel to tell of it."

While I don't say anything, I sit up straighter when Miss Rebecca starts to talk about centers and life. I find it mighty amazing to hear talk about centers with the Son of God in them when I have spent so much of the last year trying to sort out my own center and what to put in it. Another thing to puzzle over when my mind is not so cluttered with the business of my life...

"God has been so good to bring us both together," she says, and Reverend Wilder smiles tenderly at her as they exchange glances across the room, "both with the same passion and desire. I can tell that you do not like us to use words like *civilize* and *savages*. James and I have talked about that, and we realize that you may be right. Words like those are not complimentary and they imply that we disapprove of the Indian and that way of life. It is not correct to say that we *disapprove*, but it is correct to say that we *fear* for the Indian."

"Fear!" I say in surprise and confusion. "You *fear* for The Real People? I do not see that. I see only that you wish to make them white. You wish to change them from one thing into another."

Miss Rebecca sighs and stops to rearrange her thoughts, I suspect. "We fear for them because we see how the whites are taking advantage of the kind and unselfish way of the Indians. The whites have not been fair with business dealings, and in many instances the Indians have suffered greatly because of it. James and I believe that if we can educate the Indians with white words and white customs, perhaps they will be better prepared to deal with the whites in the future."

"It is not so much that we approve or disapprove of the white or Indian way, Bear," Reverend Wilder tries to explain. "More accurately, the Indian way is disappearing. No longer are there enough animals left in the wild to feed an entire village. No longer is there land enough to spare so that whole villages can migrate and move at the whim of the seasons and the migration of the animals they follow. And like it or not, more whites are coming each day. Here. To this place. They are gobbling up all available land, and guess where they will go once all of the available *white land* is taken?" He does not wait for me to answer, but looks sad and says, "They will come here to Dark Cloud's village and, eventually, to your village in The Maple Forest as well. And if The Real People are not equipped to deal with the whites properly, they will simply loose more and more of what is rightfully theirs."

"I had not thought of such a thing ..." I say and then hear my Pa saying, *The savages had their time. Their present circumstances are not our concern.* Our homestead is on what used to be the red savage's land. Bought by the government with cash and signed away by the savages free and clear. Made available to families like ours. Suddenly I've a powerful sick feeling in my gut.

"Take you for instance," Reverend Wilder says smiling, "you have not told us how you came to be in an Indian village, wearing Indian clothes, and talking the Indian tongue. Yet, at some point you had to decide whether you were going to adapt – *go along with things* – or not. You could have refused to cooperate or change, could you not have?"

I nod my head and think of Old Woman and her fury should I have tried such a thing.

"Your life would have been even more difficult as a result, correct?" Reverend Wilder continues.

I nod again.

"You adapted, Bear. Changed to fit your circumstances. Reinvented yourself to survive. Rebecca and I are not saying that one was good or one was bad, we are simply saying what you did was a wise choice." Reverend Wilder looks at me, I suspect, to see if what he says is sinking into my thick skull.

I sit up straight at the "wise choice" words for I for sure would like to be thought of that way.

Miss Rebecca waits for a moment or two and then touches my arm so that I look at her. "But there is something else that is even more important that brings us here, Bear. Yes, we love The Real People and yes, we want them to be better prepared to deal with the white man and their immediate futures. But more importantly than all of that, we fear for the Indians because we know that they have not heard of the Truth and the Love of Jesus Christ and *not been given the opportunity to choose*. It is primarily because of this Truth and this Love that we are here. Perhaps we can teach *The Real People*," she smiles at me hopeful that she has used the proper term, "how to survive in a white world *and* teach *The Real People* of God's Great Love and Faithfulness."

I decide, as I think about what the Wilders have told me, that I believe *them* and what they say is their reasons for coming. But that's because I've seen their insides, they have shared with me their centers. I'll give Miss Rebecca and Reverend Wilder my trust about what they say being true. Their words match their actions, which is just how those in The Maple Forest proved to me the same thing.

Over each meal we bow our heads, and I listen to the Reverend Wilder pray to God. He speaks loud and strong and sure and I think, those times I whispered, could God even hear me? I ask about this and tell them how Ma told me about whispering close and personal to God. They exchange looks across the table, and it's Reverend Wilder who says, "God can be so close and so personal Bear that He can be *right inside you* and even hear your thoughts. You can talk just in your head and heart and He will hear you as loud and clear as I am talking to you now."

I'm glad about that for I'd like to be sure that the things I've whispered have been heard, as many or as few as they have been. "What do you pray for, Dear?" Miss Rebecca asks quiet like.

I'm careful with how much I tell, but I can see that they want only to know of my concerns and are not interested in learning things I still wish to keep secret. "I pray sometimes that my white family is safe and healthy and that the braves who took me did them no harm." The words said out loud make my heart pound and my stomach clench with the worry of it. It's more fearful said out loud for some reason. "I pray that they know that I'm happy and strong and healthy and safe."

"Why is it that you will not tell us who you are so that we can return you to this white family that you are concerned about?" Reverend Wilder finally asks.

I sigh and look down at my dinner plate with my fork held tightly in my tan, white hand. Despite Miss Rebecca's best tries I've refused to change out of my Indian clothes. I must always be ready to go. When I look up at them both sitting, patient like, waiting for me to answer, I must give them a bit of a smile. I decide that I like these two people. *Always look for the good in a dark situation,* I hear Pa say to me. *Here it is, Pa. I've found it.* I look at each of their troubled faces. "The only people I feel I can trust here are those I eat with now. And you do not hold the power in this village, others do." That's all I'll say.

The weeks creep slowly on, and the questions in my head never stop. Why do I need guards if they are just worried about getting me home? Why all the delays? What are the secret pieces that I don't understand? How does Weasel fit into all of this? Why can't they find two men to travel and take me back in a village this size? Where are 'Martin's people' located, and why must I go to the French rather than an American outpost? *Where are they really taking me?*

I pose some of these questions to the Wilders, but they are as in the dark as I am about my situation. And probably a great deal more, I realize. Their great fault, I think, is that they are too trusting. They accept kindnesses without taking the time to understand or even see where it comes from and why. It's with some shock that I realize that they are in perhaps more danger than I am! When I try to voice these concerns they smile their sweet smiles, and Miss Rebecca gives me a hug. "Aren't you sweet, child, worrying about us! We have always followed God's lead and trust that He will keep us safe as we forge ahead to do His Will. *Though I walk through the valley of the shadow of death, I will fear no evil…5,*" she quotes to me, and Ma comes flying into my head in a memory of the Bible words.

"Psalm twenty-three," I say to Miss Rebecca. "My Ma liked that, too."

At long last, the morning comes for me to finally leave. Miss Rebecca has shed many tears over my departure. She does not fear for my safety I think as much as for my soul. I realize, I, too, will miss these two people. I struggle with a powerful sense of loss that I've not remembered since Ma's death. It's different from the fear of both takings by the Indians, it's more like a careful scraping of all my soft insides like when we gut an animal we have killed. It's not a fear so much as a terrible empty loneliness. I work to not shed any tears, but find I don't have the hate and hardness ready for these two and it's powerful difficult to stay strong. As I mount up on Willow, Mrs. Wilder rushes out in the bright sunshine and takes my hand as the tears slide down her plump, flushed cheeks. "I will pray for you, Bear. I will pray that God becomes close and personal inside you. I will pray that you still continue to whisper in God's ear and listen for His answering voice. You must trust that the Lord loves you and that He cares for you and watches over you in all you do.

> *'For I know the thoughts that I think toward you,' saith the Lord, 'thoughts of*
> *peace, and not of evil, to give you an expected end.*
> *Then shall ye call upon me, and ye shall go and pray unto me,*
> *and I will hearken unto you.*
> *And ye shall seek me, and find me,*
> *when ye shall search for me with all your heart.*
> *And I will be found of you,' saith the Lord:*
> *'and I will turn away your captivity,*
> *and I will gather you from all the nations,*
> *and from all the places whither I have driven you,' saith the Lord;*
> *'and I will bring you again into the place*
> *whence I caused you to be carried away captive.* ᵇ *"*

She carefully wraps a faded pink ribbon around my wrist, smiles through her tears and ties it in a bow. "You are no longer white. You will never be red. I think you are just a beautiful shade of pink."

I look down at the pink ribbon tied carefully tied around my wrist, and I feel a wave of love for these two people. How did they know? For I'm no longer white; I will *never* be red. It makes me happy that they were able to understand, and I smile through the few tears that blur my eyes. They have given my center a color: pink. I look back only once as we leave Dark Cloud's village to see the Reverend Wilder with his arm around Miss Rebecca as she sobs against his shoulder. He raises his arm in a farewell salute.

At last we are on the trail. There's Martin and Weasel, me, and two braves named Running Feet and Two Doves. As soon as I see Running Feet and Two Doves I understand the wait; they are the same ones that took me the first time from Pa, Henry, and Eli. If they are not brothers of Weasel, they should be. The first time I see them I look at them from the top of their heads to the tip of their toes as I sit on Willow and Miss Rebecca sobs in the background. Then I look them right in the eye and say nothing, but I think many unkind things. Very slow - like I fan the anger in my belly just to make sure the coals are ready when I need them. They look away first and turn to Weasel. Before they can say any thing, he says sharp like, "It is time to leave." He heads toward his horse and mounts up.

It's so good to be riding Willow. Me and my horse have not had a chance to be together in many, many weeks. I could only view her from a distance in the herd kept outside the village and heavily guarded by white soldiers. In her own horse way she seems as glad to see me as I am to see her.

On the trail I'm always watched with someone ahead of me and Weasel is always behind. I note that we are traveling south, a direction that brings me still farther away from everything I know or care about. In Dark Cloud's village, Weasel kept his distance from me, but on the trail all that has changed. He's always the one that's with me, guarding and watching. It's he who I am tied to at night as we sleep. It's he who takes me for my not so private moments in the woods. And it's he who insists after the first day on the trail that my hands must be permanently tied again as I ride, and even as I sleep. This makes it necessary for someone to help me onto and off of Willow, which Weasel does as well, too. I look down at the rawhide strips over my pink ribbon and think about me and the much more "savage" than "civilized" thoughts running through my head. It seems as if each time he must touch me he becomes more brave and bold. I find his eyes on me at all times; they bore into my back as we ride and they are the last and first things I see each day. It makes my skin feel scratchy and my stomach feel sick.

My anger for him is savage and hot, but I keep it tucked away careful like for when I'll need it most. I think, *A person is what they are inside,* and I feel my center fill with a hate that's almost too big for me to keep inside. There are things to fear on this trek to Martin's people that I realize are fears I put away long ago in Great Elk's village and have had too many things on my mind these past weeks to truly think about until now. Weasel is not the only one I have this fear about. *Remember, it's spring,* I think. Then I look at Martin and Running Feet and Two Doves, and I realize that I shouldn't be fast to dismiss anyone. Weasel watches me like a man watches a woman besides like a captor watches his prisoner.

On the third day of the trail we stop at noon near a stream to water the horses and ourselves. As Weasel helps me off Willow his hand touches my breast and this time it stays there. He smiles a lazy smile and gives me a look that says, *Who's in danger now?* I work hard not to let him see fear in my eyes but my heart feels like it might burst right out of my chest. I think of that night that he took me from Pa and how I wet myself. I take a deep breath to calm my shaky breathing.

I'm not Elle. I'm Bear. I'm wiser. And more powerful.

I don't have my knife. I don't have my bow and arrow. I look him right in the eye and spit in his face. He lets out a howl of anger and, grabbing me by the back of my hair, hauls me off towards the woods. He shouts instructions over his shoulder as Martin and the braves look in our direction. "Leave us be!"

He drags me kicking and fighting and shouting into the woods. I call him Dirty Feet and remind him how his mother hides her head in shame and all who know him laugh at the joke of what his is. I tell him of my hate for him and my hopes and dreams of burying my knife in his back or his neck or his heart. The words that pour out of my mouth help me forget my terror as he drags me deeper into the woods, and I wonder what he has in mind.

Weasel finally gets tired of my words and reaches down and grabs a handful of moss that he shoves deep in my mouth. I choke and gag as bits of dirt trickle down my throat, but I'm quiet now. We walk a good long distance from the others, and he shoves me to the ground and I fall hard, unable to catch myself with my hands tied.

I curl up in a ball in case he plans to kick me, but he rolls me on my back and with a flash of delight on his face pushes my tied hands up over my head and hooks them on a tree root sticking out of the ground. Then he sits on my stomach and with a Woof! the air leaves my lungs. I gasp for breath from my nose and choke and cough at the moss in my mouth and now trickling down my throat.

The "Woof" sound makes me think for a flash of Raccoon and the smile on his face when he came to me standing over my elk. Raccoon makes me think of Otter and Little Bird and Red Fox and Cloud and even

Bright Feather, and I blink my eyes to keep from crying. I let my white hot hate swim up behind my eyes and eat my tears.

He waits until my breathing slows a bit and then he gets real close to my face and starts speaking. "You are good for *nothing*," he says, "nothing but *this*. You are not a good white woman, you are not a good Indian squaw. You have caused me nothing but grief since I first saw you. It is because of you I had to leave Great Elks' village and return to Dark Cloud in shame. I should have killed you just like we killed your father and your brother," he sneers.

His words rip me wide apart with a sorrow so awful that I forget all but what he says to me.

"We used our knives," he says so close to my face that I feel his spittle rain down on me, "but made sure that what we did to them made them die slow and painful. Do not worry, Bear," he grinds out my Indian name, "I will give you a small taste of what we did so that you will have no doubt."

I look at him desperate like and search his eyes to see if what he says is true or if I can see he's lying to me. He looks smug and like he's the winner of a fight. The white hot anger has more tears to feed on and bigger aches in my heart than I ever thought there could be. "We take you to the *Francois* to *sell* you," he says. "At last there will be something good from you. A white woman trained to be an Indian squaw can bring much gold. Enough to make Dark Cloud happy, enough to make Martin happy," here he gets so close to my face I can only see the hate in his eyes, "but not enough to make me happy."

With a smile, he takes out his knife and cuts open my tunic to my waist and touches my bare breasts with his hands and with his knife. He laughs low when I try to struggle, and cough and choke on more moss as it trickles down my throat. He lowers himself down my legs and then I feel his mouth on my breasts and then his teeth. I feel a terrible pain as his teeth close on my breast as he bites down hard. The white hot anger has more to feed on as it works on the pain of his teeth and his knife.

A blackness comes down on me, different from the blackness of the hurt of my arm, different from the blackness of my last capture. This blackness is the kind that happens to a house late at night when you know a terrible storm is coming; you close the shutters tight, you blow out all the lanterns and you crawl deep under the covers to escape it all. I feel my shutters close, and I feel my lanterns get blown out. The last bit of darkness comes over me like my favorite heavy quilt I remember at my house with Pa, Henry, and Eli. *Elle, will you sleep with me tonight? I'm scared of the thunder* ... I hear Eli ask me. I leave Weasel outside like a mad wolf that no one has had the fortune to kill yet.

I don't hear anyone approach. And I don't hear anyone shout or yell. And I don't even feel Weasel move away. All of sudden my hands are free, and I feel my tunic painfully pulled over my breasts and I'm lifted and carried away. I feel the moss scraped out of my mouth and for a moment things stop while I cough and retch at my feet. It's not until I hear a familiar whistle that I peek my head out from my blackness. I'm passed up to someone on a horse and wrapped in a rough blanket, and I open my eyes just quick enough to see a raccoon tail dangling from a dark shiny head.

We ride and ride and ride for a long while before we stop. I hear splashes in water and then finally we stop on the far edge of a stream. I'm lifted down and feel two strong warm hands on either side of my face, and I hear someone say very soft like, "Bear."

I open my eyes and I see three stripes on each brown cheek and three stripes drawn down the chin, and I see three bright feathers, one red, one blue, one yellow, and I say with the last bits of strength I have, "What took you so long?" The dark eyes that stare back at me are filled with worry.

"We will take a moment to see to your wounds," Bright Feather says as he reaches for his pack of supplies. I sit still as he opens my torn tunic wide, and I stare straight ahead into the wild forest, afraid to look down and see what he's looking at. I feel a wetness trailing down my belly and know that I bleed in many spots. I look once at his face, but he's too good at showing nothing.

Bright Feather quickly but carefully washes the bites and cuts. With great tenderness, he puts a strong smelling salve on each spot, and even though I still do not look, I count eleven in all on my breasts and stomach. He also takes the time to wash the new sores on my wrists. I'm too tired to make a sound even though the pain is something fierce. He helps me take the top of my cut tunic off my arms, and then from his pack he pulls a soft leather shirt over my head that I recognize as Otter's. Then we pull my torn tunic back over the clean shirt. I watch the pink ribbon float down the stream, a small bit of color covered in blood and dirt and sweat.

Bright Feather takes my face in both his hands and looks at me real serious like. "That is all there is time for now," he says and I nod. He gives me water to drink and dried venison to chew. He looks over my shoulder, and for the first time I realize that Raccoon must be standing directly behind us tending to the horse. Waiting. Watching.

Bright Feather looks at me again. "We must keep riding."

I nod my head. "I know."

He studies my face for a moment, touches my cheek softly with one finger, and then says the strangest thing. "Can you whistle?" I take another sip of water and then let out a piercing sound. I hear hoof beats and a familiar whinny. I look at him with surprised eyes. Willow! "Good thing she never learned to listen to *only* your whistle," he says.

Bright Feather stands and talks low with Raccoon. They will split up to confuse anyone that might follow. They talk about directions and each reminds the other of things along the trail. Then Raccoon is bending down in front of me looking more serious than I've ever seen him before. And he can look powerful fierce when he wants to. He works to soften his look and then says, "Don't make him too tired now, Bear. You both need all your strength for a while."

We look at each other for a moment or two. I manage a quiet, "Woof."

That seems to be exactly what he wants to hear for he gives me a small smile. And then he's gone.

Bright Feather lifts me up on Companion, and I make noise about riding on Willow. He shakes his head, looking up at me. "There is not time to argue or ask questions. We will travel for a long way the rest of today and for a time tonight, Bear. You do not have the strength. Willow will follow us." He looks as movable as a mountain.

But I have to ask just one question. "How far are those that will follow Willow?"

He looks up at me for a moment seated on Companion's back. I can look mighty fierce, too. He sighs. "Our trail will be very cold by the time anyone from Dark Cloud's village begins to follow us – if they ever do," he says. I understand what he does not say. *There's no one in the woods here alive that will follow us today.*

He mounts up behind me, pulling a woven Indian blanket across my lap and carefully wrapping his arm around my waist so as to not cause me anymore pain. I nod in answer when he asks if I'm warm and comfortable. *Funny,* I think as I feel my eyelids droop shut, *this is the most comfortable I've been in many weeks.* And then I'm asleep.

We travel all the rest of that day and long into the night until the moon sets, and it's too dark for us to ride safely. We camp by a fallen log without a fire. I look down at myself and Otter's shirt is soaked through with my blood. Bright Feather must help me remove it to wash things more proper like and seems to know that I cannot bring myself to look down again just yet. I sit on a log by a fast moving stream, and he once again takes care to wash and clean each and every spot. From his pack he gently applies an ointment to each and every cut and bite. It smells something awful but makes some of the sting less. "This ointment is from One Who Knows," he says to fill the silence, I suspect. "She told me that should you be injured each and every cut must be carefully cleaned and then to put this salve on." He looks up into my eyes, no smile of course, but I seem to sense some humor, "I hope it is as good at healing as it is at smelling."

As I sit there like an honest to goodness bump on a log, he rinses Otter's top and lays it careful across a low branch to dry. Again he fills the silence with his own words, "Otter packed most of these things for you. She was very afraid for you."

I feel the questions bubble up in my head but am just too tired to get the words out. Bright Feather helps me put my torn tunic back up on my shoulders. "Can you sit here while I get camp ready?" he asks and I nod, feeling dumb and useless.

In a short time he's back, helping me stand and guiding me back away from the river bank, hidden behind some brush, near the horses. "We will share a pallet," he says. "One Who Knows said that you might get a fever and that I am to watch closely for that. I am to not let you catch a chill either, and to keep you warm at night. Since we can not risk a fire, this seems like the best way to stay warm."

I look at him and blink slow. If he thinks I'm inclined to fight or argue or ask questions he's wrong. I curl up on the pallet he has made, and he slips in behind me drawing the blanket over us. He slips his arm under my head for a pillow and wraps his other arm careful like around me, pulling me close against him. He's like laying with a pile of hot coals. I'm asleep, in moments, warm and safe.

We travel north and west the next day, I'm riding in front of Bright Feather with Willow following behind. She seems just as happy to be free as me. Bright Feather says it's north because it's away from the Dark Cloud's village, west because it brings us further away from the whites. We will not travel closer to Great Elk's village and The Maple Forest until we have gone a number of days of just traveling *away*.

"Dark Cloud told me that there has been talk about the search for a white girl who was taken captive. He also said that it was those of The Maple Forest who wanted me to be taken away because they were afraid my presence would cause trouble."

"What did you think of those things when you heard them?" he asks me quietly from behind.

"I decided that even if there was a concern in the village, they would not have had Weasel take me a second time."

Bright Feather, I learn, never talks quick. He always takes a thoughtful moment before he decides to speak. "You are right," he says after a moment or two, "Great Elk would never have allowed you to be taken like that." He pauses and then says almost as if he doesn't want to, "I have heard talk about the search for a white, captive girl. But there is no one in The Maple Forest that has fear because of that."

"Why was I taken again, I wonder..."

"Greed causes people to do frightening things, Bear. Things that are dark and terrible and ... hard to imagine sometimes. Maybe you were to be traded for guns or gold."

"Who would they trade with?" I say in a voice that's small and scared at the thought of it all. There's a place where you can trade a girl for a gun?

I feel Bright Feather shrug. "The French, other tribes, ... trappers. There is much greed in the world, Bear. Some people will do anything to get what they want."

"Does all of this have something to do with the time Weasel lived in One Who Knows' hut?" I ask.

Bright Feather rides in silence behind for a time, and I've learned that I must wait and see if I will hear an answer. Finally, I hear his voice above my head, "Yes. Dark Cloud's son," he says, unwilling to call him by name, "brought you to One Who Knows' hut to end a debt that can never be paid. He was angry that things he thought should be easy for people to forget were still there to haunt him whenever he was in the village. He spent the first half of his life making mistakes and the last part of his life running from them."

I think about what Weasel has done to my life. "It would seem that Weasel has debts with many people that can never be paid." I decide that the hard topic of Weasel is best not talked about anymore for a bit.

I'm surprised when long, long moments later Bright Feather says, "Yes, Dark Cloud's son has many debts with many people that can never be paid. Even from the grave."

We stop for lunch, I suspect more for me than for Bright Feather, and we sit by a stream and eat from supplies that Bright Feather carries with him. When I make moves to start the fire and get the meal going, Bright Feather pushes me down to sitting.

"I do not need you to cook for me," I say. I'm a powerful woman after all.

He does not look up at me as he starts a fire with sure hands and begins the process of setting out the meal. "I cook for myself," he says matter of fact. "You are welcome to join me if you wish." Then he glances up at me. "After you go to the stream," he gestures to the left, "and clean your wounds." He hands me the special salve in a small pottery bowl. I stare down at his bent head and think that for someone who is always alone and almost always silent he has sure become bossy all of a sudden.

I walk to the water, wading into the stream to sit on a rock by the fastest moving part. I've changed my torn tunic to a deerskin skirt and top that Otter has sent me. I slowly take off the top and stare down at the mess that's my body. It's the first time I've really, truly looked. Eleven bite and cut marks, some still bleeding, all terrible sore. *We used our knives but made sure that what we did to them made them die slow and painful.*

I suddenly feel so cold I start to shiver. Did Pa get cut like this? A moan crawls out my throat as I think, *and my Eli...?* I can't stop shivering and I wrap my arms around my bare self and rock and moan and cry with the cold that's more inside me than out. I can't get warm. I can't... I never will...

I don't know how long I sit, shaking and crying but suddenly strong warm arms scoop me up, and I'm no longer sitting on a rock but in Bright Feather's warm lap. I can't stop my sobs, no matter how I try, and Bright Feather sits right there with me in the middle of the stream and holds me like a baby. "You are safe now, Bear," he says over and over in a soft voice in my ear. He copies my movements and soon we are both rocking back and forth. "You are safe, Bear. I will see to it. The wounds will heal. The scars will not be noticeable. You are safe from those who took you. Never again," he whispers sing-song like over and over, "never again."

For long moments, I let him think I cry for my sorry state, and once again take advantage of the warmth of him. He does not know what

Weasel has said of Pa and Eli, I realize, and I try and try but can't get the words out to tell. They are so awful just in my head, what will they be like said out loud by my mouth?

"Weasel ..." I manage and he leans in close to hear my words. I swallow, suddenly feeling sick as well as sore. "Weasel .... told me of Pa ..." I start to rock and cry and moan again but I manage to get out, "and Eli ..."

"Ahh," he says rocking and holding me tight. "You carry more wounds *inside* than out. And we do not have a salve to put on them, hmmm?" He tucks my head under his chin, cuddles me close in his arms, and we sit on the rock in the middle of the stream for so long that the shade and the sun patterns change around us.

"These inside wounds," he says finally as if no time has passed at all, "they cause more hurt than any knife can. I know. They will, with time, heal a bit, but these inside scars ..." he sighs, "sometimes show more than the outside ones."

He's One Who Is Always Alone, I realize, because all of *his* inside scars have made him so. *At a time long ago he was called Hawk because he was such a great hunter,* I hear Otter tell me.

At last Bright Feather helps me clean my eleven wounds, careful and easy. Out comes the bad smelling salve and I wrinkle my nose at the stench of it. "It seems to smell worse and worse with each day," I grumble as we dab it on all my sores. He keeps silent, and I wonder at his mood. Have I stirred up his sorrow and pain now with all of my tears? "I suspect you will be happy when I can ride on Willow instead of with you on Companion." Nothing. So I add, "Behind you. Down wind." He does not look up from his work but he grunts at me. Not only do I tear at his old inside scars but I also smell worse than a bad piece of meat. "I could ride on Willow until we stop for the evening meal, if you wish," I suggest.

It's then that he looks up at me with eyes so sharp that I lean back a bit at their force. "I would have you riding in front of me on Companion smelling twice as bad and talking twice as much," he grinds out and I'm stunned to see what might be a tear in his eye. He stands and I look up at him standing in the swift flowing stream. "I have no room inside for more scars, Bear. I am very glad that you are here. Come, dinner is ready." And he wades to shore without a backwards glance.

He would like me smelling twice as bad?!

And, an even bigger thought to ponder. He wouldn't mind me talking *twice as much?!*

I shake my head in amazement. He's one mighty strong warrior to be able to handle such things.

"How did Weasel of Dark Cloud's village come to be at One Who Knows hearth in The Maple Forest?" I ask Bright Feather as we ride once again, both on Companion, after we have eaten and rested a bit.

"At one time, the villages of Dark Cloud and Great Elk were closer together. Hunting and trapping areas were shared, braves married and lived in the hearths with their mates and there was a strength in the harmony that the two villages shared.

"The white man brought more changes than just what you can see with your eyes," he explains. "For some Real People, the opportunity to own white man's rifles and other possessions they considered of value began to interfere with the way things had always been. There were disagreements among The Real People over how things should be. Should we make changes that will make the white man happy? Should we fight to stay the same? Should we sign another treaty and give up still more hunting and trapping areas? Should we allow ourselves to be moved to unfamiliar places? Who knows the right path? Who should be listened to? Suddenly the way we had always done things, to talk and come to an agreement could not help us solve some of these concerns. For who knew if just one person was right and all the rest were wrong?"

We ride in silence for a time, and I think about the hard choices The Real People had to face. It was hard, Pa told me once, to move our whole family out to the Virginia homestead. What would it have been like had Pa tried to convince an entire town to move with him?

We talk about the neighboring Indian tribes. I'm surprised to learn that there are many reasons why the Indian's regret the white man's arrival.

Distrust and even battles between The Real People and their neighbors have been a sorry result. "You fight amongst yourselves?" I say in surprise. I remember the words about harmony and balance and the center of the world needing to be right.

"Some tribes are eager to gain white man's possessions," Bright Feather tells me, "guns, metal pots and pans, and," he says as though he has dirt in his mouth, "*liquor.* Some tribes do not agree. Disagreements lead to fights. As you have seen with Dark Cloud's village and Great Elk's village, it has reached the point that we even disagree among ourselves."

I tell him what I know about liquor. I remember a corner in Cooper's General Store and the jugs and how the men would crowd around and laugh and talk and drink. I remember Pa again saying, *"It burns your belly when you drink it, but it's your brain that carries the scars."* I tell Bright Feather.

"He was a wise man," he says, and I wonder just how wise Pa really was and what he would have thought of Bright Feather. Would he have been able to see past the skin and the feathers and the permanent lines on his face and be able to see what a good man he is – *red or white?* Would he think only savage?

The savages had their time. Their present circumstances are not our concern. That sounds as if Pa knew about the things that Beaver and the Wilders and now Bright Feather are telling me and the hard way of things for The Real People. Then I wonder, does minding your own business and keeping your head down and your mouth shut stop you from learning new things? Keep you from seeing the truth? I suspect it does. For it's only since I've made the effort to pick my head up, pay attention, ask questions and make hard choices that I've gotten to be this wise and powerful.

From my memories of Pa, he seemed fair and true. But he did not let much into his life and worked hard to stay as far away from the world as he could. He was loving and kind and true to his family. But only his family. *Would that extend to his daughter mated with an Indian brave?* I wonder. That's a question I can't truly answer.

Bright Feather does not know my thoughts and continues to explain that while the Indians desire white men's possessions, the white men desire the Indian's furs. I ponder this for a bit, and then must finally say that it sounds like an easy matter of barter and fair trade.

I feel him shake his head 'no'. "These woods and the animals in it are a good supply for the people who live here, but not for a whole world across the ocean which is where many of the furs go. Already the whites come further west to hunt, because the forests to the east are empty."

I think about Pa, Ma, Henry, Eli, and I and try to recall us traveling to the place I remember that used to be my home – Ward's Mill, Virginia. The memories are small and few, tiny flashes of moments; a white wagon, a bear and Ma's frightened screams, Henry holding a small baby rabbit he found in the woods. "Pa was a white man, but in some ways he lived like an Indian," I say after a while. "He had no desire to become rich or to hurt or kill. He just wanted to be left alone to live a life with his wife and children on a piece of land he could call his own." Memories of how things changed after Ma's death are clearer for they are more recent. "When Ma died it seemed that Pa lived only for each day. There was little talk of times before nor was there any talk of future dreams." I realize that made him even more like an Indian.

"Dark Cloud argued very strongly in those early times that we should accept the white man's offers," Bright Feather explains. "He traveled to see the land they offered to give us if we would move from the forests, and he said that the land was fertile, the forests full of animals, and the rivers jumping with fish. He embraced many of the white man's ways, had already agreed to move to the village you saw, and was happy to accept many gifts that were offered to him: guns, clothing, cooking utensils, seed for planting. Great Elk felt less certain about the decision. He counseled with those in his village he respected: Cloud, War Woman, One Who Knows, and many others I cannot name. No one from Dark Cloud's village had seen what War Woman had seen in The Great War. No one felt that a move would bring us balance or harmony. We already knew the woods and the mountains, the streams and the animals. Our ancestors' spirits roamed the land and guided and protected us. Great Elk decided to stay in The Maple Forest, and so the villages became two places great distances apart rather then two places a day's quick ride away."

I feel Bright Feather shrug as I lean against him. "Great effort was made to maintain contact, but the differences became greater with each passing season. The white men had great hunger for the deer hides and furs that our forests provided, and Dark Cloud and his people began to hunt for more than just themselves. They forgot, I think, about the important role a hunter plays in the forest. They no longer respected and appreciated the animal for the gifts it gave us, but saw it only as a way to acquire more things." He shook his head and said almost to himself, "There is no balance in a life that lives to only get more things.

"In a final effort to keep the contact between the villages, it was decided that braves from each village should be encouraged to marry women in the opposite villages. It was something that had always been done in the past, but with the great distance it had not happened in many seasons. There was a great outcry from both places, I understand, neither wanting to move to the other's village." Very quietly I hear him say, "Maybe they were right...." He offers no more information, and I'm left to guess and sort out ghosts that neither one of us can name.

Finally I say, "Dark Cloud's village did not have the same feeling as The Maple Forest. When I was there I felt ... mixed up. It was like before I found my center and decided what I would be. Only it was a whole village of people like that."

We ride in silence for a bit, and I wait. At last Bright Feather says, "The Maple Forest fights to keep the harmony and balance that we know is so right. But it is very hard to find harmony and balance anywhere else."

I begin to doze to the rhythm and sway and warmth of the ride. "And what is in your center, Bear?" Bright Feather asks me as his arm tightens around my waist and Companion works his way careful down the sloping path.

I realize that I've let some things into my center that I shouldn't have. Weasel's cruel words for one. I'll have to work hard to get them all cleaned out. I think about the Wilders' words and about this soul of mine that they seemed so powerful worried about. Perhaps I should put that in my center to protect it, too. I'll ponder that. "Me," I finally say to Bright Feather. "A wise and powerful woman named Bear. She loves to learn, and she is working hard to keep only the good things in and the all the bad things out." I turn to look at him behind me. "And she has a color. She is not white. She will never be red. She is pink."

"Pink," he says and grunts.

By the second full day on the trail, I insist that I'm strong enough to ride Willow. I suspect Bright Feather travels slower and stops more often than he would if he was alone, but I don't say anything. My cuts and bites have stopped bleeding and some have begun to heal. There are two bites, one on my left breast and one high on my right hip that cause me much pain and show signs of festering. At each stop Bright Feather makes certain I go and clean all of my wounds carefully, and I continue to spread the ointment on them. It's bear grease, he suspects, with special herbs that One Who Knows mixed up before he and Raccoon set out in search of me.

I'm surprised to hear that there are some in Great Elk's village who thought at first that I'd made a run to go back to Virginia and Pa, Henry, and Eli. It's Otter and Raccoon, and most surprising to me, One Who Knows, who steps forward and say no to this, but precious time was lost in the arguing. Bright Feather and Raccoon found the place in the woods where I fought and understood the truth of things. Red Fox and Beaver wished to come along to search as well, but Great Elk had them stay in case the village needed to be protected. I'm amazed to learn that all those weeks I waited in Dark Cloud's village Raccoon and Bright Feather were camped no more than a day's ride away waiting and watching patiently for a good time to rescue me.

"Raccoon was certain that you would escape, and we only needed to wait for you to show up," Bright Feather said. He studies me for a moment. "You may make him tired with all your questions, but he thinks greatly of you."

"What do you think of me?" I ask, and then wish I can suck the words back in my mouth before they reach Bright Feather's ears. What made me ask such a thing I wonder?

We have finally stopped for the night, and I'm tired and sore from a full day of riding, even if we are going at a slow pace. He stirs up the fire that we have started to cook the rabbit he has caught. The sparks shoot up into the night and look like stars in the night sky. When I look at him he's watching me, "You are someone who despite all the things that have happened to you can still find joy in life. You change people who are close to you with the person that you are. That makes you very strong. When I am with you, I feel like my name is Bright Feather instead of One Who Is Always Alone." I've no more questions to ask and nothing to say.

Towards the end of the third day on the trail, I find myself achy and tired. The bites on my hip and breast pain me, and I'm looking forward to getting down off Willow and washing in a cool stream. Bright Feather startles me by saying, "I can take you back to Virginia if you wish."

I'm so stunned that Willow and I just stop on the trail while Bright Feather and Companion continue on ahead of us. He knows I've stopped following him, but he continues on a bit before he has Companion stop. With his back still to me he says, "Great Elk said I was to do as you wished if I found you."

My precious box with memories of Pa, Henry and Eli bursts open, and they fly all around me like the bees around a flower. I've trouble remembering their faces I find, but I remember Pa's laugh and the silky feel of Eli's brown hair. I can feel Henry's strong arms around me as he hauls me up over his shoulder and dumps me – clothes and all! - into the stream. I can see one of Henry's rare smiles as I sputter and try to stand in my clumsy wet skirts and splash him. I can see our cabin in the woods and the flower garden that Ma planted and that Pa and I worked hard to keep alive. I see Eli's big blue eyes and those eyes float up before me, and they become the dark eyes of Little Bird and Pa's laugh becomes Otter's as we giggle over something silly. I see Cloud sitting in the warm sunshine with my Elk's antlers tied to the front of his hut. And I remember the night Elle went away and I became Bear, a powerful woman, and how the village cheered a welcome. I think of Miss Rebecca and her words to me, *You are no longer white. You will never be red. I think you are just a beautiful shade of pink.* I come back to the here and now, and Bright Feather is still sitting on

Companion with his back to me waiting patient as ever to hear if he will get an answer.

My knees tell Willow to move up the trail until I'm alongside Bright Feather who is staring straight ahead at the tree line in front of us. He looks tense to me, like he's ready to go into battle. I reach out to touch him and hesitate. I realize I've never touched him before. *He* had touched *me*, but never the other way around. I suddenly have such a powerful strong urge to do just that that my fingers twitch, and so I do.

His arm is warm and solid, a deep reddish brown compared to my white, tan hand. I feel the muscles in his arm jump, and he turns to look at me. I loose my words and my thoughts as we stare at each other in the late afternoon sunshine. As usual, his face is careful to show nothing, but I wonder what mine shows. *I like this Bright Feather I'm learning to know,* I think loud and clear in my head. Bright Feather looks down at my hand still resting on his arm and then back to my face.

I take a moment to find my voice and then say, "I was happy when I lived in Virginia with Pa, Henry, and Eli. My life with them was not easier or harder, it was just different. I was happy in Great Elk's village, too. I found a person that I didn't know I could be." *I'm pink now,* I think to myself. "I don't think I can go back to being Elle. You cannot put a plant back into its seed. I like the person that I have become in Great Elk's village. I like this powerful woman, Bear. I think I want to keep watching and see what else she will do." He has a moment where I can almost say he looks pleased, and then he frowns at me, suddenly furious it seems. His hand reaches across and covers mine that's still on his arm. His touch is wonderfully cool.

"Bear ..." he begins and makes hasty moves to get off Companion and come around beside me still seated on Willow. I puzzle over his sudden change in mood. "Bear, you are very hot," he says with real concern in his voice. He reaches up, and I protest as he makes a move to help me down.

"Don't!" I shout, afraid he will touch my sore hip or breast.

He hesitates just a moment and then turns into a stubborn mountain right before my eyes. "I will," he says. His strong hands reach up and lift me gently down with only a brief twinge of pain. He leads me to a spot of shade, has me sit down, and then squats before me. "Let me see," he says fiercely, and I know not to argue.

The two wounds are wet and oozing and have stuck to the soft buckskin of Otter's shirt. As the fabric separates from the skin, I feel a sticky wetness trickle from both places and a bad smell rises up from them that has nothing to do with One Who Knows' salve. "Bear," he says in a very angry tone, "you told me that they were healing!"

I feel angry a little and tired a lot. "Most of them are!" I say strong like back to him. "Except these two," I say a little less strong.

He makes a moaning sound in the back of his throat and makes quick moves to set up camp and get a fire going. When I try to help he shouts at me, "Sit and stay!" like I'm an annoying child. I glare at him for a bit, but he takes no notice. I doze, lying on a blanket as he moves about the camp. I'm far too hot to cover myself, and the cool evening air feels good on my burning skin.

When Bright Feather comes to squat beside me and cover me I throw the covers off. "It's too hot," I grumble. If he treats me like a child, I decide, I'll act like one.

He makes me drink from a water skin. "I go to find some more water," he says. "We have not camped close to a stream."

"You chose this spot, not me," I say, fanning myself with my hand. "Why did you start a fire? It is *so hot.*"

He touches my neck with his wonderful cool hand and moans again in the back of his throat. "Stay here, Bear. On your pallet. Do not move. Do not get up. Do you hear me?"

I give him an angry look. "No wonder you are always alone," I say with a smart lip as I close my eyes. "It is because you are so bossy, no one can be bothered with you."

He grunts and stands up holding our water skins.

I don't know when he returns, but when I next open my eyes he's squatting by the fire tending to our birch bark bowl we carry for cooking. *He's a handsome man,* my head thinks as I watch him working. Then he turns to look at me and gives me a fierce frown. I sigh and close my eyes again.

I struggle mightily with Bright Feather when he comes to clean my wounds. "I can do it myself," I insist, but he's back to his silent self and ignores my words as if I've not even spoken.

He sits besides me grimly with a birch bark bowl and a deerskin cloth. "I must work to clean the bites that are the most sore, Bear. You will not like me for a time."

I can't help but say, "What makes you think I like you at all?" but then I smile a bit. As usual he does not think I'm funny. *I miss Raccoon,* I think sudden like. At least he teases me back.

Finally he says, "I will work as quickly as I can, but you must let me do what I must do? All right, Bear?" When I just stare at him without answering, because my words are a bit confused in my head, he leans down and looks into my eyes, "Did you know that all powerful women each have their own special war cry?"

I blink at him, and try to focus, but the heat that's rising off of me is making things blurry. I shake my head 'no'.

He nods as he puts down his bowl and dips the rag into the liquid. I see that it's steaming too, with heat. "Yes," he says and takes a deep breath. "Powerful women scream their war cry when they are most angry, most sad, and most hurt." He touches my cheek with one cool finger. "Tonight you will find your war cry, hmm?"

Despite the fire Bright Feather builds, by the time it's dark I'm so cold I can't stop shivering. My throat and voice, sore and tired from my war cry, moan at the pain that the shivering causes to the rest of my hurts. *How can a body be so hot one moment and so cold the next?* I think in my misery, along with, *I'll never, ever be warm again.* Finally, a very hot body and strong arms surround me and hold me tight and share a warmth that my body can't make on its own.

I have busy dreams that mix up my lives and make them one: Bright Feather trying to pull a blanket over my head and take me away from where I want to be. Pa and Raccoon hunting. Eli tied on Little Bird's cradleboard and swinging on a tree hung by a pink ribbon. Henry teaching me how to shoot a bow and arrow and looking close in my face and speaking *Francois*. Bear John with a burning stick that he touches to my hip and to my breast and me screaming with the pain of it. My Ma comes to me and she cradles me in her arms and sings to me a lullaby in the language of The Real People. Sometimes Bright Feather is there in my dreams forcing me to drink cool water, but sometimes it is Weasel and I fight powerful hard to get away. I hear Miss Rebecca's words over and over, *For I know the plans I have for you, to give you a future and a hope.*

I open my eyes, and they focus on Bright Feather who is sitting against the opening of a small cave, his long legs stretched out in front of him. A small fire smolders just at the cave's opening and sputters now and then as drops of rain hit it. His eyes are closed and his breathing peaceful, yet he has an alertness about him that makes me know he's not full asleep. It's pouring rain outside; a mighty thunder of water crashing down all around us. Inside this little place we are warm and dry. I study his face and I think he looks mighty tired. I make the slightest move and his eyes snap open and he looks at me. He looks close at my face, and I see him relax a bit. He draws one leg up and leans his arm across it. "How do you feel?" he says quiet like.

I shift a bit and feel a little like the time I fell off Willow when Raccoon was first teaching me to ride and tell him so. "You have been sick for a while," he says.

I struggle to sit up, and it takes great effort and my head swims round and round like pieces are loose inside. He comes to me and squats down. With both hands on my shoulders he steadies me. He seems to know not to let me go or I'll fall right over. "How long have I been sick?"

"You have been with fever for three days," he says.

"Three days!" I shout. He grunts.

He shifts and moves so that he's behind me, and I'm leaning against his chest, sitting between his legs. I hear him yawn, and he reaches up a hand to rub his face a bit. "Raccoon knew what he was talking about when he said you could make a body more tired then anyone else he knew." I turn to see his face, and he bends down so I can look at him. His dark hair and colorful feathers swing loose behind his shoulder. His eyes are so dark brown you can't really see the black centers in the light of the cave. *Here is a good man,* I think loud and clear and strong in my head. I reach up to touch a yellow feather. *The goldfinch is hard to see even in the best of seasons. You can search all summer and hardly catch a glimpse of him.* Bright Feather has dark circles under his eyes. "Are you hungry?" he asks quiet like.

My stomach rumbles loud enough to be heard over the rain, and before I can speak he reaches across to hand me a bowl of warm rabbit stew. I hold it in my lap and take a small taste. It's delicious, and I gobble it all down. "Sleep some more," he finally says after sitting quiet behind me while I eat. As he moves away and I lay down again, he sounds very far away to me. "Tomorrow we must move from here to stay safe." My last thought before I fall asleep is, *I always feel safe with you.*

I feel much better in the morning and with Bright Feather's help I'm able to wash at the stream. Both bites look much better and no longer ooze or smell. There's a good scab over the top of both and some of the other knife cuts and bites itch something terrible. Bright Feather says that's good, too.

I once again ride in front of Bright Feather, too weak to ride far on Willow on my own. I notice we travel east, the first time we have gone in that direction since we have left Raccoon, and say so.

"Unless you tell me different, we return to Great Elk's village. We will be there in five days at a fast pace, six otherwise." He rides silent behind me while I once again think about what he has said about taking me home to Virginia.

"It would be dangerous for you to take me back to Ward's Mill," I say.

"It can be done," is all he says back to me.

"I have been gone a long time," I feel inclined to point out.

"Not so long," Mr. Talkative answers back.

"Do you think I should go back?" I ask, powerful curious to hear what he will say.

"No one can choose your own life path but you."

"Weasel did," I say with a bit of anger.

"Did he?" Bright Feather asks, "Or did he just bring you to another place to start making new choices once again?"

I think back to the time when I knew that the only thing keeping me in The Maple Forest was my own self and what I couldn't or wouldn't do. I keep quiet because Bright Feather is right about Weasel. My thoughts of The Maple Forest make me excited to see Otter and Little Bird and Cloud and even, maybe, One Who Knows, and I know I won't tell Bright Feather different. I think then of Red Fox and Beaver, and I feel tired again. I must make a sound like a sigh. "You are not happy we return to the village?" Bright Feather asks.

I tell him about spring and mating and Red Fox and Beaver. I tell him about Otter and the basket of apples. I tell him about sitting up on my quiet spot the day they came and took me, and why I'd gone there that day, and that I was thinking about all the choices I have as a powerful Indian woman. I wait to hear what he has to say, and I think about how much I like to talk to Bright Feather, because he always seems to listen and tries to understand.

"All I wanted when I was a boy was to be a great hunter," he says after a time.

"It seems you got your wish."

He shrugs his shoulders. "When you are young you are stupid, too. You don't always know the best things to wish for."

"I never even knew I *could* wish for anything," I tell him. "For almost all of my life I have done what was needed or expected. There was not a time ever, until I became Bear, that I was told I could decide what I wanted to do with my life. *Having choices!* There is a magic in just that, you know … More than I thought I could even dream of."

He thinks on this for a while. I can tell I've given him a new taste to try in his mind. "So what choices are there for a powerful woman to consider?" he asks. I know he's not teasing me.

"That's part of the fun. I don't even know them all yet." I say. "All of a sudden I am no longer the mule, I am the driver. Who knows where I can go or what I can do? I guess the only choice I must make right now is when do I stop looking at the choices and start making some?"

"Choices are a little bit like weeds," he says at last. "Some left to grow can have beautiful flowers. Others might be important for healing. But if you aren't careful and choose some to pull out now and then, they'll take over your whole garden and you won't have any crops to harvest come fall. You'll die from starvation. You never have to *stop looking* for choices, but always, at the same time, you must never *stop making* them. That's life."

We ride in silence for a very long time as I think about all the choices I've to consider. "When we get back to Great Elk's village," he says as the sun begins to set, "you must choose a mate. Otter is right."

"That's the one choice I don't want to make yet!" I shout, and his arm goes tight around me to keep me from jumping off Companion and moving away from his words.

With his arm tight around my waist and his mouth close against my ear he says, "The only way you can keep your other choices is to make this one. Choose a mate who will let you keep looking for other choices *or* the choice you've made of staying with The Real People may be taken from you instead."

I twist in the saddle to look at him and feel the pull of the scabs at my hip and my breast but I don't care. "Why do you say that?" I shout.

"Because," he says calm and quiet like, "you will always be more tempting to be rescued and brought back should you remain on your own. Remember, they look to rescue a 'captive white girl'. Once you take a mate and establish a family and blood ties, things will be much more difficult to unravel. You may think you are Bear, and to many of us you are, but you must realize that to some - red *and* white - you will always be *Elle*." My white name sounds funny in his mouth.

I'm more quiet than ever as we set up camp for the night and prepare the evening meal. Bright Feather leaves me alone with my thoughts, and we work and eat in silence. My brain works and works to put all my choices in a pile, and I sort through them one by one trying to make everything fit just like I want. No matter how many times I try, it always comes back to the same way of thinking; Bright Feather and Otter saw what I did not. If I'm a mate of an Indian brave and a mother of Indian children, there will be many more strong reasons for me to stay where I want to stay than if I stay Bear, a powerful woman on her own. The Indians might understand this way of thinking but white folk never ever will. As I fall asleep under the stars I make a choice that really is no choice; I understand that I must choose a mate.

I spend the whole next day riding on Willow lost in more choices. I don't see the beautiful forests, I don't hear the conversations of the birds, I don't taste the cold venison we chew for lunch, and I don't notice the place we choose to stop for the night. I think about Red Fox and his kindness and patience as he taught me to shoot a bow under Cloud's directions. I think about his shy smile when I ask many questions and his willingness to answer and explain everything I ask to know. I think about us taking turns being the hunter and the hunted and the laughter and fun we have together. I think about his offers to take me hunting, to go riding with me. I remember discovering through Otter that I seem to be the only thing in the village he watches closely, and how she said that I was the first girl in the village that Red Fox has ever seemed interested in.

I think of Beaver, tall and sure and proud. He's War Woman's son. For the first time I think, is he Great Elk's son, too? I compare the two and realize they are the same height, they have the same muscular build, and they have the same proud bearing. Yes, they are of the same blood, I conclude, and another piece to the puzzle of life in the village slips into place. I'm amazed that of all the young women in camp, Beaver has looked at *me*. I can become the mate of one of the most powerful men in the village it seems. I think about him and his patience on our hunts, teaching me how to track animals and tell one apart from another just by what they leave behind. I think about him working patiently to teach me how to light a fire. I think about his sitting with Otter and Raccoon and me the many nights he visited our hearth and talked. I think about the wonderful stories he tells that bring the way of The Real People to life in my mind.

The silence between Bright Feather and I is comfortable. He seems as comfortable with my silence as he does with my questions. After almost two weeks on the trail with only each other for company, we have found an easy rhythm. He's not at all surprised it seems, after almost a full day of silence between us, when I finally ask over our evening meal, "How does a woman choose a mate?"

"She begins to spend time with him, she accepts gifts from him and does kindnesses for him in return, and at some point they choose to set up a hearth together."

"White folks have to have a preacher – a special man of God - say special words before you call yourself joined," I volunteer.

"Is that so?" he says. "There is often a celebration in the village at the time, but there is no other person that says 'yes' or 'no" to the joining. It is the couple's choice, and often they live together for a time to see if the choice is right."

"What happens if a baby comes?" I ask.

He looks surprised at the question, "Babies are always considered a wonderful thing." I realize I still have many thoughts in my head that are white.

"What happens if a woman is interested in a man who doesn't seem interested in her?"

He shrugs. "She makes her interest known, and he must decide what his thoughts are."

I sigh. "I am certain Pa married Ma 'cause he loved her," I say remembering. I see flashes of laughter and smiles between the two of them. I hear him calling her "Lizzie" sometimes instead of her proper name, Elizabeth. I know for sure that the only times I ever heard Pa laugh was when Ma was around to cause it. I can hear her voice say with soft love, "Oh, Andrew," over something he has said or done that I can't remember. I remember a sadness in Pa that never went away after she died. He became a different person. I look at Bright Feather and think, *Pa would have changed his name after Ma died had that been our custom, too.* But Pa had me, Henry, and Eli, and he couldn't become One Who Is Always Alone. A wave of missing Pa washes over me that I haven't felt in a long time. I work hard to close my memory box.

"There are many reasons to join with another, Bear," Bright Feather says after a time. "Some join for love, some to make tribes and families stronger – like Great Elk and Dark Cloud's villages, some to gain more respect in the village," he looks to me, "and some for security and wise choices for the future."

I make a face at him. "That is an old song I have heard too much of these past days."

He shrugs his shoulders and becomes silent again, eating the last of his meal. I study him and remember. Bright Feather, the hunter, sitting silent, alone and nigh on invisible in the woods, waiting. Bright Feather the night he brings me Willow in the council circle and calls me "Bear". Bright Feather helping me train Willow and answering question after question I ask. Bright Feather holding my face right after my dark time with Weasel and saying my name and the look in his eyes. Bright Feather holding and rocking me as I talked about my inside scars. Bright Feather sitting in the cave tired and exhausted from caring for me while I was sick. I have a thought, and I decide to speak real quick before I change my mind, like jumping into a pond you know will be ice cold so you do it fast to get it over with. "I have spent time with you and have received gifts from you and have done kindnesses for you in return, and I have even kept a hut with you."

"So you have, Bear," he says, and he waits patient like, his brown eyes staring at my face and the breeze blowing his colorful feathers and loose flowing hair around his head.

"And you will let me keep looking for choices even while I keep making them," I say quiet like, almost at a whisper.

"So I will, Bear," he says, and still he keeps looking at me with nothing moving but his hair and feathers.

"And you don't seem to get as tired as Raccoon when you are with me, and you seem willing to answer my questions and teach me things that I still need to know to become a more powerful woman," I say in a whisper that's hardly louder than the breeze.

"So I do, Bear," he says.

I feel the tears pool in the corners of my eyes and begin to wander down my cheeks as I look into his face, and I see things that he has never, ever let me see before: caring, loneliness, need... There's no hate to eat these tears I realize, and I can't stop them. He reaches across the fire to catch one tear with his finger, and I speak again so quiet he must lean forward to hear me. "And I think," I say almost more to myself than to him for he must surely know the answer already, "you must like me just some small, small bit."

"A powerful woman is good company for One Who Is Always Alone," he says, and he takes me in his arms and holds me very tight.

You are part of me now, you touched me.

With your kindness and love so enchanted.

Your soft lips are kind. Your eyes glow with life.

I'm glad you touched me. You're part of me now.[7]

~Lloyd Carl Owle

Mate

"I think," I say to Bright Feather much later on as I watch him add more wood to the fire, "that this mating thing is much more complicated than I ever dreamed."

"How is that, Bear?" he asks as he comes back beside me, lying on his side, propped up on one elbow with his silky dark hair collecting on the pallet behind him.

"Well," I say, "I just had no idea that you mate with your head and your heart as well as your ..." I clear my throat and suspect I blush a bit, "well you know what I mean."

"No," he says serious like, "I don't. Try to explain."

I start to open my mouth and explain, and I catch Bright Feather's look. I sit up and study him for a moment in the firelight as he looks right back at me. "You're teasing me!" I say in absolute wonder, for as best as I can recall he has never done or said anything but serious things for as long as I've known him. He grunts a sound that I suddenly realize is as close to a laugh as he can manage. He reaches out to me and runs a finger from the top of my forehead, down my nose, slow across my lips and then down my neck between my breasts to my belly and beyond. I feel my nipples tighten and my stomach clench and goose skin runs wild all over my body, and I decide to stop talking for a while again. I suspect I need to learn a lot more about this mating business before I'll be able to explain anything.

Nine days later, we enter Great Elk's village of The Maple Forest amid great shouts of welcome. It seems we have traveled slower than even Bright Feather planned. Otter and Raccoon stand outside their hut with grins that just about split their faces apart. Toddling at their feet is Little Bird, walking on two very fat, sturdy legs. There's great commotion in the village, and after we care for our horses we are fair rushed to the council circle before we have time to even wash, eat, or drink.

Seated in the bright spring sunshine are many faces I'm familiar with; Great Elk, War Woman, Raccoon, One Who Knows, and Beaver among them. But I'm stunned to see a white man dressed in some Indian style and some white, sitting comfortably next to Great Elk, laughing and talking with much ease. I feel my steps slow and fear shoot like lightning all through me. I hear Bright Feather's words of delight from a distance further than where he truly stands, "Deer! My brother! At last you have found time to return to your home!"

The white man stands, wraps his arms tightly around Bright Feather, and says in perfect Indian words, "One Who Is Always Alone! What are you doing here? You should be out hiding by yourself in the woods like I hear you always do!" There's much back-slapping and good natured shoving, and Bright Feather shows a joy that I've seen only in the last few weeks.

I stay silent and apart during this time, but Bright Feather finally turns to me and says, "Bear! Come meet my brother, Deer. He has been away from us for a long time, and it is good to have him back!"

I step forward, awkward and fearful, but somewhat better having watched Bright Feather's mood. *Would he not have a worry if there is one?* I think. "Welcome, Deer, brother of One Who Is Always Alone. I am glad to know you," I say carefully.

"No you are not!" he laughs good-naturedly. "You look terrified! Has anyone not told this child of me?" he shouts to the crowd as he reaches out to grasp my hand and hold it firm and sure.

I feel my back go up like an angry camp dog. "I am not a child," I hear myself growl, furious at the first thoughts I've caused in his head. I stand tall and push the fear away, reminding myself that I am a powerful woman. "I am Bear, of Great Elk's village, of The Maple Forest of The Real People. I have earned the name and the right to say that." I firmly remove my stiff hand from his warm one.

"Whoa-ho!" he shouts with delight, and makes a motion to count all the fingers on his hand to see if I've bitten one off. He turns to Raccoon and says, "You were right about her! She is much more than she first appears." I glare angry eyes at Raccoon who gives me his innocent look. Deer bows respectfully towards me, but his eyes as he lifts them to look at me twinkle with mischief and delight. "Please, accept my apologies if I have caused you offense, Bear, of Great Elk's village, of The Maple Forest of The Real People. You must know that all Raccoon has learned about the seriousness of life and all that One Who Is Always Alone has learned about the dealings between others, they have me to thank for."

I can't stay angry but also can't keep myself from saying with a flip tongue, "Then I add another man to my list of who I must retrain." But I smile at him just the same.

"I look forward to the opportunity," he says with a wink.

I've many, *many* questions boiling in my head for Bright Feather, but they must wait. Questions are directed to me and Bright Feather instead about our travels and time away. Much information is exchanged, and I'm surprised to hear Bright Feather report on what seems to be the borders of Great Elk's territory. It has not occurred to me that he would be expected to do such a thing. Could I have been so complete with my descriptions had they asked me the same questions? I disappoint myself because I know the answer is 'no'. They ask him questions about animal patterns and human activity and finally a few brief questions about Dark

Cloud's village. Weasel is never mentioned. *They must have talked with Raccoon just like they talk with us now,* I realize.

They ask me questions, too. How large is Dark Cloud's village? How many braves? How many whites? How many soldiers? How many huts? How many horses? Do the people look healthy and strong and well fed? Did I see any sickness? What did I hear and see that I think is important for them to know? I try very hard to tell them as much as I can remember.

I tell them how there's a different feeling in Dark Cloud's village. People behave differently with each other, the men to the women, the women to the men, the adults to the children. I try hard to explain but it's difficult. "There is more secrecy, more fear, more distrust it seems between everyone. Every face works hard to tell a different story than what really is."

When I speak of the white men who seem so comfortable in Dark Cloud's village there's great interest. I'm able to answer their questions in most cases. How many white men? What kind of weapons did I see? I tell them of guns and metal pots and pans for cooking. I tell them of the white clothing on the Indian people and even how the white men have places to sleep in the village. I tell them of two white men style homes, one for the preacher and one for Dark Cloud, and the large building that's used as a church, school, and council meeting place with chairs and tables. I talk of more building that's planned and how I understand it's to be for a large school.

They hear about Reverend Wilder and his wife, Miss Rebecca, and their plans for a mission school as well as the farming and weaving projects. I remember that they spoke of money from the Government of the United States and from the American Mission Board. "I believe that Reverend Wilder and Miss Rebecca are filled with good intentions." I tell them. "They seemed at all times to have nothing but good thoughts for The Real People who they help and teach. But they are the only white people I saw there that I can say that about. I have fear for the Wilders for they seemed to be in as much danger as I was."

I tell them of the French that I heard spoken and how I understood the Indians better than some of the whites when they spoke. I tell them how it seemed that both languages fit in the village, and it seemed to be only me who couldn't speak the French white words.

Finally, War Woman addresses me. "One Who Is Always Alone spoke with you and the choice you had to return to Virginia." It's a statement, not a question with an odd accent on the English word.

I nod my head yes. "One Who Is Always Alone told me of this offer," I say. "But I am eager to get to know more of this powerful woman that's called Bear who I now am. I choose to stay here in Great Elk's village in The Maple Forest."

"It is possible that your presence can bring trouble to this village," she says, and I feel my heart begin to pound loudly in my chest and in my ears. This is what Dark Cloud had said as well. Will they make me leave now that I've chosen to stay? I glance at the faces around the circle and look longer at the new face of Deer than any of the others. I think, why has he not been spoken of before? Has he brought news that I'm the only one who does not know? He looks back at me with an Indian face; it tells me nothing.

War Woman and I look at each other across the council fire. *Are you white?* I hear her ask me. I choose my words careful like and speak with great respect, "It would seem you speak only of my skin color because I have made my best effort to be a powerful woman of The Real People in every way but that," I begin, stopping for a bit to let my words sink in. I try to calm my pounding heart by remembering her kind words so many months ago. *I watch you because I try to see how you are coping with the blood on your hands. It is not an easy thing to become accustomed to.*

No one speaks. I swallow and continue. "But there have been others in this village who I will not speak of who have had the right skin color and yet seem to have brought more trouble and sorrow than I can even think of.

"I was taken from my home in Virginia by force. Over this past year, I have struggled with who I am and where is home. I look at my skin and I think, "Am I red? Am I white? Is one right? Is one wrong? At one time in my life I would have called you all red savages." I look at each of the serious faces watching and listening to me speak here at the council fire. I remember wanting to have wise enough words so that others would want to hear them. I swallow with worry. When does a body know when that time has come? I for sure don't. But I will tell them the truth of the thoughts in my head and let them decide for themselves. "That was all that my head knew about skin color: black was slave, red was savage and white was everything else." I shake my head. "It was not much to know, that is for sure."

I sit up straight. Proud. Tall. "But I am older, now. And wiser. And more powerful because of it. I know that the color of my skin has nothing to do with whether I am a slave or a savage or anything else. It has everything to do with what is inside my head and my heart. It has everything to do with what I choose to make my center."

I look at War Woman. "You told me once that life has always pulled you forward faster than you felt ready for." She does not nod, but she blinks. "It seems that will be the way for me, too. This past year has not been easy, but I am better for it. And that is why I wish to stay here in The Maple Forest. I would see what else this place can teach me and help me to become.

"One Who Is Always Alone has shared with me the dangers this village faces in having me live here with you. Even Dark Cloud spoke of it to me. But tell me this: should I leave, will this village cease to face dangers? Who is to say that as the white man comes further west – and we all must believe that he will – that I will not be a help to this village; a woman who has lived in both worlds?" I've a flash of Rebecca Wilder and realize that I, too, love these people now and want them to succeed, just like she and her husband do. *They are my people now, and I want to be theirs.*

I put my hands out in front of me, palms up, where they are the whitest even with my summer brown skin. *Let them look and see,* I think, *one last time and let this all be over – who is white and who is red.* "Is this all you see of me?" I ask quiet like. "I have learned that there is so much more to a person than just what your eyes can see." My gut clenches with the need for them to understand this as I do now. "*I am so much more, you know*," I say to them with pleading eyes.

I glance at Bright Feather sitting silent and still. The look he sends gives me strength to finish. I clench both my hands into fists and rest them in my lap. "There are dangers at all times in life! Let me tell you the story of my life so far to prove my point! I have learned that life is filled with choices, some of them very hard to make. I have made the choice to stay here. I am ready to become a part of this village and all that that means."

I stop and am quiet for a moment. I look at Great Elk, War Woman, One Who Knows, Raccoon, and Beaver. I make my eyes meet each one of the people that sit around the circle. "But should this village wish for me to leave because they feel that it is a better choice for all, then I will go, for I want only what's best for this place I now call home." I take a breath to calm my stomach, head, and heart, and look down at the hands in my lap that I'm now holding tightly together. "Thank you for listening to my words," I say quiet like, full of worry that I've said too much. Or not enough. "I have finished speaking."

Bright Feather reaches out and places his hand on my tightly clasped ones, warm and strong. It's a motion that stuns even me for it's not his way to even speak, much less to show how he feels with a touch in front of all. I look up at him in surprise, but he's looking at those around the council fire. "And should you ask her to leave, I will go with her," he says, quietly but firmly to all.

I catch Raccoon's look of wonderment that says, *Otter was right again.*

I feel a warmth seep from mine and Bright Feather's hands right through my body to my heart. *Pay attention to all of us wise and powerful women!* my look says back to Raccoon when he glances my way. I take another deep breath and get ready to hear what else will be said this day.

There's much silence around the council circle as everyone chews on the words I've said, sprinkled at the last with Bright Feather's surprise. Finally, Great Elk speaks to me. "You are well spoken, Bear. For one that struggled so long to learn our language it is obvious that you no longer have trouble."

I look at Raccoon who has made a small sound in his throat but has an innocent look on his face as he meets my glance. "It is surprising that you speak of the white man coming further west," Great Elk continues in his deep, smooth voice. "Deer has only arrived this morning and is here to tell us more of what he has learned about the white man's plans regarding where he wants to put his foot next. It would seem that there is talk of still another treaty and another attempt to gain more land from us. He feels that very soon we will be asked to attend a great council to discuss this. Speak to us Deer and tell us what you know."

Deer addresses the council circle in serious tones. "I hear many things at the trading post when I walk in my white life as William Holland Thomas. Some things I know to ignore for I consider the source, and some I know to follow through on. I am most fortunate to have some powerful friends in the white world some through the accident of my birth and others through the course of my schooling in the law. Some share my passion for The Real People," here he shrugs, "and some do not. But it is always wise to know what your enemy is thinking as well as your friend. I am known throughout the area as one who sides regularly with what is in the best interests of The Real People."

White life? School of Law? Accidents of birth? My head whirls with all that's being said while Deer, or *William Holland Thomas*, continues to speak to us. Oh, the questions I want to ask!

"I speak to you today as a full a son of War Woman's hearth, of the Wolf Clan, of The Maple Forest of The Real People. Brother to a precious few," he looks around the circle and makes eye contact with Beaver, Bright Feather, and Otter, "and your chosen eyes, ears and mouth in the white world. I will remind all of you of things as they were and as they are, for there are some who do not know and some who may need to be reminded. It is always important not to forget the good as well as the bad. That keeps us wiser.

"The last treaty between the government of the United States of America and The Nation of The Real People was one that gave more than half of the tribal lands to the whites in exchange for money and other lands across the Mississippi River."

Deer draws a circle in the dirt. "If we were to divide all of The Real People into three equal pieces," he cuts the circle into three big pieces of pie, "one piece would be to the west of the Mississippi and two pieces would still remain in the east on the small piece of land that the United States Government allows us to call our own. As you know, a delegation of representatives from The Nation of The Real People traveled out west of the Mississippi River at the time that this treaty was being considered and selected lands they agreed to accept in trade for what they planned to give up here. Many promises were made by the United States Government to help make the move and the trade favorable and profitable for The Real People."

I look around the council fire at those sitting listening to Deer talk, and they wear the same sad face that Deer wears. "We now know that many of these promises have not been faithfully kept."

Deer looks right at me when he says, "This 'Nation of The Real People' that the United States Government deals with and talks to is different from what you know here in The Maple Forest, Bear. When I speak of 'The Nation of The Real People', you must understand that I am not speaking of people in The Maple Forest."

I frown my confusion and work powerful hard to keep my questions to myself. In the council circle it's not proper to interrupt speakers until they are finished. "Those who support The Nation of The Real People argue strongly that the only way to survive the encroachment of the whites is to adopt their white ways. But in an effort to gain recognition by the United States government, the ways they have adopted are greatly contrary to the way things have always been, our *Old Ways*. It is as if they wish for The Nation of The Real People to be like the white world in every way but skin color."

Deer looks at War Woman and One Who Knows and then back to me. "In The Nation of The Real People, the advice of powerful and wise women such as War Woman and One Who Knows is no longer welcomed in important decisions nor is their counsel sought or listened to. They are no longer allowed to express opinions nor are they allowed to help choose the men who go to the treaty councils to represent them."

He looks at the entire council group and gestures wide with his arms, "This council circle here in The Maple Forest no longer holds power in The Nation of The Real People as it once did. They no longer wish to hear our words of advice or caution. They wish our children to be schooled in the ways of white children: they wish us to worship their God and to learn their language. They wish to encourage all men to become farmers, not hunters, for farmers need less land than hunters do. The government of The Nation of The Real People accepts and welcomes these changes while here in The Maple Forest we do not."

Deer looks at me again. "Bear has seen this in Dark Cloud's village. She has just spoken of it. Many of these 'new' ways have been a fact for so long that youth do not even know there has been a change or another way.

"In this last treaty I spoke of, The Nation of The Real People conducted a census – a count – of all of their people. The Government of the United States needed to know our numbers, they needed to know how many of us wished to go across the Mississippi and how many of us wished to stay.

"Besides the many promises and land trades they offered, the Government of the United States offered all The Real People who were displaced by the changing boundaries an amazing thing: *citizenship*. They said to you, 'If you are not happy with these promises and land trades, then we will offer you something else instead. We will give all of you the chance to become citizens of the United States of America. Should you do this, you would no longer be a part of The Nation of The Real People; you would be a part of the United States of America. And you would be entitled to all the rights and privileges that go with that title. Any new citizens were promised land, each household – six hundred and forty acres!"

Deer shook his head. "When I first heard of this offer, I did not believe it. It could not be possible. I insisted that the person who told me of this show me proof, and he did. I saw the treaty and read the words that made these promises to all of you. I spent much time thinking and asked many people their opinions – those I considered my friends and those I considered my enemies."

Suddenly, Deer looks older, more tired. He sighs and says quietly, "In the end, I encouraged you to accept the offer of citizenship. Weapons and might no longer will win this fight, so I wanted us to put a wall of words around us as protection. I know that there were many of you in this village who were unsure of this advice. 'How could separating ourselves from our own people make us safer?' you asked me. But in the end you trusted me and my words. I am greatly honored that you thought about and then listened to my suggestions." Deer takes the time to look at every person sitting around the circle and nod respectfully to each of them.

With a bitter laugh, Deer asks, "Who could believe that leaving The Nation of The Real People and becoming citizens of the United States of America would allow you more of a chance to continue your Old Ways than had you stayed? But it is so. Sitting here in The Maple Forest and hearing about the way things are in Dark Cloud's village in New Echota is proof."

Leaning forward, his face fierce, Deer says, "You chose to accept the citizenship offered to you by the United States Government in an effort to keep your heritage, your land and your Old Ways. You did not take the white man's money, possessions, and promises. You understood what was the most precious thing."

I can't believe what I'm hearing! I look around at the faces sitting silent and unhappy around the council circle, and my head says with amazement, *You are all citizens of the United States?! Just like me and Pa, Henry, and Eli?!* And then I have another thought. *You left your own nation so that you could keep living the way you felt was true and right.* I hear Beaver saying to me, *"It is a struggle that The Real People have been fighting with for many more years than you have."* And then I look at Beaver and the look on his face has nothing to do with sorrow. He looks angry. Angry enough to kill.

"The Maple Forest," Deer continues speaking to this silent group all wrapped in sorrow and bright bits of anger as well, "where you have always lived and where our ancestors who have gone before us still walk, is on land that is now part of the state of North Carolina."

He laughs another bitter laugh and shakes his head, looking down for a moment at the ground and then back up at the group. *Does he look ashamed?* I puzzle. "The United States made the offer of six hundred and forty acres and citizenship in the treaty, and you accepted it. It was only later, after the treaty was signed, and after all agreements were made, that the *State of North Carolina* told the United States government that there was no land to give you, whether there was a treaty or not, whether you were a citizen or not, and whether you were homeless or not.

"This land that we sit on, that you made such hard, hard choices to keep, had already been put up for sale to be bought by white settlers. There was no land in North Carolina free for the giving, not *six hundred and forty acres* for each family, not even *one tree.*"

As I look around the circle, I see many different feelings on the faces. I see no surprise on Great Elk's and War Woman's faces and I think, *They know this already.* I look at the dark look One Who Knows shows, and I know it's not a surprise for her either. But Beaver's face shows an expression of such anger, such *fury* that for a moment I can only stare and watch the emotion grow as Deer keeps on speaking. "It was in this last treaty, the Treaty of 1819, you also appointed me your agent. You officially told everyone that I was your spokesperson in the white world. I have been doing *much talking.* I have talked with the Government of the United States in Washington, and I have talked with the Government of the State of North Carolina. I have talked loudly and fiercely and at great length. I will not be stopped. I will not be made silent. I will not surrender this fight of paper words and broken promises.

"I have used my family money and profits from my trading post, and I have been buying land as it becomes available for sale. I have finally secured an agreement with both governments, that the Treaty of 1819 is *binding.* That means that they cannot go back and change what has been said and written. *They must honor it.* It has been agreed that the land offered to you, your 640 acres, was *fair.* North Carolina, admits its mistake in not having land to give you and has offered to give you money instead." Deer sighs. "I have accepted on your behalf the offer of this money in lieu of land. I have received several large payments towards this debt North Carolina owes you."

Deer looks at Beaver, and I know that he has seen the anger that's pouring off him like a raging fire. "Beaver, you wish to speak?"

Beaver struggles to keep his voice calm as he speaks to Deer, "What good is white money?! What good are these Treaties?! What good is this *citizenship?!*" he spits the word out of his mouth just like I remember Bright Feather saying the word *liquor.* "What has it brought us but separation from our brothers and sisters and a hatred from all people both red and white?"

Beaver looks at Great Elk and War Woman, his voice strained. "You said you trusted Deer! You said you believed this was the way to choose; to go against all that we have ever stood for and side with the *whites* against our own people! Do you still believe that we have made a better choice? Do you still believe we should sit here quietly and wait for the white settlers who *purchased our land with their white money* to move in and tell us to get off their white property? Do you think that severing ties with our nation and our people has given us a strength now when we find that there is *still no land for us?*"

Beaver looks around at all those sitting at the council fire wearing faces that show no thoughts, giving nothing of their inside feelings away. "Our brothers and sisters still at least have land to call their own! I cannot believe that the whites will *ever* treat us fairly, that we will *ever* be given the respect that we deserve. There is no harmony in these choices! I believe we need to return to our people and stand firm beside them in this *fight.*" The word "fight" is thrown down into the council circle, just like Beaver has taught me to throw my knife. Beaver looks at Deer, and through teeth gritted in anger says, "I have finished speaking."

Deer waits in the silence of the circle for a time. He seems to me to be gathering his thoughts and carefully arranging his words so that each one that's spoken is perfect. He looks at the group and says at last, slowly and softly, "After these many seasons, *over seven summers,* I still think you have made the right choice. When I step into this village, I see the Old

Ways everywhere I look. I sit within this circle and am honored to accept the wise counsel of *all* elders in this village. I am pleased to feel harmony and balance with all those that walk in this center of the world."

Deer looks at Beaver, still steaming his fury. "While I know that there are some at this council circle who are not happy with the advice and the choices that have been given, I must tell you that the part of The Real People who live west of the Mississippi are in a sorrowful condition. I tell you these things so that you can understand that your choices, as hard as they may have been, were the right ones." He runs his hand through his hair, a very white movement I think, and looks at each one of us in the circle, including me. "The Real People west of the Mississippi live on lands that are part of the Territory of Arkansas. Even that far away, they fight with the whites for the land that they were promised and battle with the other Indian tribes that were there before them. They are suffering great degradation and misery and have already sought relief from the Government of the United States. They request money, better lands, protection, and the fulfillment of promises made but never kept."

I feel the sorrow travel around the circle even as I ponder the fact that these *savages* as Miss Rebecca and Reverend Wilder called them *are citizens of the United States of America* just as I am! But looking at the faces around the council circle and listening to Deer and Beaver's words, I know there is little comfort in that.

"As for those of The Nation of The Real People here east of the Mississippi," Deer says, "I do not like the talk I hear at the trading post and beyond. I fear for the safety and security of the two parts that remain. I fear that the land they claim to be theirs will be something the whites will want. I believe that soon The Nation of The Real People will be approached once again with another treaty and more promises in exchange for the land they still claim as theirs. This is the land south of here, at Dark Cloud's village and beyond, in New Echota, in the white state known as Georgia.

"I have come here to you, having traveled many miles, having spoken many words, and having spent much time trying to stay ahead of what is coming this way to The Maple Forest. I will not betray your trust.

You must be prepared. You must be informed. Hard times are coming for The Nation and for The Maple Forest. I cannot stop it, but I will be here right alongside you as we *deal with this together.*" Bowing his head, Deer says, "I have finished speaking."

"I cannot believe that even Dark Cloud would settle for less land again," Great Elk says with great certainty. Many others around the circle nod in agreement.

Deer looks powerful sad when he says, "Then the United States Government may use force to help him make the choice that the Government wants."

"What are you saying?" Beaver says, the anger in him sparking and crackling now like a log exploding on the fire.

"I am saying," Deer says slowly and carefully, "that there has been little bloodshed over these past years because an agreement has always been reached between the United States and The Nation of The Real People. But should an agreement prove impossible this time, it does not mean that the Government of the United States would not use force. I do not for one moment believe that the Government of the United States will accept 'no' as an answer from The Nation of The Real People."

"And we would just sit here while this happens?" Beaver shouts to Great Elk. "You would allow soldiers to come in and remove our people by force and you would not step forward to help?!"

With a tired voice, Great Elk says to Beaver, "The Nation of The Real People separated from *us*, long before we made the choice to accept citizenship with The United States. These choices we made here in this village were not ones that we made over night quickly just to keep our land. We sought to save our *entire way of life:* the Old Ways that continue to honor our ancestors and those spirits that have gone before us."

Great Elk uses the same quiet voice he always uses no matter the feeling surrounding him. But he holds out his hand to Beaver, reaching out it seems to calm him. "My son, when a village is viciously attacked by an enemy, you seek to gather those closest and dearest to you and try to save a *small few.* It is only a fool who thinks he can save a whole village all by himself."

I think of Bear John the morning he came to our village and how I only had care to save just one small baby I called Owl.

Beaver stands no less angry and no more calmed by Great Elk's words. "It is thoughts like that, I believe, that have divided our people. You are right to say that only a fool thinks he can save a whole village all by himself, but it is also a fool who puts himself in the position to be *alone* rather than in a trusted group. I will gather my things and return to The Nation of The Real People. I will not be a fool who is alone, but a warrior who is with my brothers." In the silence of night, I hear the noise of the crackling fire, the breeze blowing the leaves above our head, and the footsteps of Beaver walking away from The Council Circle.

No one speaks for a time. I think of the important things I know are at Beaver's center. I remember his serious ways and how much I learned about The Real People because of all of the wonderful stories he shared with me. Much of the peace I carry in the center of who I am and what I've become and where I plan to go is thanks to Beaver and his wise words.

I wish I could give him some words of peace or calm back, but I'm at a loss.

Deer says at last, "I respect Beaver's opinion. I too have great fear for The Real People of The Maple Forest, for I know that our walls of safety are not as strong as I would like them to be. The United States Government cannot be trusted to deal fairly when the prize is the land they want so desperately. It will lie, it will cheat, and, finally I'm afraid, it will steal.

"But I still believe that The Real People's only way to be victorious in this battle is to fight and *win* with the white weapons of words and laws. I cannot agree with Beaver. Our chance of victory through might and warfare is long, long gone. I have been buying up land with my profits from the trading post as I said, and I have been using the money I have received in the capacity as your agent to purchase even more land. This land we sit on I have already purchased; it is *in my name* and is already owned *by us*. Every chance I get, every penny I receive, I buy more precious land. Each family head within this village, because he has not received the promised allotment of six hundred and forty acres of land is receiving money instead. All the money that I receive, I immediately use to purchase more land in my name for this village. We will fight this fight quietly and carefully and win in the end with the weapons the United States Government has given us. While we cannot ever claim land with confidence that we have been promised in *any* treaty, we *can* claim land that we have purchased outright, legal and proper, with *real white money.*"

Great Elk nods in agreement as does War Woman and a number of people sitting around the council fire. War Woman finally says, "We have worked in this village to remain separate from the white world even though we are now legally a part of it. We have worked in this village to remain separate from The Nation of The Real People even though we will always be linked with it through our heritage and our history. We must do a careful dance between both of these worlds and watch over the careful barrier of words that Deer has put around us to always see what is coming towards us, be it with red or white skin."

Deer smiles a smile that's more fierce than friendly. "What I hear makes me have concerns and urges me to ready all those white weapons we have to protect us. Only this time I fear that both The Nation of The Real People and The Government of the United States will have to be carefully watched." He looks at each face within the circle. "I owe you my life." He touches his chest with a closed fist. "The person I am is because of you. *I will not forsake you even from my grave. I will make sure that you are taken care of.* You are my people and my family. Again, I am finished speaking."

Great Elk looks at the council circle. "Your words are not a surprise to many of us, Deer. And I have long been aware of Beaver's opinions of the choices we have made as a village. It is right that children listen and learn and develop their own beliefs and opinions. He knows that whether he lives in this village or elsewhere he is always a son of this hearth, and we are always happy to welcome him. Maybe it is good for him to go and see what Bear has seen." He looks at me for a moment. "Sometimes words cannot do justice to what our eyes must see and our heart must experience.

"We do not need to be One Who Knows to understand the way of things with the white people and their constant desire to have more and more land. What is more distressing to many of us is this division within The Real People that could not be avoided. I feared the response that we have seen with Beaver. Those that are young still believe things can be solved with might and weapons while those of us with gray hair know they cannot."

He turns to Deer, "You are a treasured friend and son of this hearth, and your concern for us is a weapon that the whites cannot match. We will take your words to heart and look forward to more words that you can send our way or bring us yourself."

Great Elk looks at War Woman who nods her head ever so slightly. War Woman looks at me. I sit up straight and realize that me and my white skin have not been forgotten. She begins to speak. "Although you are young, you are clever with your mind and with your words, Bear," she says. "You watch and listen and learn. You are quick to see the way of things."

With her head, War Woman motions to One Who Knows and I look at her. Her dark eyes stare out at me from her dried apple face. I remember my time in her hut and how I was Mouse, always scurrying to do my chores hoping no one would notice me. While I'm still looking and lost in memories, War Woman says, "One Who Knows feels strongly that you bring brightness to this village rather than dark." I look at War Woman in surprise and shock. *One Who Knows thinks good things of me?* I shake my head. Surely I must not have heard correctly. When I look at her she gives me a look I've seen many times before: it's impatience at my stupidness.

War Woman's words draw me back, "It would seem, Bear, since you *are* a member of this village and you *are* one of only a few able to speak both the white man's and our language, that you are indeed very important to us. We of The Maple Forest would be foolish to think that we would be better off without you here. And when the time comes to go and talk with the white men and our brothers and sisters in The Nation of The Real People about a new treaty," here War Woman stops and looks at all those sitting around the council circle, "and we all know that time will come soon," her stare finally rests on me, "you will be one who will go as a voice of The Real People of The Maple Forest."

I feel a flush of pure joy rip through my body. It heats my face and neck and arms and body. *I'm truly a part of this place,* my heart sings. *I've known it for a time now, but they seem to know it, too!* I look at this collection of people sitting and looking at me, and I'm speechless with the wonder of what is being said.

Then my heart begins to jump and pound as what they are telling me sinks into my slow head. They wish me to speak for them?! They trust me to do such a thing?! *I can't!* my terrified head says in a scream, *I'm just a ...*

And then I stop myself from saying what my head is going to say. I push any of those 'I can't' thoughts out of my center and make Bear sit up straight and tall in the council circle. *I'm Bear,* I force myself to think, *of The Real People of The Maple Forest. I'll do what needs to be done. And do it well.* I look up into the unsmiling, wrinkled face of One Who Knows, who now has the same satisfied face that she did that night I stared down Weasel and his friends.

Great Elk turns to Bright Feather, "And it will also seem, One Who Is Always Alone, that since you are inclined to go with her – even were she to be put out of this village," he pauses and waits for Bright Feather to nod that that's so, "then you will not be alone so much anymore." I catch a brief movement from Deer; he winks across the circle to Bright Feather. Or was it to me?

Later that night, Bright Feather and I lie close in our hut, and I ask some of my many questions. I struggle with what to ask first.

I learn right off that he thinks little of the citizenship. "Deer felt it was the right choice, and we trusted him in the end. We were having such a difficult time trying to maintain connections with Dark Cloud's village with all of the changes they were embracing and encouraging us to embrace as well. Dark Cloud eagerly accepted the money, gifts, and promises that the white man offered The Real People. He willingly moved his entire village within the new boundaries drawn in that last treaty and assumed a position of power within the leadership of the Nation of The Real People that was recognized in the white world as well. We talked among ourselves and realized that to align ourselves with Dark Cloud was not any more appealing than aligning ourselves with the white man's government.

"It was One Who Knows again who agreed with Deer and spoke out to follow his advice." He shrugs his shoulders. "She said there was no choice really, and she was right. We chose to keep the land of our ancestors where their spirits still walk and where we can still practice the Old Way that we know brings harmony and peace. The offer of money, white man's things, and different land to live on did not interest us. In the end, we became separate from both worlds by our choice. We are the better for it."

After a moment's pause, he adds, "I hope that Beaver will find a peace," and I feel his sorrow.

The topic of Deer takes much longer to explain. Deer has not been to Great Elk's village in many seasons, but that does not mean that some in the village do not see him regular, I come to find out, including Bright Feather. "We all know that things are very serious if Deer left his family and the trading post to come out here to speak with us.

"Why was he never spoken of?" I finally ask.

Bright Feather looks at me in the darkness of our hut. "I am sure he was. You just never thought of a white man's face when you heard his Indian name spoken." He touches the white skin on my neck below my ear with a gentle finger.

"How did he go from being *William Holland Thomas* to Deer?"

He grunts. "The better question is how did he go from being Deer to *William Holland Thomas*. He was found in the woods by a hunting party from the village many years ago when he was just a boy. Back then there were fewer whites and more land claimed by The Real People. Yet it was still impossible for them to bring the boy back to his people. What white man would believe that no harm had been meant? He was a pitiful, scrawny, frightened white boy, found terrified and lost in the woods. Because we spoke different words, he could offer no information to the puzzle of who he was and how he came to be where they found him. The village welcomed him, and he became a son of War Woman's hearth. Yet even after he became able to speak and understand our language, he was never able to remember what brought him to be in the forest alone and so full of fear. He could not even remember who he was were he to go back to the white world." Bright Feather's silent for a time, lost in thought I suspect, fiddling with my hair and touching me here and there.

"He had flashes of memory," Bright Feather explains, speaking softly against the top of my head, and I can hear his voice rumble quiet like in his chest. "He described it to me once like keeping your eyes tightly shut all the time and then, very briefly opening them up quickly to take just a peek of what might be there to see." He sighs. "But there are no memories of anything that will answer the questions he always wonders most about. He became known as Deer for he was a swift runner, and just like the white tail deer that can give brief flashes of whiteness now and then, so does he. He is a member of The Real People of The Maple Forest through and through. He, Raccoon, and I grew up together, best of friends, inseparable.

"But as Deer grew older, the curiosity of who he was in the white world began to eat at him. Who was his white family? Where were they? Was there a need for revenge? Were the answers to these many questions only to be found in the white people's towns? Would there be family or people that knew him? I think," Bright Feather says in the quiet darkness of our hut, "that even though his mind could not remember what truly happened in the forest and before, his spirit could and that was why he could not find peace.

"The village encouraged him to search for answers recognizing the need for him to balance both sides of who he was. So he was taken back to where he had been found in the woods, and Raccoon and I traveled with him as far as The Real People's territorial land to the east. There were still those in The Maple Forest who remembered the old territorial hunting grounds and were able to give guidance as to what direction he should head once Deer was on his own." Bright Feather sighs. "I missed him so once he was gone.

"He was gone for almost a season, and we had great concern for him," Bright Feather says. "I, being young and foolish and quite full of myself, wanted to cross territorial lines and go looking for him, but even Raccoon would not support me much as I tried to convince him. At last, late one summer evening he rode into camp on his Indian pony dressed in white man's clothes. 'Have I missed the Green Corn Celebration?' he asked like nothing was different and no time had passed."

Bright Feather grunts at the memory. "We sat around the council circle fire that first night he was back, Raccoon wearing Deer's white man's pants, me wearing his white man's shirt, Otter wearing his fancy hat and even Beaver stumbling around in his white man's shoes while Deer sat there in his breechcloth looking much more like we remembered him."

Turning on his side to look at me, he fingers my robin's feather. "He was never able to find out about the death of his parents or how he came to be alone and lost in the woods, but he did discover who he was in the white world: William Holland Thomas. The last information his white family had had of him, according to the slaves his family kept, was that his father, a prosperous farmer and landowner, had traveled to seek out some business interests and had taken William and his mother along on the trip. A sister of his mother welcomed him back with great enthusiasm. Even more surprising, he discovered that there was family property he was entitled to and quite a bit of family money that was due him. In the white world, it seems, he was quite a wealthy man.

"But he returned to his true family, The Real People of The Maple Forest, to seek their guidance," Bright Feather says, his voice filled with approval. "He was still filled with indecision. Should he stay in the white world or the red? The sister of his mother offered him the opportunity for some white schooling. Should he accept and live with them and learn their ways?" Bright Feather says with real sympathy, "After spending time in the white world, he seemed almost more eaten up with the way of things when he returned to us than before he had left.

"It was One Who Knows who stepped forward and told him what to do. I remember that night as she stood there and told him that he was forever destined to be a person with two spirits that would never be at peace with each other. 'You are Deer to us and always will be. You know him as well as do we. But you must go home to your white family now and become *William Holland Thomas*, for you will always be that, too, and you need to know him better.'"

"I know some of what he struggled with," I say quietly after a time. "That wondering of the choosing." I hold up one hand in the dark, "Should I chose this?" and I lift my other hand, "Or this? Which is the way to go? Which is the way to leave?"

"But you were able to weave your two selves together," Bright Feather points out. "Like a twisted piece of rope, you bound them tightly together and became stronger because of it. Deer could never seem to do that. He has always been two pieces that cannot be joined together."

"Maybe because he couldn't remember."

Bright Feather nods. "Yes, I believe that to be so. He was always more haunted with what he did not know, than what he did." He cups my face and says, "Your strength is in your remembering and in your ability to take the best of both lives and use them to be the powerful woman you now are." He kisses me once, twice, three times in the dark.

He lays back down on his back pulling me beside him, and I feel him shrug. "So Deer listened to One Who Knows. He put on his pants and his shoes and his shirt and his hat, and he left the next morning to find *William Holland Thomas*. He visited us regularly and often, but he never lived with us again." In the silence of the hut, I hear Bright Feather's breathing grow slow and steady, and I know he's falling asleep. Questions are still crashing around in my head like the children outside playing at first light. I'm not tired at all. Not one bit.

"Do you know," I say in the silence of the night as I lay snuggled against his side with my head on his shoulder, "that there are some in the village who would like to call me 'Never Stops Asking Questions?"

I listen to his breathing, and it does not change, not one bit but at last he says, "Besides being a powerful woman, I was warned by a number of others that that was so."

"You told me that you never go east into Virginia and white territory. If he hasn't been here to this village in so long, how is it that you see him at times?"

He begins to trace slow lazy circles along the plane of my face as he speaks. "Just like Great Elk recognizes your value to the village in your ability to fit in both worlds, the whites recognized his value as a white man who can speak with The Real People and travel between the two worlds. On more than one occasion he has been asked to interpret council sessions between The Real People and the white settlers. Over the years he has become a prosperous trader on property near the red and white border on his family's original land which the whites call *North Carolina.* He is faithful and fair to all Indians who deal with him. It is to Deer that almost all those of Great Elk's village – and many other villages of The Real People - go whenever there are furs to trade or goods to be bought - me included. His is the only place I go to to trade my furs and get supplies. I trust no other and deal with no other." It turns out that Bright Feather and Deer have contact at least once each season.

His hand continues to caress my face and then begins to trace the outline of my lips and the lines of my eyes and angle of my jaw and the bend of my ear. I struggle in my head to recall the wide awake questions that only moments ago were running wild in my head, but they have all of a sudden slipped far, far away. He gently eases my head down on the pallet and raises himself on his arm to look down at me, his hand still making their lazy travels. It's pitch black now in the hut, and I can't see anything, despite the fact that I feel like every single piece of me is straining to pay attention. I feel and smell and hear him bend down over me, and his hair tickles my bare shoulder and pools at my neck. I feel his lips brush against my forehead, not in a kiss so much as just in a feel, and I hear him breathe deep the smell of me. His hand moves down and rests firm and sure in the curve of my waist and the heat of it is almost – but not quite – enough to distract me from his mouth that has felt its way down the bridge of my nose to stop just above my lips, untouching. Every single piece of me is aware of him hovering like a hawk silent above me in the dark, watching and waiting. I barely breathe; waiting, waiting...

"Your questions are wonderful to me," he says oh so quiet, and I feel the heat from the breath of his speaking, "because they come from this mouth of yours that is *so sweet* to taste." At last I stop asking questions.

Deer joins us at Otter and Raccoon's hut the following evening for dinner, and I listen to many stories as they talk and reminisce far into the night. I begin to draw a picture in my head of what Bright Feather was before he was One Who Was Alone, when he was known as Hawk.

"He was always the most serious," Deer moans with Raccoon nodding in pained agreement. "Always the voice of common sense. Always concentrating on the hunt or the trapping or the faster way to ride or the quicker way to shoot or the more accurate way to shoot. The first to hunt all night alone, the first to make a kill, " Deer looks at me with great seriousness as he holds out his hand, keeping count of all the firsts, "the first to master trapping, the first to own a horse. He was never any fun at all." Raccoon nods again.

Bright Feather listens to most of the stories and comments as I expect him to; in silence. But he has a casual air about him as he leans back against a tree with me sitting close by listening. Maybe not casual, maybe peaceful is a better word - and content.

After a time, I have to finally ask the question and no one seems particularly surprised when I do. "Have you heard of me? Of my family that lives in Virginia? If you have a trading post then you must surely see people from all over. It has been said that there is talk of a missing white girl from Virginia ... named Elle ... ?"

I find there are times as Deer talks to us, and in particular to me, that I realize he puts on his white face that speaks sometimes when his mouth is quiet. But at other times, as now, he puts on his Indian face; the one that doesn't talk at all. "I have heard word at my place of the search for a white girl who was taken captive some time ago. But you are not the only captive, Bear, so this is not necessarily about you."

I study him for a bit looking close at his face and think, *Why has he put his Indian face on if he has nothing to hide?* Surely the search for a white girl – whichever girl they're searching for - will be careful to give details so to tell each captive white girl from the next – if there are so many of us. Then I realize, if there were details about me specific like, there were probably details about my Pa and Eli, too. Pieces of another puzzle slip into place, and I know all of a sudden that he knows things of Pa and Eli. I know this even though when I stare into his eyes I see only blueness like the skies. I think of Weasel and what he told me in the forest outside of Dark Cloud's village. I remember his eyes as he spoke to me close to my face with such great anger, and I remember I saw no sign of lying. I swallow for I know all of a sudden that what I must hear is what I wished never to hear.

I look at him serious with *my* Indian face and I say, "I will have you tell me what you know. I will hear the truth of the way things are. I wish to hear *all* the words you have in your head, not just the ones you think are those that I can swallow easy."

Raccoon snorts loudly. "Watch and learn quickly, Deer. The most powerful asset we may have in this village is that little *girl* sitting across from you who has got a mind sharper and quicker than a rattlesnake's bite."

Deer begins to speak and my mind struggles to keep up as my heart gallops in my chest. "In the late spring of last year, word was sent out around the surrounding territory, in particular to trading posts like mine in Forest City that have a great deal to do with the Indian trade. The words spoke about a white girl who had been taken captive in the early spring and who answered to the name *Elle*."

I sit and wait in the silence that wraps around us just like the darkness of the night. I know there's more. Besides my white name, there had to be other things the "words" spoke of. I finally lift my tired green eyes up to meet his unblinking blue ones and let them talk to him, for all of a sudden I'm far too tired to speak with my mouth. *And???*, my eyes say to him, *what else must you tell me that my ears must hear?*

Deer sighs deeply and finally says, "The actual description, if I recall it properly, was," here he speaks in white words that sound hard and rough to my pink ears, "'*Orphaned white girl whose mother has died and father and brothers have been murdered by marauding Indians, who answers to the name of Elle.*'"

The only sounds around us are the sounds of the night forest and the crackling of the fire before us. No one speaks. At first I feel the ache grow and the tears burn behind my eyes and I think, *Hurry hate, get busy with those tears!* But who is there to hate now? Weasel is dead and so are the other two braves who took me that night, Bright Feather and Raccoon have seen to that. Whatever one killed my Pa and Eli and … Henry, is gone now.

I stare at the fire, and I remember Pa looking so terrible tired sitting by the fire; I understand all of a sudden that the look was *powerful sadness* over the passing of Ma not tiredness at all. I see Henry working so hard in the barn that his face is flushed beet red and the sweat is dripping off his nose, and all of a sudden I know, *that was tears*, not hard work. I feel Eli's dirty, sticky, sweaty hand in mine as we walk out to the field to bring Pa and Henry their lunch and all of a sudden I'm certain, *that was true love*.

I think sudden like, *What happened to Ma's Hope Chest?* and that's the silly thought that makes the tears spill down my cheeks. I make a deep, deep sigh; it seems to come all the way from the darkest bottom of myself, and I'm all of a sudden so powerful tired that I can't sit up any longer. At that very moment I feel Bright Feather stand, bend over, and scoop me up like I'm a tiny child rather than a powerful woman of The Real People. I bury my face in his neck and try to escape my sadness with the good smell of him. Sometimes, it seems that a powerful woman must yell her war cry *or* shed many a tear.

Bright Feather and I ride out very early the next morning in silence. He seems to know my need to be away from the village to think and to mourn proper, and then with a start I realize, *Of course, he's One Who Is Always Alone.* He knows all I feel and maybe a pile more. I think about his first mate and child and wish I could ask him questions, but the dead are never spoken of. Then I think about Pa and Henry and Eli and I'm brought up short. Can I no longer speak of them? I'll not like that.

"Why do the Indians not speak of their dead?" I ask as we crest the first hill and all signs of Great Elk's village slip away behind us.

"The Real People believe that the spirit world is the next place we go on this journey of life," Bright Feather explains. "It is a nearby place much like this one, and those who become spirits are much more powerful than those of us who are living persons. Spirits of the dead can return and have been seen in times of great good and in times of great bad. Their presence in this world can create great disharmony or great peace. It is believed that to mention the name of someone who has passed on to the spirit world calls them back here to this place. It can cause the spirit to become lost and confused to see the world he or she once knew rather than the new world where he or she now belongs. It is always best to allow those in the spirit world to make choices to return to us on their own rather than with our interference."

How many times have I mentioned Pa and Eli and Henry to those of the living? I think about my time since I've been here in Great Elk's village – and farther - and how many times I've heard Pa's voice in my head like he was standing right next to me. Each time it has happened it has brought me great comfort or good advice and never has it been bad. Has Pa been a spirit with me all this time as I continue my walk here in living? Have Henry and Eli also spoken to me quiet like with their remembrances I often have of them in my head? In my speaking their names have I caused them confusion or for them to become lost?

Bright Feather knows my thoughts. "Whether their names are mentioned or not, sometimes the spirits of those we love and care about choose to watch over us and follow us and guide us all the while we are here in this place of the living." I follow him through the beautiful green forests bursting with summer life wondering if I'll always fill this gaping hole of sadness. "They wait quiet and patient for us to join them in the spirit world so that the walk can be continued on together." He reins in Companion and waits until Willow and I ride up to be beside him, and he looks over at me. "Or sometimes they wait just long enough until they are certain that those of us left behind are safe and secure and headed on a path that they know to be right."

We sit side by side on our horses looking at the beautiful valley stretched out before us. As far as the eye can see are green tree covered hills. I think of what Miss Rebecca and Reverend Wilder have told me about God and prayer and living forever depending on the choices that are made about believing things or not. I tell Bright Feather about this Jesus and God and how they say He's so close that he can hear words that are in your head before you let them out of your mouth. "Miss Rebecca told me to always talk to God for He's always ready to listen and help. She called Him *personal.*"

"What do you think of that?" Bright Feather asks, and I think again how much I like to talk to him.

I let my Hope Chest of memories open up and think on what I remember. "When I lived with Pa, we read from The Bible, a great big book that was filled with the wise words from this God. Ma's favorite verse she used to say to Henry and I when we were scared of something was, *'Thou preparest a table before me in the presence of mine enemies: thou anointest my head with oil; my cup runneth over. Surely goodness and mercy shall follow me all the days of my life: and I will dwell in the house of the Lord for ever.'*[8]

I smile at Bright Feather, "I remember Henry saying, 'Who'd want to eat dinner with an enemy, Ma? That sounds like powerful foolishness to me."

"What did your Ma say?" Bright Feather asked quiet and thoughtful.

"She said, 'Well, there can't be much fear in you if you can sit down and enjoy a meal with someone, now can there?' I liked the 'goodness and mercy' part following me all my days best." I laugh a little. "Henry used to say to me, even after Ma died, when we were scared of something, *'Shall we start cooking dinner, Elle?'* to make me laugh and stop me from being frightened. I wonder if it helped him, too..." I ride for a few moments in quiet and then finally say, "I'd forgotten that until now...."

We ride again in silence, deep in thought. Then I finally say, "I think maybe I like the idea of this Personal God always willing to listen and hear what we think and say. I like the idea of putting Him in my center where He will always be close."

Bright Feather looks at me with great seriousness, "Maybe I do too, then."

We ride for a long while in silence, taking in the sights and sounds and smells of the forest: chirping birds, rustling breezes, deep green ferns curling in the shade, and the rich scent of damp earth. At the top of a ridge we stop in a spot of the forest where I don't think I've ever come before. I realize that we have been riding most of the morning as I look at the sun. We are quite a distance from the village. *No matter how loud your thoughts are Elle girl, you should always be sure to listen and know about the things around you. That's called "survival,"* I hear Pa say in my head. *I'm still not so good at that one yet, Pa*, I think to myself.

"I have spoken often of my Pa since I have been away from him. And Eli and Henry, too. I hear his voice in my head, and I talk back to him, too. His words are always wise and good and kind," I tell Bright Feather and search his face for his thoughts, for I'm worried that I should no longer speak of Pa or mention him in the way of The Real People.

He's quiet for a long time, and we watch a hawk soar high above the trees down in the valley below swooping and diving in the warm air. He does not look at me, but stares straight ahead for a long time before he finally says, "I have a quiet voice that speaks to me in my head, too." He sighs and looks down at his hands holding Companion's reins. "It, too, speaks of good things. But sometimes," he makes a slight face, "it shouts at me to do things other than to live up to my name of One Who Is Always Alone." He looks at me then, searching my face and says at last, "It speaks a lot of you."

"Me?!" I say in puzzlement and great surprise. "What does the voice say about *me?*"

He reaches across and cups my cheek in his palm. His thumb strokes me soft and sweet. "It says to love you," he says, and he gives me a look of such great tenderness that it melts away large pieces of my grief and pain. "And so I do."

Two nights later there's a celebration in the village. I remember a time over a year ago when I was terrified of the whoops and screams and shouts of joy from the returning hunters and how I was just like a mouse scurrying around in the shadows trying hard to go unnoticed. Now it seems I'm right in the center of it, for the celebration is for our return and, more than a little bit, I suspect for the joining of me and Bright Feather and for the visit of Deer.

I'm given a new tunic to wear. It's of soft deerskin and decorated along the hem and the sleeves with the tails of an animal whose fur is so soft it feels like warm butter. I ask the name of the animal but can't recall ever having heard of it before when Otter tells me its Indian name. I try on the tunic and the tails swish against my bare arms and legs in a way that reminds me of Bright Feather's softest touches. Ten bear claws shiny and black are carefully sewn around the neck. Down the front in a "V" pattern to my waist and all around the hem are detailed stitches that as I look closely I see are a robin's tracks. "The tunic is from One Who Knows," Otter tells me, "she made it just for you." She hands me matching moccasins, each one decorated with two bear claws and robin's feet stitches. For the third time I'm taken aback and puzzle over One Who Knows and her thoughts of me.

I run my hand over the detailed stitching that would have taken even the fastest person many, many days to do. As I look at Otter, my head is so full of questions that I screw up my face to decide which one to ask first. Otter bursts out laughing, "Well, first off," she starts, guessing already my first question, "that is how she got her name!"

"Why these great kindnesses to me?" I ask in wonder. "First, she speaks up for me when I am taken, then I learn she has told Great Elk and War Woman that she believes I will bring brightness to the village, and now this," I hold my arms out and look down at my beautiful tunic and moccasins.

Otter ponders this. "I think for many reasons," she begins. "First, she wants to make a point with you and the entire village that she thinks highly of you despite how things first started out between the two of you. Second, she has always known things that the rest of us do not. And last, I think she wants to send a message to Bright Feather that she is happy for him and gives him her blessing."

I look puzzled. "What's between One Who Knows and Bright Feather?"

"Bright Feather was a son of her hearth for a time," Otter says quietly.

My head spins this information around slowly and then faster and faster as I see the bigger picture. Bright Feather's mate was One Who Knows' daughter … Weasel was also a son of One Who Knows hearth for a time … So One Who Knows has lost at least two daughters and at least one grandson … "Such sadness she has known," I say finally.

"Yes," Otter says, "more than most people can bear."

We hear a crashing sound as a basket is tipped over, and Otter jumps up. "Little Bird!" she scolds, "put those down! They are special!" Big eyes begin to drip enormous tears. "Well," she says, "then bring them to Bear as your gift to her." Flat, wide, brown feet pad happily to me, and I take from each tight fist some feathers. One big gray brown robin's feather, "To replace the one you lost," Otter explains and two small dark red feathers – also a robin's. "New ones to add," she says with a smile, "two because there are two of you now." She helps me comb out my hair which has gotten quite long – almost to my waist – and we wrap it with deerskin strips in a tight tail down the back. One Who Knows has sent two more tails of the same soft fur to the tunic to decorate my hair, and we add the feathers at the side in the same style that Bright Feather wears his. Otter surveys her handiwork and claps, "Perfect!"

I find Bright Feather near a clearing you can see from the hut where Willow and Companion are hobbled. Both horses knicker a greeting, and I take time to scratch Willow in the favorite place behind her ears and to rub Companion's soft muzzle and blow my scent up his nose. Bright Feather is looking at me with the silent look that I've already come to know is a look of great caring. I smile shyly at him and touch the beautiful new tunic that I wear.

"This is a gift from One Who Knows," I say, still with wonder in my voice.

He takes in all the details, touching the bear claws, fur tails, and robin's feet stitches. He touches the feathers in my hair and the tails that hang there, too. "It is fine work," he says, but his eyes look at me, and I realize he speaks of me and not so much my clothes. I sigh a great sigh and lean against him and his arms go around me. I breathe deep his wonderful smell of the outdoors, and wood smoke, and Companion, and sweet sweat.

"I do not know the animal that has fur as soft as this," I say after a time touching one of the tails.

"White men call it *mink*," he says. "Those both white and red who trade with each other do not always know many of each others' words, but they almost always know the word for *mink.*"

I search my mind for words to say because I feel a sadness in him as well as a happiness. Does he think of other times and One Who Knows' daughter that he joined with? Does he have a voice in his head that speaks to him today? I struggle with what to say that's just right.

It's finally Bright Feather who speaks first. "One Who Knows thinks like I do of a time just as this long ago. She remembers the joy and the excitement and the dreams of good things to come. She must know better than we do of the happiness you and I have and the great things that are to come for us. She knows that it is good that I am no longer One Who Is Always Alone and am instead Bright Feather." He takes my chin in his hand and bends down and kisses me on the mouth, soft at first like the brush of a bird's feather and then again a little harder. I wrap my arms around him and feel the mink tails swish against my arms and legs as he scoops me up and carries me to a more quiet spot in the woods.

Before the celebration begins that night I make my way to One Who Knows' hut. She's waiting outside in the last rays of the setting sun as if she has been expecting me. The girl who took my place, Turtle, is working carefully on a hide stretched out on cross poles. All around One Who Knows are her precious herbs, some newly gathered, some dried and carefully tied together, and still others in the process of being carefully ground into small bits. I sit down beside her and am at a loss for words. I take a deep breath and remember the smells of her hut; memories of my first months in the village creep through my head along with the smells that creep through my nose.

"Thank you," I begin, "for many things."

She's silent, staring straight ahead. I can't help but think of my time with her when I knew her as Old Woman, and I force myself to remember that things are different now, that I'm a powerful woman, the mate of Bright Feather, and no longer called Mouse. "Thank you for speaking up for me more than once during important times," I say, and for once words seem to be missing from my head and from my mouth.

One Who Knows grunts and says, "I am far too old to worry about what people will think of me or my words. I speak only truth, and those who hear can decide to listen or not," she says. "I saw your destiny in this village the night you stood outside my hut filthy and tired yet strong and proud enough to stare down those who meant you harm. I knew the truth of things, then."

My mind goes back to the night with Weasel and his companions as they laughed and made fun of me. I murmur, "My Pa used to say, *Why waste your breath on something unworthy?* I'm not quiet often, but there are times when silence speaks more than words, I think."

She looks at me then and studies my eyes and my face and I stare back at her and all of a sudden I realize I'm right comfortable sitting with this woman who has a face as lined as a dried apple. "And the older you get," she says at last, "the quieter you will become." I think I see a twinkle of fun in her eyes.

"Thank you for my tunic. One Who Is Always Alone says that you know of the happiness he and I have and the good things that are to come," I look down and trace the robin tracks along the hem.

"You are tiny to look at but strong like a stone inside. One Who Is Always Alone is strong to look at but with many cracks inside his heart that make him weak." She looks at me, and I feel goose skin go up my bare arms. "There is much difficulty as well as joy to come for both of you, but," here she weaves her old and narrow fingers together in her lap making a sturdy bridge, "together you will be unstoppable."

I stand to go, and she motions for me to help her up. The bony hands grip my arms with a strength that's surprising, and she holds on tightly to me even after she's standing. "Your first place when you came to this village was my hearth, as hard as it was for you. Despite the things that have happened to you, you have remained strong and good and true. Never think that what happens to you is by chance, for your destiny began with your start in your mother's womb. You embrace our ways here with The Real People of The Maple Forest because you say they have made you a powerful woman. But," she says pointing a bony finger at me as she bends very close to me so that I see deep into her dark brown eyes, "*you were always a powerful woman even before you knew it.* I was proud to claim you as a daughter of this hearth many months ago," she says and then turns and goes inside her hut.

Daughter?! She claimed me as daughter months ago? Bear. Daughter of One Who Knows. Of The Elk Clan. Of The Maple Forest. Of The Real People.

I stand there in the evening twilight outside One Who Knows' hut for a long time watching the movement of the village, listening to the voices and sounds, smelling the smells. I feel a connection here that's so strong that for a time I imagine I'm rooted to the ground like a great tree with roots that extend under all I see and branches that tower over and shade each and every hut. *My village,* I think, *my people, my life, my choice!* I hear steps behind me, and I know they are Bright Feather's. He does not disturb me but waits until I turn and look at him and I can't help myself as I give him the brightest of smiles even as tears make fast trails down my face. We search each other's eyes for long moments and then he nods and gives me a gift I'd never thought to expect. He smiles, a quiet, beautiful smile that fills me with a rush of warmth.

I know, his smile says, *I know.*

There are food and games and laughter and story telling late into the evening. We are given gifts to celebrate our joining. Raccoon gives me my knife that was lost to me almost two months ago. "Found it in the woods," is all that he will say, but I see it's cleaned and sharpened and polished, and it's in a beautiful new sheath belt to wear around my waist. He gives Bright Feather two very small balls of black fur that we all puzzle over for a time. "For your ears," Raccoon finally volunteers, making motions as if to block out sound, "I am certain you will need them." Bright Feather grunts and the village howls with laughter. I try to look angry but can't keep the face for long.

Red Fox steps forward, shy and awkward, but also with a gift for me. It's a beautiful new bow, quiver, and thirty arrows. "I know your others were taken," he begins. "I made the quiver and arrows, but the bow is a gift from another." I search the crowd for Cloud and it's Bright Feather who reaches out and places his hand on my back gentle and firm. *He's not here anymore*, the hand says. I feel my eyes fill with tears. "Thank you, Red Fox, for your kindness," I say. I rub my hand along the smooth lines of the beautiful new bow and think of the old and crippled hands that made it. I touch the quiver, with no outer decoration but beautiful in its own way, and hear Cloud's voice, *Let your shooting speak for you, not the designs on your quiver.* Arrows peek out from the top, and from the weight I know there are arrows with special tips and new things for me to learn of now. "The time I spent at your hearth last winter learning all I know about shooting was one of the happiest times I've had in this village." I make a point to meet his eyes with my tear filled ones. "I will hear wise words in my head each time I prepare to draw my bow." He looks happy at my words.

As he turns to step away, I say, "Red Fox, I am thankful for this friendship that we have that I treasure more than this gift."

He smiles a sweet smile at me, "As I treasure it too, Bear."

War Woman stands to speak and even children's voices hush. "There are many reasons we celebrate tonight. We celebrate the return of our daughter, Bear, who was taken from us by force and returned to us by choice. We celebrate her joining with One Who Is Always Alone who now we shall call Bright Feather. We celebrate the time we have with our son, Deer, who spends so much time away from us." She looks out at the crowd, and despite the large number of people – young and old – there's a strong feeling that each one is noted. "Let us all realize the power of choices good and bad and make every effort to always be wise."

She turns to look at us, "Bear, daughter of One Who Knows of the Elk clan and Bright Feather of the Wolf clan and son of my hearth, The Real People of Great Elk's village of The Maple Forest look eagerly toward the future and the good that you will bring us." The people shout and cheer and laugh and talk and the noise around us rises up like the heat of a great fire that has just caught.

I look at Bright Feather as he speaks and nods to well-wishers who have crowded forward. *I'm the mate of the son of War Woman,* I think in wonderment, for in all this time I did not know who Bright Feather's mother was. *I've joined with the chief's son. I've joined with the brother of Beaver.* My head tries to fit these new pieces in my mind, but I realize that they are far too large, and I'll have to clear a powerful bit of space up there before they fit right comfortable. *Not so quick again, Pa,* is my last quiet thought to myself before I'm caught up in the celebrations.

With the first morning light the questions begin for Bright Feather, who seems not at all bothered to open his eyes and find me sitting waiting to ask. "The position of chief is traced through blood," Bright Feather explains as we ride out to do some hunting in the company of Deer. Strapped across my back is my new bow and arrows and my fingers itch to try them out. "While a child's heritage is traced through the family line of its mother," he tells me, "the position of chief is always traced through the line of the chief through his sons."

The fact that he's the *oldest* son of Great Elk and War Woman's hearth does not mean he must be chief. "It is a decision the entire council makes since it affects the entire village," he explains. "Over these past years when I was called One Who Is Always Alone, more and more often people looked to Beaver and consider whether he would be chief. But Great Elk has many years of leadership ahead of him. The time to decide is not yet." He does not speak of his feelings or desires. I remember his words, *All I wanted when I was a boy was to be a great hunter.*

"I, too, am a son of Great Elk," Deer says in seriousness. "I was adopted into their clan and welcomed into their hearth in the same way that

One Who Knows now claims you as her daughter. Remember, Bright Feather first introduced me as his *brother.*"

I do remember our first meeting and realize that I'd thought the term "brother" to be only a kindness and say so. Bright Feather nods, "Yes, that is done, but Deer speaks the truth; he is my full brother just as Beaver is. He has every right to be considered for the position of chief as I do."

"It is not my calling," he says quickly, and I turn back to look at him and see him use his white face to make a silly look. "Everyone knows that I struggle with who I am even today – White? Red? A chief must be certain of many things, including who they think they are. Of that I am quite certain."

"So," I say after thinking quite a while and trying to arrange these very large pieces in my head that feels smaller by the moment, "if you should become chief and we should have a son…" My voice trails off with the huge understanding of it all.

"Were I to become chief, it will be my sons who will follow in that path." Bright Feather voices my thoughts out loud.

I've more pieces to add to the puzzle. I think about War Woman's questioning of me and the answers I gave her when we returned from Dark Cloud's village. I think that this Indian village has willingly accepted me and welcomed me as a daughter even after Bright Feather chose me for a mate. I think about One Who Knows and what she said to the village about me and what she told me in private. I see her bony fingers weaving together to make a strong bridge. *There is much difficulty as well as joy to come for both of you, together you will be unstoppable.*

"Will there be a time when I know all the things I need to know?" I ask out loud to anyone in particular after my head grows weary from trying to make sense of all this.

"No," Bright Feather and Deer say both at once without hesitation. *I didn't think so,* I think to myself.

Before Deer leaves he speaks to us both privately. Looking at Bright Feather he says, "Learn the white man's language. Have Bear teach it to you. Do not tell anyone even in this village that you know it, or even that you are practicing. It will be a hidden weapon that will always be ready and can only mean good things for The Real People of The Maple Forest. Bear and I may not always be available to help, and your only true chance at winning future battles in the council tent over the treaty table is for you to understand and know how the white man thinks and plans. Learning his language is the first step."

He looks at me, "Can you read?" When I nod 'yes', he looks relieved. "Good. Many things are often written that are never spoken of, and once a treaty is signed in the white man's world that is all they care about. Do not let *anyone* sign *anything* until you are certain you have read and understood everything that is written. And if this one," he gestures his head toward Bright Feather, "shows that he might have the skill for it, teach him to read the white man's word, too. But that is really too much for me to hope for."

He looks again to Bright Feather, "You may be surprised and disbelieving, but there are *some* whites who are speaking out about the poor and unfair treatment of the Indians. There are some who feel that what has happened has been nothing short of theft. With the new government of *The United States of America*, there may be hope that things will be different." He looks to the eastern horizon and squints his blue eyes against the rising sun. "But it will be like walking barefoot through a nest of ground bees; *possible*, but highly unlikely that we might not get stung at some place along the way. *We just don't want to be stung to death, that's all,*" he mumbles almost to himself. He meets our serious stares with his own. "Both of you are the brightest hope for this village," he says. "*It just may be possible* we will be able to get through this to the other side with only a few stings to show for it."

It's a good summer for me. I work hard, learn much and smile most all of the time.

I help with the village chores, in particular the garden, and delight in watching it grow to wonderful summer fullness. I spend much more time at Great Elk's and War Woman's hut in the circle of leaders each evening. I wish to become familiar with the workings of the village and maybe more so, understand the many thoughts and beliefs and ideas that make up the face of this place. I listen to the wise words and interesting discussions, no topic more talked about than what Deer has told us about the white man, the census, the new treaties to come, and *citizenship*. Debates range far and wide. There are some in the circle who hate the white man and believe he should be destroyed. There are some who don't believe that the white man is as great a threat as others believe, and can't possibly succeed for their lack of harmony in their life and with the world around them. Stories are told of mysterious powerful white magic that has killed whole villages in a moon's time. I watch the faces of those around the circle as the white man is discussed and see fear, anger, disbelief; each face shows different thoughts.

In the privacy of our tent, Bright Feather tells me that such stories are true. "There were great tribes in the north and east that shared the woods with my people's ancestors, and they are no more."

I learn many things about The Real People and their history. We hear nothing specific from Beaver, but from others who travel to Dark Cloud's village for trade and business we do get small bits of news We know he has settled there and has a position of authority in the council circle. I miss his stories.

Many summer nights are spent listening to stories of bravery told at the council fire. The Real People have been part of this land for longer than my brain can understand. But some stories are from times even before they lived in this place and are filled with adventures of travel and ice and great mountains and rivers the likes of which I've never thought of. And there are stories that go back farther still to the beginning of the earth and what was before.

I discover that there is a greater story teller in the village than Beaver; it is One Who Knows. While she does not speak often at the council fire, when she decides to the gathering always is its largest. "In the beginning of time," One Who Knows tells us one evening as we sit around the council fire, "Mother Earth was a celestial body floating in the universe among the stars, like a great island floating in a sea of water. The island was suspended by invisible cords at four places or directions in the sky vault and was a solid rock that had special energy and power. The old ones tell of the cords being delicate, and they feared that one day these cords would break and the island would sink into the ocean of the universe and become part of the flow of water energy for all time."

"All spirits were in the sky vault in a place called The Father's Place. During one of the councils with the Great One, the animal spirits asked for more room, since it was getting crowded in The Father's Place.

"Water Beetle was the first to go see what was below. Because she was Beaver's grandchild, the animal spirits thought she would be able to fly and land on a surface in the water. She flew and flew but found no place to land. Finally, she dove into the water to discover that it was mud which clung to her as she moved back to the surface. The animals were so excited that they provided what we know as gut string to tie the dried mud in the four directions to provide balance to Mother Earth.

"Great Buzzard, one of the Bird tribe, was sent to find a place suitable for each of the tribes to locate. When he flew over the area, he found that the mud was still very soft. Being tired, he let one of his wings dip into the mud which created valleys and mountains. Today, we know that as the place of The Real People because of the beautiful mountains that seem to always smoke and the other beautiful mountains that always have a blue misty haze across their ridges. There are still places in the valley called Buzzard's Place.

"At last it was time for the four-legged ones, the winged ones, and all of the Great One's creations to come down from The Father's Place to this new place in the sky vault called Mother Earth. The Great One sent the Thunder Beings to give a special life energy to Mother Earth. He also asked Sun to be the father over this new land knowing that the Great One was very busy with everything in the Universal Circle. Also, the land was dark until The Sun and Grandmother Moon agreed to watch by day and night.

"While this was the beginning for Mother Earth, the early Real People knew that there were other worlds out there in the Universal Circle, and others such as the Sun, the Moon, and Thunder beings oversaw those worlds.

"All living things on Mother Earth were to be brothers and sisters to one another. As there was opposite energy, so there would be balance and equality for all. The wisdom of The Real People and all the tribes would protect that balance so that all creatures on Mother Earth and in the Universal Circle could live in harmony.

"And so it is that all the animals and creatures, big and small, would live in peace on Mother Earth."

I think about *all living creatures* living *in harmony* on Mother Earth. I've a powerful strong understanding of why The Real People have such a distrust and fear of the white man. I know that for many white people *harmony* is not the first thought of the day.

I hunt with Bright Feather and become so familiar with my bow that I can feel it even in my sleep. I work on my shooting with a variety of new arrow tips, and Bright Feather encourages me to determine the kind I like best and forget the rest. We both agree after a time that I'm best with the plain arrows fashioned to a sharp point; I just don't have the arm strength to handle the heavier ones and make them fly true. We practice my shooting from Willow as she runs, and I try to hit a moving target. We both know my skill still needs much work, but it doesn't need to be spoke out loud. I'm happy that Red Fox joins us on these times and after many weeks have fun teasing him for I see he watches Turtle now with as much care as he watched me at one time. It's hard to see it, but I'm certain that he blushes now and then from my teasing.

I become a teacher, and Bright Feather becomes my student. I'm surprised at how many white man's words he does know, even if they are all related to hunting, trapping, animals and trade. It's a starting point, and we work each free moment we have away from the village. He has a good mind for the language, and more than once I'm surprised at how quick he is to pick it up and remember it. With the ending of summer and the excitement of the fall harvest, I'm amazed that Bright Feather and I can spend an entire day hunting in the forest and speak only white words if we choose. One late summer afternoon he says to me, "I think it is time that we go visit Deer and see if we can find out any news about things." He has spoken in perfect English.

But lastly, as the summer heat slips into brief catches of autumn's cool, my most favorite parts of the summer are those times I work on this way of being a mate. I grow to love and cherish the man that less than one and a half years ago I'd have called a *red savage* just as Miss Rebecca and Reverend Wilder did. And I ponder sometimes the knowledge that all who knew me as *Elle* still would call him *red savage*.

I enjoy this role of mate and of knowing things about him that no one else knows. I treasure our time together as we learn what it is like to be two who work as one. I delight in the skill we seem to have of being able to talk to each other without too many words but with just simple looks or gestures. I'm well and truly honored that just as *I* chose him, *he* chose me. I realize that while I was a Powerful Woman before I met him, I'm more powerful now that I'm loved by him.

I hear One Who Knows' words, *Together you will be unstoppable.* And it causes me to smile.

Listener

The trees slip into their bright autumn colors and just as Bright Feather said, we head out for Deer's trading post, also known as *Forest City, North Carolina.* Our trip to Deer and Forest City is in a very roundabout way. Bright Feather explains it's to make sure we don't travel on any white settler's lands.

"But isn't this the land of The Real People?" I ask, confused.

"Yes," is all he says. I'm left to conclude obvious answers.

We travel for five days, and I'm jumpy and nervous the whole time despite Bright Feather's best efforts to calm me. Is it safe for me to travel? Is Bright Feather safe *with me?* What will people think if they see us together and with me dressed as I am? Will they shoot first and ask questions later? Mouse thoughts crowd my head. I miss the feeling of safety that I have in my village and at my hearth. Those feelings of fear that I had leaving The Maple Forest on the way to Dark Cloud's village bubble to the surface. More than once I think that I want to go back to where I know I'm safe. More than once Bright Feather reminds me that we are traveling to a *trading post,* and many people of all kinds come and go with safety. But that does not make me feel much better.

Some powerful woman I am, I think with a big dose of disgust. How am I expected to be a voice for The Maple Forest at a great council circle if I can't overcome my jitters about traveling to a trading post owned by friends?

My first thoughts riding into the cleared space in the woods that is Deer's trading post is just one surprise after another. It looks more like Cooper's Store back in Ward's Mill, Virginia, than I'd expected. Then, as Deer steps out grinning from ear to ear to welcome us, I think he looks nothing like Deer and everything like William Thomas dressed from head to toe in white man's clothes: boots, button fly trousers, white shirt, suspenders and all. Then he greets us with the words of greeting of The Real People, and I relax a bit.

I meet Deer's mate, and she introduces herself to me as "Possum of the Turkey clan of The Real People of The Maple Forest, but you can also call me Mary," she finishes with a laugh. "It does not matter," she says serious like but quiet just to me, "as long as they speak polite and respectful to me." She's shorter than me with bright dark eyes and long, long dark hair. She, too, is dressed in white clothes, including an apron dusted with flour. I see bare feet peeking out beneath her skirt.

We are welcomed with great enthusiasm into their sturdy wood-frame home that sits separate but within a few quick steps from the trading post. Sipping on cool apple cider and eating warm corn fritters dipped in maple syrup, I struggle with the strangeness of it all. The wood plank floors and the sturdy chairs and tables are not what I'm accustomed to anymore. Looking at Bright Feather sitting casually talking to Deer, I realize how silly it is that he seems more at ease than I do.

Bright Feather and Deer go outside to examine the hides and furs and other items we have brought for trade. Deer is happy to hear that aside from the usual things, we have had an excellent season in the garden and have even brought along many seeds good for next year's planting. He's eager to examine them, too.

I smile at Possum as she gives me more than one shy smile. I think we will have fun talking on this visit! Before we have time to speak in burst three children of different ages.

"Is One Who Is Always Alone here yet?" says the oldest boy.

Possum smiles the same smile I see Otter give Little Bird. "Bear, this is our oldest boy, James, *Red Bird.* He is seven." Possum puts her arm around a girl looking at me with wide, interested eyes. "This is Eliza, *Sleeping Rabbit.* She is five. And," peeking out from behind Eliza's skirts is another small boy that Possum grins at, "and this is my smallest bit of trouble, Richard, *Small Turtle.*"

Richard holds up a filthy hand. "I'm thwee," he says with no small bit of pride.

I study them, an amazing mix of white and red, and see my future staring right back at me with dark Indian eyes and hair, yet fairer skin. They greet me with Indian faces and polite Indian words, yet within moments are shouting white words and greetings to Bright Feather and their father outside in front of the trading post. The boys eagerly follow Bright Feather, asking if he has brought his bow and arrows and can they ride Companion and will he take them hunting? Possum looks at me and rolls her eyes as I giggle.

Eliza can't seem to take her eyes off me. She's keenly interested in my dress, for I'm in full Indian clothes, including my weapons still strapped to my back and waist. She's in full white clothes. In no time she's close enough to me that I can see the freckles sprinkled across her nose. I recognize a kindred spirit, for the questions just bubble up and never seem to stop coming. "Are these real bear claws?" she asks as she fingers my necklace from Great Elk. "Did you kill the bear yourself? Is that why they call you 'Bear'? Pa's teaching me how to shoot a rifle. Can you shoot? What kind of knife is that? Pa says I'm too young to learn to throw a knife. Is that really your very own bow and arrows? Will you let me try? What is your horse's name? Can I have a ride on her? How long are you staying?"

Oh, how I remember! A time before Ma died, when I was just a little girl running wild with Henry, everything and anything I saw or did always led to a question. Or three. Or ten. I grin at Eliza and work hard to answer every question she can dream up.

Finally, Possum can stand it no more and shoos her out the door. "The questions never stop!" she says in mock frustration as Eliza makes her way outside, but on slow and not so happy feet. "And she's the most opinionated child you'd ever want to deal with!" She sighs and takes a sip of apple cider. "It is good to finally meet you. I am so happy that you came. Deer said that he thought you would come with *Bright Feather*," she tries to hide a grin as she makes an effort to call him by the new name, "when he came to trade next time." Possum studies me and seems to see what she likes, for finally she says, "Only the most special of women could have caused the change I see in him. He has been alone for so long, I feared that he would never find a new path."

She asks of the village and the people and is quite happy to hear any and all things I can remember. She's familiar with many people, and we laugh over things that never seem to change. I finally ask her how long she has been away from The Maple Forest, the mate of Deer.

She answers after thinking for a bit. "Close to nine summers," She smiles and shakes her head slowly in memory. "My family was not happy when I told them I wished to come with Deer to this place so far away from them and so close to the white world," she says. She sits up straight and tall in her chair and grins a wide, mischief-filled grin. "But they could not stop me!" She leans forward and whispers, "I was the most opinionated child you'd ever want to deal with!" and then laughs with me at her joke.

Possum shakes her head at the memory of it all. "I had my eye on that man from the moment I knew to look. He would visit for the summer and for a week or two in the spring and fall. As a child I would follow him around like a puppy and was a sheer annoyance. As a young woman on the hunt for the man of her choice, I completely terrified him." That made me laugh out loud and Possum grinned again, nodding. "Poor Deer, he always wanted so to do all things right and proper, especially once he began living in the white world and only came to The Maple Forest for short stays. He was so respectful and helpful, always listening, offering suggestions, making promises about what he could try to do when he was with the whites.

"His life made it impossible to do as it was always done when two people mate: join with my clan, set up a hut in my village, provide honor and protection to the village. How could he do such things, he argued, when he planned to live in the white territory as William Thomas and establish a trading business? It was the same fight each and every time."

"Didn't you ever think of giving up? Of choosing another?"

Possum laughed and shook her head no. "Oh, my family agreed with Deer and told me to choose another. So I just started a new argument and said I would go with him to live in the white world and help him with his trading business. That made Deer even more crazed. He said he feared for my safety and refused to even consider bringing me with him to live.

Possum smiles a sweet smile and looks at me. "Do you know, every single time we argued about whether or not to join, he *never* told me he did not want me for a mate, he *never* said I should choose another. He only ever gave me arguments why it would not be proper or why it would be dangerous." She nods with certainty. "He loved me."

She shrugs. "Despite what my family thought and despite what Deer said was right and proper, I was bound and determined to go with him. He had come to the village to tell Great Elk and the others that he was finally to a point where he was opening up this trading post and how he hoped they would come where they knew they would be treated fairly. He spent a week with us that time and on the morning he got ready to leave I was seated on my pony packed and ready to go! I had made my choice, and there was no one who could stop me."

She sighs a deep, deep sigh. "I was young and foolish and had no idea what to expect. *Deer knew*, he'd tried to tell me, but I was in love and that was all I could see." She smiles at me sadly. "It was terrible hard for me those first few years. James came along and then Eliza… Things were better by the time Richard was born. I had grown accustomed to the life of a white trader." She looks at me for a moment and says quietly. "Perhaps you know a little of what I felt…"

We stare at each other and seem to speak without words for a time. Finally, I say, "The Indian way is easier, better ..." I shake my head in annoyance for I can't find the right word. "I chose the Indian way," but I look out the window and see Bright Feather helping Richard up onto the back of Companion as he squeals with delight.

I turn back to meet Possum's eyes again, "I made that choice, though, before things were the way they are now with Bright Feather and me. I know, now, I will follow him anywhere he needs to go and wouldn't think twice about it."

"Ahh, so you do know," she says with a smile and a nod. "That is called *the path of love,* and it can be as difficult as the path of war!" She shrugs, "I adjusted slowly to the life here. Deer was good; he tried so hard to help. The children kept me busy and gradually I began to feel confident with the language and the people and the business. Slowly I found my place here. Now, I am happy. Now, I fit. I can be Possum of the Turkey Clan of The Real People of The Maple Forest one moment and turn around and be Mary Thomas, of William Holland Thomas Trading Post of Forest City, North Carolina the next. *Just as long as they speak polite and treat me with respect,* everything is just fine."

She stands and begins making preparations to cook dinner. "Can I help?" I ask. "At one time I made a pretty tasty venison stew with dumplings..."

Possum turns to me. "Now I am *really* glad you are here!" she says with a laugh.

I learn that the trading post is not on the family land that Deer discovered he owned as a result of being William Thomas, and while the trading post is on land that's close to Indian boundaries, it's carefully placed in white territory. The family land, I gather, is sizeable, as it's supported by the work of black slaves. Profits from this land helped to purchase the land for the trading post. "Deer's aunt and her husband have been seeing to it from the time of his disappearance, and when he returned, it really was not something he felt he wanted to take over," Possum explained. "He wanted to keep contact with the Indians and this," she gestures with the sweep of her hand, "offered that chance.

"This trading post helps him hear new things that will impact The Real People. He takes his job as their agent in the white world very serious and listening to all of the folks that wander through is a perfect way to hear what needs to be heard. Through his law schooling he knows people in government here in the state of North Carolina and even in the United States Government. Now that James is older he helps quite a bit at the trading post. The last time Deer had to go to Washington to discuss business about citizenship and such, James and I were able to handle things here all on our own." There is great pride in her voice when she tells me this.

The trading post is a busy place with a steady flow of people – red and white – coming by. I have fun wandering around the place; looking at the bolts of colorful cloth, stacks of furs and hides, tools and pots and pans, sacks of grain and seed and jars of fruits and vegetables stacked neatly on the shelves. It's a family effort and all are involved, large and small. I help Possum with the various chores of sorting and cataloging and organizing. I listen to the steady flow of conversations, some white, some Indian, and despite reassurances of my safety, try very hard to remember my life as Mouse whenever strangers come in to do business.

Something makes me work especially hard to be invisible on our second day there when I hear a group of people enter. By the sounds of their sturdy boots I know it to be white men, and it's not just their skin color but their numbers that make me skittish. I'm a powerful woman, but I've already learned two good lessons in my life about being *powerless*. With my back to the group I know I look like an Indian squaw, and I concentrate on the containers of thread and buttons and needles in front of me making a show of great interest.

"William," a voice says in way of greeting, and I try hard to determine how many pairs of feet I hear. Four? Maybe Five?

"Samuel," I hear Deer say in a cordial response. "What a surprise. It's been quite a while since you and your men've been by this a-ways."

"Got orders to do some patrolling of the western perimeter. Seems the Injuns have taken offense to some of the new settlers west of here. No violence yet but there's been reports of stolen horses and such, and Nancy Jamison of Pine Ridge claims Injuns broke in to her home and stole a ham right out of her oven!"

"Is that so?" I hear Deer respond. "Seems like settlers who make a point to set up a homestead on Indian land are only asking for trouble, wouldn't you think?"

Samuel snorts at this comment. "Should know better than to discuss this with you, now, shouldn't I, William, being how we all know how you feel about Injuns and all."

I try so hard not to move or breathe. White men are one thing but soldiers, too! I'm certain that Deer and Bright Feather may not have concerns about any others visiting the trading post and seeing me, but *soldiers* are a mighty different story. My heart pounds so loud I know that it must be heard by everyone. I make myself breathe deep and concentrate on calm thoughts rather than panic. I realize I've been holding a spool of blue thread for longer than it will take to make it, and I put it down with a clump louder than I'd like and look up at the shelves in front of me.

"Better keep an eye on your goods," I hear Samuel say. "The squaw's awful quiet over there and might be helping herself while you're distracted with me. Those Injuns are a thievin' lot, you know."

"I thank you for your concern; I'll be sure to keep a watch," Deer says. "Can I help you with anything?"

"Have you heard or seen anything that we should know?" Samuel says, and I hear other footsteps of the men in his party beginning to wander around the store. *Think*, my head says to me. *What should you do now? What will you do if they notice you are not as much an Indian squaw as they think you are?* I look up at the rows of trinkets on the shelves, and at the end of the shelves are papers and bits tacked to the rough wood of the wall. Good ideas escape me, and trying to look calm instead of a frozen Indian statue, I wander a few steps further into the darkness of the corner and start reading the faded scraps of paper, some yellow with age. I think tiny mouse thoughts in my head.

"It's been quiet," Deer says, "although John Henry from up the river brought me the best damn ham steak I've had in months a few days back."

"John Henry?" Samuel puzzles aloud. "Ham steak...?" and then he gets the joke and laughs uproariously. "Oh! I see! Did he steal it from Nancy Jamison's oven do you think? Ha! Ha! Ha! That's why I always like to stop by here William, even if you are confused in some of your political opinions. I always get a good laugh!"

I hear Deer chuckle as casual like as possible. "Actually, got some excellent apple cider that Mary's just made, cold and sweet outside hanging in the cistern if you'd like a cup. She might even have some of her apple pie, too. I think I remember your men liking it last time they were here..."

The wandering boots stop and make a hasty return back to the center of the store. "That would be right kind of you, William," I hear Samuel say. "The men and I have been a long way aways from good cooking and treats of such like for quite a few weeks."

The thought of fresh apple pie is enough to make them even forget about me. In the cool dark of the trading post, I feel my heart begin to slow and find it's natural rhythm. My eyes focus on the edge of an old paper peeking out beneath some new notices that have been tacked over it and I see the words, "- of Ward's Mill, Virginia." I reach up pulling the newer papers away to see the old page beneath, and I see a rough sketch of a white girl with "ELLE GRAVES" written in big letters below. My heart begins to pound again as I take the paper down to read it.

"On the evening of TUESDAY, the 22nd of March in the year of Our Lord 1828, the peaceful homestead of Andrew Graves, Esq. of Ward's Mill, Virginia was violently and savagely attacked by a marauding band of blood thirsty Indians. No surviving witnesses were found to provide an accurate account, however it is with the Utmost Hope and Desire that the person of Mistress Elle Graves might still be Alive and with the Most Extreme Care and Speed be found and returned post haste. All leniency will be afforded to those cooperating with authorities in the positive outcome to this tragic occurrence. April 10, 1828, Cornelius Cooper of Ward's Mill, Virginia." Beneath the writing is my picture, roughly drawn with the description: "Orphaned white girl whose mother has died and father and brothers have been murdered by marauding Indians, who answers to the name of Elle.."

"Don't suppose even if you held that up right next to you, they'd recognize you, you've changed so much," Deer says quietly behind me making me jump almost high enough to bump my head on the ceiling. "Bright Feather said to tell you to stay quiet and out of sight for a bit until the soldiers are long gone. He's gone off to follow them to make sure we know what direction they're choosing to follow."

I turn around to search his face, "Will he be safe doing that?"

"No one has ever seen Bright Feather – on foot or horse – unless he chooses it to be so. And a whole passel of white soldiers, talking and clanking and crashing through the woods are not going to notice one quiet Indian trailing them from behind. Yes, I'm sure he will be safe." He shows me his white face and lets me search it thorough until I'm satisfied.

I touch the picture of me on the yellowed paper. "It would be better if they thought I died with my Pa…" I say quietly. "I don't want to bring any harm to Great Elk's village, for they had nothing to do with it."

Deer looks at me for long moments and then sighs. "Ah, but there you're wrong, Bear, for it was under Great Elk's instructions that you were taken."

The look I give Deer seems to alarm him, and he reaches out to take my arm and steady me. "I'm sorry, Bear," Deer says to me with real concern. "I did not mean to have that come out as blunt as it did. I have a reputation of being frank and forthright in all of my business negotiations, but that does not always work so well on the personal level." He rolled his eyes. "Just ask Possum."

"Here," he says, "walk with me a while, and I will tell you a long story." I notice his son, James, in the shadows by the counter busy with his ever present whittling. "Can you handle things for a bit, son?" he asks. James flashes him a quick smile and gives him a nod. "Fetch your Ma if anyone comes, hear?" And we walk out the back of the store into the cool shade of the bright autumn forest.

"First off, for reasons that will be clear very quickly, I speak to you as William Thomas, not as Deer. Possum and I spoke for a long time about whether I should tell you things *I* know that Bright Feather never will. At last she made the wise suggestions that I speak with Bright Feather and ask *him* whether I should tell you or not." He sighs and looks at me serious, "Last night I spoke with him about telling you things you should know that he will not speak of. I speak to you because he said I could.

"To understand how you came to be in Great Elk's village you must go back many years even before I came to be a son of War Woman's hearth, and I must speak of people who are no longer alive," he says. I feel a prickle of goose flesh up my arms as we walk into the forest full of bright reds and golds and oranges. I struggle to slow my head and my heart down and just listen and take it all in. "I ask *you* before I go on with any more of the story. Do you want to hear what I have to tell you?"

The pieces to the puzzle that I'd never thought to see, I think as I look into Deer's serious face. *The chance to understand all the whys.* There are so many pieces to the puzzle that are missing. Had I lived my whole life in Great Elk's village there would be more understanding. Do I want to know the whole picture? I must admit that I do. "I think that I must trust you and Possum and Bright Feather and hear what you have to say," I answer, but my voice is quiet and unsure.

"Weasel was the son of Dark Cloud and would have been one of three sons who would be considered for chief." Deer shrugs his shoulders, "It is easy knowing the things we know *now* to think that Weasel would have *never* been selected to be chief, but at the time I speak of, there was no such certainty. Some sons of chiefs do not have a great desire to take their father's place. They look at the job as something they must face should the time come." He looks at me certain that I know, "Bright Feather is one such as that." He looks away and continues, "Other sons hunger for it like a starving man hungers for a warm bowl of tasty stew. Weasel was one such as *that.*

"It was during the time when Great Elk's village and Dark Cloud's village were still struggling to maintain a bond. They wanted to remain close in spirit even though they were no longer close in distance. Marriages were arranged, between the two villages in the hopes of keeping the bond tied with blood. I do not know how Weasel's village came to choose him to come to Great Elk's village and join with One Who Knows' oldest daughter, Raven. I do know that Raven considered it an honor, for she told me, but in fairness she was not traveling to a new village, and the two braves that traveled to Dark Cloud's village from The Maple Forest were not overly happy about the move.

"For you see, by then already there were difficult feelings between the two villages about the white man and how much involvement we should have with him. Those differences had made each place a very different world to live in." We stop by a peaceful spot that I sense he comes to at times, and he motions for us both to sit down on a massive tree trunk covered in moss. Deer searches my face, "Bright Feather has told me that you have talked about these things," and I nod my head 'yes'.

"Weasel arrived in Great Elk's village angry, and he stayed angry for as long as I knew him. He disagreed with those who sat around the council circle on almost everything that was discussed, and he challenged those who had differing opinions rather than trying to understand their thoughts.

"One of his greatest continual battles was over the decision of whether The Real People should go west of the Mississippi, stay east on smaller tribal territory, or accept the offer of citizenship. Weasel married Raven in the spring of 1818 the year after the treaty was signed that commissioned the census of The Nation of The Real People. The census was begun in the summer of 1818, and it was during the census that one was to be counted *and declare their intentions* about what they wished to do. The Treaty of 1819 contained a list of those who requested citizenship. Weasel was present for the census in Great Elk's village that summer of 1818 and I made a point to be there when the agents for The Nation of The Real People and the representatives of the United States Government arrived." He looks at me with a sorrowful and serious face. "I so feared the outcome with Weasel there. I did not know how he would react.

"Weasel supported the views of his father, Dark Cloud, and was passionately vocal about it. His arguments fell on deaf ears, for there was no one seated at Great Elk's council circle that had any desire for the white man's money or the white man's possessions. Weasel simply could not understand that.

"He made great efforts to discredit those of us who were sons of Great Elk, and at every opportunity sought to show that he was better, faster, smarter and wiser than we were. Bright Feather, Beaver and I chose not to respond to him, for all knew it was useless to argue with a person who could only see one side of things. As more and more people felt that the path of citizenship was the right one, Weasel had more and more people to challenge and argue with. He succeeded only in making all those who dealt with him unhappy, none more so than One Who Knows' daughter, Raven." He sighs and runs his hand through his hair, and I realize that try as he may to be speaking only as William Thomas, the man that's called Deer is there, too. "There was no harmony in Great Elk's village from the moment Weasel arrived.

"Many people were at the council circle that night when The Real People Agents and the United States Government Representatives arrived. Great Elk spoke as did War Woman. I think he made every effort to explain the facts fairly the way he understood them to be. Great Elk said, 'I do not tell you all these things to upset you or to make you angry. I tell you all this *so that you know the way of things.* There are many different people who believe they have only the best interests for The Real People at heart, and there are many different choices we are faced with. Some will choose differently than our neighbors or our friends or even our brothers.' He said his greatest fear was the eventual division of The Real People.

"War Woman explained about the census," and Deer smiles with the memory. "She was harsher and made less of an effort to speak in the middle. She said, 'Why does the United States of America want to know our numbers? My first thought is it is always best to know the size of your enemy.'" Deer chuckles. "I can still see the nervous faces on those United States Government Representatives.

"She told all about the offer of citizenship and what she understood it to mean. It meant that they would not be considered part of The Nation of The Real People anymore but would instead be considered part of the United States of America. She said that with the promise of citizenship came the promise of land – six hundred and forty acres for each household."

Deer smiles at me. "War Woman also reminded everyone of promises that were never kept fully in the past and others that had been outright broken. And she also reminded them about the fact that The Nation of The Real People *no longer recognized* anything that they decided within the council circle but instead depended solely on the decisions made by Dark Cloud and his village of advisors.

"The hardest thing she tells them, though, is that the land they are sitting on, the land they have always considered theirs, was not part of the new tribal boundaries that would be drawn. She said, 'The Maple Forest is not within the new boundaries of The Nation of The Real People. Your choice is this: stay with The Nation of The Real People and loose the ancestral land that has always been ours or leave The Nation of The Real People and claim citizenship with the nation we have always considered our enemy … and the right to land that we are *told* comes with us.'" Deer looks at me. "It was not much of a choice, was it?" It's easy to admit that it was not.

Deer pauses and lets the many words he has said slowly seep in. "I sat there in the firelight with all of the people whom I considered my brothers and my sisters, and even though I knew everything that was going to be said, to hear Great Elk and War Woman say them aloud was devastating. There were many who sat there in that circle that night crying silently for they knew, *they knew* much of the Old Ways were disappearing right before their eyes."

He shrugs his shoulders. "So, the Government Representatives stayed and counted each and every person in the village. Everyone stepped forward and made the decision whether they would move and stay with The

Nation of The Real People or not move and become citizens of the nation they considered their enemy; the nation they did not trust.

"Weasel went just about mad as they all made their decisions, and he was counted as one who wished to stay in the east as part of The Nation of The Real People and accept money and goods in trade. He was the only man in the village who did not request citizenship," he pauses for a moment in memory and deep thought, "although I wondered for a time whether Beaver would decide to go with The Nation of The Real People rather than stay in Great Elk's village." He looks me right in the eye, "And Raven is the only woman who is counted as wishing to stay with The Nation of The Real People for he forbade her to go against his wishes.

"Raven was a good woman: strong, independent, smart, and loving," and for long moments he's quiet with his memories. "She was full of life and mischief. She could charm you to do just about anything that suited her. All the braves were in love with her at least just a little," he smiles a bit shy like. *Including you*, I think and know it to be true when I look into his eyes. "She was proud to be chosen, and she entered into the joining with Weasel willingly; not for love of a man but for love of her people. *Braves fight*, she said to me the night before he arrived, *women love.*" He laughs an embarrassed laugh. "I tried to convince her to leave the village with me rather than join with Weasel. There was no one else like her," he said with just a whisper and then looks at me. "Except her younger sister, Black Fox." *Black Fox*, my heart jumps at the sound of the name. I feel a shiver run up my spine, Bright Feather's mate when he was called Hawk and the mother of his son was Black Fox.

"Weasel was cruel to Raven in his manner and his speech and his behavior. He showed her no respect, he did not recognize her goodness and he was quick with his hands in his anger. One Who Knows and Black Fox," he snorts with bitter humor, "never ones to be quiet in the face of difficult situations *ever* were silent about Weasel. It *had* to be at Raven's insistence; nothing else could have kept them still. She was quiet and tried to do everything he demanded. She never spoke ill of him nor did she do anything to discredit him. It soon became apparent that he was destroying her spirit, and as they entered their second winter together all in the village wished that come the Green Corn Ceremony of the summer she would end the union."

He stands and begins to pace about in the small area where we are; the memories of it all make him restless. "That would be good for her, but bad for him, for he would have to return back to his village in a less than favored status, while she would be free of his anger and frustration to start fresh." Deer pauses, quiet for a while, and I can almost see him sorting through the words he will say to me and those he will not.

"Weasel convinced her to visit his village at the end of the winter just before the trees began to bud. It was not unusual to visit other villages, and Dark Cloud's village was certainly one we traveled to often yet One Who Knows was insistent that she not go. She spoke with great passion at a number of council circles against the visit - I was present at some of them - but Raven was determined to go. By then Hawk had joined with Black Fox, and they were expecting their first child. They, too, tried to convince Raven not to go, but Raven would not listen to anyone.

"The morning they left, One Who Knows tore at her clothes, painted her face black, and cut her arms in mourning as though Raven was already dead. I was leaving to go back to the white territory and can still remember standing there watching Raven and Weasel leave while One Who Knows wailed her sorrow."

He shook his head. "I never spoke to Raven about it. I never asked her. No one has ever shared with me her thoughts. Many times I have wondered, *Why?* Why did she feel so strongly about going, especially with One Who Knows' objections?" His sorrow sits with us like another person in the forest, huge and big.

We are there in the silence of the forest for a bit, pondering the reasons that we can never really know. "Maybe she just wanted to have a piece of the puzzle that might help her understand Weasel," I say at last. "Maybe she thought if she met his people and saw his village, she could understand his anger better. Maybe she cared for him one small bit. Maybe she thought she could see goodness in him where others couldn't. Maybe she wanted the joining to work for the sake of her people."

He nods his head and shrugs. "Those are as good reasons as any, I suppose."

He sighs. "No one ever saw her again. Weasel returned to the village a full month later without her with a story none of us ever believed. He claimed he had been set upon by a group of white trappers who had beaten him and left him for dead, and that they had taken Raven as a captive. He claimed to have traveled to Dark Cloud's village first because it was closer to seek their help, and despite their best efforts they were unable to find any trace of her or the trappers." He looks at me, his eyes showing great pain. "Why didn't they send riders to our village so that we could join the search?

"Hawk came to me here at the trading post that first night he heard Weasel's story. We searched the forest and surrounding areas based on where Weasel told us everything happened, and we found nothing either. We notice that Weasel's story seems to change with every telling. We sent riders to Dark Cloud's village to speak with the braves who had come from our village, as well as others. There were different versions of his story from almost everyone we talked to. We heard everything from he showed up alone flashing a new rifle to he showed up bleeding and almost dead barely able to speak." He shrugs, "But the only thing that was certain was there was no Raven. We searched for almost three weeks for her."

He comes and sits back down by me and his speaking has gotten so quiet that I catch myself leaning in closer and straining with all my might to hear. "When we returned to Great Elk's village, Hawk and I, it was with great sorrow because we had nothing to show and nothing to tell for all of our weeks away. We arrived to a village in full mourning, for Black Fox, in her grief over her sister, had gone into labor early and both she and the baby – a son – had died. One Who Knows who's entire life had been healing and guiding had done her best and yet had been unable to prevent either of her daughter's deaths. We thought she mourned only Raven's death that day she left with Weasel, but One Who Knows knew even more sorrow was to come.

"Hawk was inconsolable after Black Fox's death. He blamed himself for so much ... He said more than once he should have traveled with Weasel and Raven when they first set out, yet he had not wanted to leave Black Fox, who had not done well in her pregnancy from the start. He knew how upset Black Fox had been when he left to search with me, and yet even she had encouraged him to go and look as best he could. Hawk blamed himself for much of the sadness that came into the village but there was, of course, no one to blame but Weasel."

He looks at his hands clenched tight in front of him, "The village was such a sorrowful place that even I found many reasons not to visit after a time. The business at the trading post became the best excuse. Hawk became One Who Is Always Alone and was hardly there either. Even Weasel was more unhappy than ever, but pride made him stay rather then go home to Dark Cloud's village for a long while."

I have a thought all of a sudden in my head and must make a sound in my throat for he looks at me. "I, I think I saw Raven once ..." I say.

He studies me for a moment. "Bear John," he says finally. "Yes, I know. *I knew him*, believe it or not. He used to come here to do business, and it would take a week to clear out the stench."

The last pieces to the puzzle begin to fall into place. "You never found any trace of her because she was with Bear John, and he was in Virginia," I say quiet like. "He must have headed north into white territory as soon as he got her from Weasel." My head is full of memories of her and me standing safe and sound with my Pa, Henry, and Eli at Cooper's Store.

Deer nods his head sadly. "I heard much talk once we gave up searching, and I got back to the trading post. Mostly from the white trappers and hunters – not the homesteaders that have one spot and stay there - but the ones who were temporary and had no place they called home. They spoke of Bear John and laughed over his 'Injun squaw'. They thought it was funny how he kept her on a rope like a dog. Each one said the same thing; he'd brought her proper like from her 'Injun brave' who traded her for a brand new rifle. Those stories made more sense than Weasel's story to most of us. Selling captive Indian enemies to the whites was something that had been going on for many years. Whites would think nothing of an Indian slave any more than a black one." He extends his hands out in front of him, "What could we do? I made many inquiries as to Bear John's whereabouts, but there was nothing solid for us ever to act on. It was not until you killed him that we had any idea for certain where he was."

He stands again and paces, "There was a scrap of deerskin cloth they found in his saddle bag after you killed him, you know," he says, and he stops and looks at me. "Bear John used to clean his rifle with it apparently. It was from Raven's tunic. One Who Knows recognized the stitching and decorations even through all the filth. After she died, he used her clothes to keep his rifle clean." I remember after Bear John's death how his possessions and all of his companion's possessions had been carefully examined and looked through.

"In those months after Weasel returned without Raven, and Hawk became One Who Is Always Alone, I think Weasel actually began to believe his own stories. He talked at length of revenge and was angrier and more filled with hate than ever before. He never tired of the debate about the bad choices the village had made and the good choices Dark Cloud's village did. Council circles at Great Elk's village were filled with Weasel's condemnations of those elders who had steered the people falsely and his grand talk of vengeance for the wrongs that had been done him. One Who Knows sat there silent and accusing, never speaking a word. Finally, Great Elk challenged Weasel to seek out his own revenge if he was so certain he deserved it, but War Woman refused to allow him to take anyone from the village with him. She told him that revenge must be a personal thing, and she would not have the village dragged into something that it had no part of. It was then that Weasel knew there was no one sitting in the council circle who did not blame him for all that had happened in the village."

Deer comes over to me and kneels down in front of me and looks at me with sorrowful eyes. "That's how you come to be sitting here with me today. I think the village hoped that Weasel would just go, and for quite a while he did. There was word that he went back to Dark Cloud's village for a time, but he did not stay. How he came to be in Ward's Mill, Virginia," he points to the paper I realize is still clutched in my hand, "on

March 22nd, 1828, on the property of Andrew Graves, Esquire I will never know."

He reaches out and grasps my hand tightly, further crumpling the notice and speaks with great emotion, "Weasel brought you to Great Elk's village and in many ways he restored the harmony there, whether he intended to or not. I need only to sit around the council circle and see the changes in every face as a result of your presence. *That* is why One Who Knows speaks of your brightness, *that* is why One Who Is Always Alone is now *Bright Feather*, and that is why you are no longer Elle but *Bear*." He laughs a strange laugh, "You have made so many choices on your own with your good heart unaware of the tangled mess of broken hearts and spirits around you, and *all your choices have been fine ones."*

I hear Bright Feather's words in my head as we rode back from my time in Dark Cloud's village. Choices are a little bit like weeds. Some left to grow can have beautiful flowers. Others might be important for healing. You never have to stop looking for choices, but you must always at the same time never stop making them. That's life.

Deer stands in front of me and pulls me to my feet. He takes his hat off his head and bows a formal bow to me in the forest amid the bright autumn leaves and bustling animals scurrying to prepare for winter. "It is a privilege to know you, Bear, daughter of One Who Knows, of The Maple Forest, of The Real People," he says solemnly. "I count myself honored to call you friend." My eyes fill with tears from his words, and I can't find any words in my mouth. He steps forward and puts his arm around my shoulders and turns me to head back to the trading post.

And now I have a puzzle I can see the whole picture of.

Bright Feather is in the courtyard of the trading post showing James how to hold his bow and shoot when we walk into the clearing. He stands and walks toward us as we come out of the forest, Deer and I, and his eyes search my face for a brief moment. *I know the name of the spirit who speaks to you in your head,* my head says. *Her name is Black Fox.* He touches my cheek gentle like, and I smile at him, my heart full of sorrow and tenderness and love all rolled into one. "The soldiers go north," he says to both of us. "That is the direction I would have picked if I could have." He looks at the two of us, "Did you have a good walk?"

"Can you believe it, brother?" Deer says in wonderment. "She barely asked one question!"

Later that night Bright Feather lies next to me in our private space in the back storage room of the trading post which is lit by flickering lantern light. "I have a gift for you," he says and reaches over beside him and hands me the parcel.

I feel like a child as I unwrap the deerskin and am flooded with curiosity. I sit up with excitement when I realize what it is. A book! *"Hymns and Spiritual Songs,"* I read aloud and touch the fine black leather cover aged but still sturdy, *"by Isaac Watts, 1707."* I look at Bright Feather in great wonder. "Why? Where?"

"Deer was very pleased with how well I am speaking the white language," he explains. "He thinks maybe *my* thick skull might be able to begin to read it now. This was the only book he had, and he thought we can practice my reading *and* maybe save my soul as well. I'm not so sure about the soul part, but the reading should be something we can work on."

I open the book and read aloud by the flickering lamp, "Teach me the measure of my days, thou maker of my frame, I would survey life's narrow space, and learn how frail I am. A span is all that we can boast, an inch or two of time; man is but vanity and dust in all his flower and prime[10]." The book feels strange in my hand, for aside from the great family Bible we used to read at home with Pa, I've never held one, let alone owned one. "White people consider books to be very precious," I say after a time. "We had a family Bible that we would read from – me and Henry – each night to practice. It had many names of our family who had been born and died from before they even came here to the Colonies. Ma's mother gave it to her when she and Pa married. Pa let me write Eli's name in it when he was born and Pa wrote of Ma's death…" My head is full of memories of sitting by the firelight listening to Pa's strong confident voice reading the hard words out loud, then Henry and finally me reading through the verses and struggling with the understanding of it all.

"We would read once Eli was in bed, and he would slowly drift off to the sounds of our voices. There were many times I had trouble understanding what it all meant. But there was one verse I remember I liked the sound of 'cause it was so hopeful." I whirl the white words around in my head trying to change them to Indian and keep them sounding good. "*It is of the Lord's mercies that we are not consumed, because His compassions fail not. The Lord is my portion, saith my soul; therefore I will hope in Him. The Lord is good unto them that wait for him, to the soul that seeketh him[11].* That is from the book of *Lamentations*, third chapter, verses twenty two to twenty five."

For many moments I feel powerful like I'm back home in the cabin in Ward's Mill, Virginia, and I expect to hear Pa's voice any moment say, *Well done, Elle, and can you tell us what your understanding is of 'mercies'?* "Pa would have us read verses, some we'd just open up to, some he'd make us find and then we'd talk about the meanings of the words and the meanings of the verses. He always was patient and kind, although he must have been powerful tired by then, for I knew for sure I was. Most nights I just wanted to curl up in bed with Eli and fall fast asleep. I remember Henry and me many nights complaining and wanting to skip lessons. *What good will this book learning ever do for us, Pa?* I can still hear Henry saying in a voice filled with tiredness. Pa would insist we practice, and it was a quiet time I must admit has a powerful good memory tied to it now."

"What is my 'soul' that Deer speaks of needing to be 'saved'?" Bright Feather asks quietly.

"Pa said the soul was the part of us that never died. He said that our bodies can last just only so long, but the soul goes on forever. Once the body is gone, the soul moves on to the next special place where God intends it to be. In those early times after Ma died, I used to think that maybe Ma's soul was in Eli and her things around the house, like her Hope Chest. Now I think about what The Real People believe and how the spirit world is the next place we go on this journey of life. I think about how I hear Pa's voice in my head and about your voice," I look across to him in the lantern light, and he looks back at me with dark thoughtful eyes. "I think about those we love who are not with us anymore, and I think about a time in the future when you and I will be separated like that. I hear the word *destiny* quiet like in my ear, and I know as sure as you are sitting here close enough to touch," I reach out and touch the warm, alive, bare skin of his thigh glowing gold and orange and beautiful brown in the flickering light, "and I *know* there is another life after this one where we will all surely be together as well.

"Reverend Walker and Miss Rebecca talked about a God that loved us so very, very much that He sent His son to die for us and take the blame for our wrongs," I tell Bright Feather. "I've pondered what they have told me, and I understand it to mean that He allowed His death to bring Harmony back in exchange for all the wrongs that we have done.

"What is truly amazing to me is that Miss Rebecca said that God's son, Jesus, loved us so much that he chose to die rather than to live without us."

Bright Feather stretches out and puts his head in my lap. "That is an amazing love," he says after a time. "I would like to ask many more questions." He gives me a tender look. "Do you think I am learning that from you?" He places his hand at the top of my head and follows my long wrapped tail of hair down my back. He wraps his arm around my back and says, "Read me more of this *Isaac Watts* and then let us make some powerful good memories of our own."

I open the book and begin to read, "We are a garden walled around, chosen and made peculiar ground; a little spot enclosed by grace out of the world's wide wilderness. Like trees of myrrh and spice we stand, planted by God the Father's hand; and all his springs in Zion flow, to make the young plantation grow[12]," I read aloud with the book resting on Bright Feather's bare chest and my hand stroking his hair as it lays like some shiny blanket thrown careless over my crossed legs. Nice new memories to mix with the old, I think in my head with a happy sigh.

"What is 'peculiar'?" Bright Feather asks.

I roll the word around in my head, and I hear Pa trying one of my dinners and saying, *This has a mighty peculiar taste, Elle...* Then I hear Eli say,

We put honey in it, Pa! Honey, Pa says thoughtful like, *honey and trout. Now that's a new pairing I'd not thought of...*

I say, "Peculiar means, I think, different, not what you'd expect."

"I like that one," he says after a moment. "'*We are a garden walled around, chosen and made peculiar ground...*' that's just how The Real People of The Maple Forest are; surrounded by the whites and the reds, '*a little spot enclosed by grace out of the world's wide wilderness.*'" He picks up one of my hands and kisses it, settling it against his heart. "Read that one again," he says. And I do.

On our third and last day, Deer speaks with both Bright Feather and me as Possum fusses about the kitchen. "I must speak to you of what news I have heard. And none of it is good. There is great trouble on the horizon for The Nation of The Real People. I have heard even more talk since I last visited The Maple Forest. It is not good that Andrew Jackson has been elected President of the United States. He will not look towards the direction of what is right, but will instead, always look towards the direction of who shouts the loudest." Deer looks at both of us serious like, "And the white man always shouts the loudest."

He smiles at Possum as she pours him some hot black coffee, and takes a careful sip. "Already the state of Georgia has asked for permission to enter Real People lands to mine for gold that has been found in the northern part of the state. Georgia has never recognized the tribal boundaries and for many, many years has sought to have the piece of paper giving rights to The Nation of The Real People destroyed. They have tried things legally, and they have tried things outside the law. I do not believe they will stop until they get what they want: the land." Deer shakes his head. "Should Georgia decide to act on its own without the Government's permission, I do not believe anyone will try to stop them. In fact, I suspect all will watch carefully and see how successful they are at getting what they want. I speak to you plainly: there will be Real People lives lost, and the land will be taken by theft."

Deer sighs and Possum sits down next to him, putting her hand on his shoulder. "For a time, the Government and the states will look toward the largest pieces of land that are held by The Nation of The Real People. They will set their hungry eyes and hands on where they can get the most with the least effort. But they *will come* to The Maple Forest. You must believe that. No matter what we do or hope. We must be ready."

Deer has a look of such powerful sadness, I feel my throat get tight with tears. My heart beats fast and furious and I look at Bright Feather's solemn face and Possum's fearful one, and I know I am not alone with my great worries. "For many of us," Deer says, "it will be a fight to the death whether we go to a war with weapons or not. Words on paper sometimes can kill more than a rifle shot can. Our greatest defense in The Maple Forest is to be ready and to continue to collect all those weapons – paper ones, wisdom ones, and" he looks at me, "people ones.

"I told you last I saw you in The Maple Forest that I thought that you two were a great asset to your village. Watch, listen, learn, and *think*. Always think.

"We must believe that it will be our *difference* that will give us our greatest strength. We have made ourselves separate and apart. We are citizens of the United States with all the rights and privileges that affords us. I have worked long and hard to sew all these paper piece walls together to protect us when the time comes. Though it will not keep us from the battle that is coming, it *must* make us victorious in the end."

The Maple Forest is chosen and made peculiar ground, I think, and I look at Bright Feather. He looks back at me, and I suspect the worry he sees in my face makes him reach for my hand. *Enclose us in grace,* I whisper prayer to God, *please!*

I'm quiet that evening of the last day at Deer and Possum's trading post as I think about all the things I have learned in these three short days to Forest City, North Carolina. Names swirl through my head: Raven, Black Fox, Bear John, Weasel, … Hawk. Are the spirits restless for the talking that was done about them? I think about Bright Feather and the great sorrow he must have felt to have lost both a mate and a son. *Truly he does know how sorrowful a heart can be.*

I think about Cornelius Cooper of Ward's Mill, Virginia, and the notice he posted about my missing. If Pa, Henry, and Eli are all gone, why should he care about me and my circumstances? Why would he go to such trouble to have a 'positive outcome' to such a 'tragic occurrence'. Is he after all this time still looking for me? Still wishing for my return? I find that thought upsetting for he has no reason to have concern about my safety.

I help Possum bake bread and work on a gift I'm making for One Who Knows. Eliza and I go for a ride together on Willow, and I let her talk herself dry. As I brush down Willow later that afternoon I think about our "garden walled around" in The Maple Forest and am so glad for it and have a yearning suddenly to get back there. I ponder over this man who is President, Andrew Jackson, who will listen to those who shout the loudest rather than those who are the wisest. *Why can't things just stay quiet and still and peaceful for just a bit?* I wonder.

Night has fallen and I enjoy the quiet moment sitting on Deer and Possum's front porch swing. I sigh and put my head on Bright Feather's shoulder. I decide to show Bright Feather the crumpled notice about my missing. I've kept it to myself for a day, but now the pile of worry I'm keeping inside me is too much for just one body to hold. I can't worry about Andrew Jackson *and* Cornelius Cooper all by myself.

He searches my face as I hold it out to him. "Read to me what it says," he says softly against my ear after pulling me into his arms. I decide to make it a sort of reading lesson saying each word slow and careful like. It takes us a while because whenever I say a white word he doesn't know he makes me stop and explain it. It takes me quite a while to realize that he's choosing the big ones I sometimes stumble on on purpose. "Mind yourself, young man," I say in the best stern white Pa voice I can manage. He grunts. White folks furniture comes in handy sometimes I think as we swing, and I enjoy the heat of his body burning through the sides of my tunic.

"The picture is not you," he says after studying it for a while.

"Deer said the same thing, just about. He said if I held the picture right next to my face those soldiers would not have been able to see the likeness."

"Your eyes are more almond shaped and your mouth turns up in the corners all the time so that you always look like you're just about smiling even when you are trying to be serious." He hesitates and then says, "I have seen this before."

I sit up and turn to look at him. "When? When did you see this?"

"Well, that's a mighty long story," he drawls out in his best white person words.

I sigh and snuggle back up against him and put my head on his shoulder. "This trip seems to be all about stories."

He waits a moment and says, "That first night when Great Elk took you from One Who Knows, I had just gotten back from visiting Deer and Possum. I had returned earlier in the day and the village was in an uproar over what had happened to you. I kept thinking, '*White girl? What white girl? Here?*' When I ask finally, all One Who Knows will say is, 'Watch and see.' Before I know it, Great Elk has given you to me to care for my needs. More than once I think I should have waited *just one more day* before I returned." I pull away and look at him with a fierce stare. "I am not always as quick to see the good in things," he says by way of apology.

"I took you hunting," he says with a deep sigh, "at Otter's insistence. 'I hunt alone' I told her over and over, but she would not hear me. I planned to leave you with the women at the hunting camp, but you looked so uncertain. You sat quiet with me that whole day and then worked so hard the next. And you still had the energy to laugh at something as we washed in the stream at the end of that day. I looked at you and you had the robin's feather stuck in your hair, and I thought, *There is something special about this girl.*

"The next time I visited Deer, it was just about this time last year, autumn time. That was when I saw this picture hanging on Deer's wall. He thought it was important I take note of it once I mentioned that there is a white captive in the village. He read to me the words, too, so I knew what they said." He felt compelled to add, "You did a good job at explaining the big words. Deer explained them almost the same way," and hugs me tight and finally gives me a kiss when I pretend to try to give him a good shove.

"But I did not know for sure it was you. I realized I had never really even spoken with you. I had every intention of finding out your white name when I returned to the village. I made a point to remember *Elle Graves* so that I could say it to you when I got back to Great Elk's village. I arrived to another big gathering, and again you seemed to be in the center of it all. I watched you sitting by War Woman that night and trying so hard to be a Mouse. I saw Otter speak sternly to you when you tried to get up and scurry and hide in the shadows like you preferred to do. I knew then as I looked at you that the drawing was not very good, but that you were the young girl in the picture, and I sorrowed for you and your loss even though you were unaware of it.

"I went and I got Willow and your things and was ready to come forward at the end of the celebration to bring you home to *Cornelius Cooper of Ward's Mill, Virginia.* I watched you tell your story with Otter to those around the council fire. I knew Deer has talked to you, so you can imagine my shock to hear *who* you killed. The very man Deer, Raccoon and I had searched so long and so hard for but never found. Then I heard Great Elk call you a daughter of One Who Knows and name you Bear, and I knew that you had a family again and One Who Knows had a daughter again. I realized that your place most certainly was now with The Real People of The Maple Forest. So instead of taking you home to sorrow and grief, I brought you your horse and acknowledged you before the village and gave you your freedom from any obligations to me.

"I worried that whole winter that I had made the wrong choice. What if you were unhappy? What if you had more family to go to? What if you felt just as much a prisoner in Otter and Raccoon's home as you had with One Who Knows or me? I returned from my winter trapping, determined again to speak to you and offer you the chance to go home to your own people. And what do I find on my return? I find a beautiful and powerful Indian woman sitting proudly on her Indian pony with her bow and her arrows, wrapped in her furs, her face flushed with victory over a kill, who put me smack in my place when I failed to address her properly and with respect. I can still see Raccoon sitting on his horse grinning like a fool at my confusion.

"That was the first time we talked. We talked about horses and shooting and the forest. When I left again to hunt, it was the first time in many years that I felt that my name did not fit me so well anymore, for as I rode into the woods the only thing I wanted to do was to come back and answer many more questions for you. I made myself stay away. I argued with the voice in my head that I was best off with the trees and the animals and Companion. I made myself do all the things that I had always done, and I made myself remember the pain and the sorrow and the tears of loosing someone. I stayed away as long as I could stand it and then rode back to the village telling myself that I was going to just be the way I had always been. But I had plans about what I would show you, and things I wished to teach you and places I thought you might like to ride to, and the voice in my head teased me about lying to myself as well as others. I returned to find the village in turmoil for you had disappeared not two days before.

"While they argued over whether you had gone on your own or not, Raccoon and I searched the woods. He knew some of the places you liked to go, but it turned out that you had shown me still others. It was at your quiet place that we saw the signs of the fight and even found your knife with blood on it. We rode back to the village to get supplies and tell them what we were doing." He shook his head, "Some were still arguing about what to do when we rode out.

"As we followed the trail, all I could think of was how could I be doing this again? Looking for someone I cared about who I was certain was in danger. It was on the trail and the wait outside Dark Cloud's village that I had to be honest with myself that you made me not want to be alone anymore." He grunts. "By then Raccoon had told me that Beaver and Red Fox had made their interests in you known. I did not want to interfere with your choices, and again told myself lies that I would bring you home and leave you again so that you could make the decisions you needed to make." He shakes his head. "I even knew I would make the offer to you about going back to Ward's Mill, Virginia, as Great Elk had instructed me to, and worried if I would have to tell you what I knew to be true about your family."

I turn to him on the swing, and I take his face in my hands and cover his mouth with mine to make him be quiet. It's a long, sweet, slow kiss that seems to go on and on and on. I finish kissing his strong mouth and kiss his eyes and his cheeks and his forehead, and he breathes a loud sigh and finally wraps his arms tight around me. He pulls me across his lap and holds me so tight I'm not sure he will ever let go, and still we kiss again for a very long time. Finally, we stop and both take a long shaky breath.

"I will not let Cornelius Cooper have you," he says after a time, and I feel my worry bow release about that very thing.

"I do not need to fear that he will come searching for me," I say without a question.

His arms tightened around me, and he pulls me close, almost across his lap. "No, you do not need to fear."

I ponder how he knows this to be so but decide I no longer wish to ask questions about this worry. "You know," I say to him, "different places, different languages, different *worlds*, and still," I can't help myself, and I draw him down to me and kiss him again longer and slower, "we found each other. What do you think that means?"

He's grown tired of the talking at last, I can tell, and he's more interested in the kissing. He has me cradled in his arms, and he kisses my neck while he touches my breasts both slow and careful like; he's in no hurry at all. "It means," he says, "we are each other's *destiny*. No person, no situation, no thing will stop this that we have." He holds my face with his hand and leans over to whisper in my ear, "And that makes me *so glad.*"

I'm up with the very first rays of the sun on the day we're to leave Deer and Possum's trading post. I walk out into the cool, autumn dawn and wander through the forest alive with colors of red and gold and orange. I walk as far as Deer's thinking rock where we sat just two days before as he filled in all the puzzle pieces I'd been missing for so long. Now I must think of Bright Feather's new puzzle pieces of life. My head is just too busy to sleep. I must take some time by myself to look at this new picture that's been made. Sitting on the rock, I shiver a bit at the coolness; sleeping beside a hot furnace body night after night causes a body to become less accustomed to the coldness of being on its own.

I feel a heaviness pressing down on me this morning. It's in my head and in my heart. My head worries about my people and those that I now consider my family and friends. The more I learn about the world, the more I fret about what's ahead. Will we win this battle that's to come of words and paper and selfishness and greed? Will the world invade our garden walled around and destroy it? Will I be able to do more for anyone than I did for Pa, Henry, and Eli? My head can't imagine how I could.

Part of this heaviness is about what my future has in store for me. Will I get pulled ahead faster once again than I'm ready for? How many times does a body have to face such a thing? I think about Bright Feather and all he told me last night sitting on Deer's swing. My heart swells big with love for him.

I realize that I've much more to loose now than when I was a white girl named Elle Graves! As Bear of The Maple Forest I've become a powerful woman, mate, sister, daughter, and friend. It'd seem that being all these wonderful things also means that I've just that much more to fear losing. Could I carry on after the loss of all those precious to me a second time? My heart beats fast with terror. I don't see how my heart could survive such a thing.

I look down at my hands tightly clenched with worry. My white hands. But I know better about such things now. With that thought my heart begins to slow and my head begins to calm. For I now know that the color of my skin's not what makes me the person that I am. There's much more power in what's *inside* a body than what's outside. I can fit in two worlds instead of one. I have a strong pink color. It's better than only white, better than only red. Suddenly, I realize that this makes me stronger than the most powerful warrior in the village.

I think of my pink center and what it holds. Standing proud and tall is a young woman named Bear, who's a part of all she's met along the path of her life: some have made her wiser and some have made her stronger. I think about this God I whisper to and decide right then and there to let Him stand beside me in my center and invite Him to put His arm around me, full of this special love that seems to know no boundaries. I feel a strong sense that I'm no longer alone in this battle for those I love and hold so dear.

I let the strength of my center push the heaviness away and I decide that I'll look forward to the future. I've made it this far, haven't I? Surely, with all I have inside me and all I have surrounding me, I'll succeed again. *How can I not?*

There're so many things that I am. But, I suspect, more importantly are the things that I *am not*. I have been a captive and an orphan. I have been alone, frightened and helpless. At one time, my only thoughts were ones about what I didn't know and what I couldn't do.

Though I hear no sound I suddenly know that I'm no longer alone sitting here on Deer's thinking rock. Looking up, I stare into the concerned eyes of Bright Feather who stands silently on the edge of the clearing patiently watching me ... Waiting ... Loving ...

I stand and make my way toward him. With each step I think about what I am now.

I'm capable!

I'm smart!

I'm brave!

I'm strong!

I'm eager!

I'm a partner!

I'm a friend!

I'm a daughter!

I'm a sister!

As strong arms enfold me I know that these thoughts are those of a wise and powerful woman.

Call me Bear.

It is never too late to give up your prejudices.[13]

~ Henry David Thoreau

Actual Facts: Book I

Every historical fiction novel has a little bit of fact and a lot of fiction. For me as a reader I always have a strong curiosity as to which is which. Believe it or not, I had close to seventy pages typed of the story of the fictional Elle Graves who becomes known as Bear before I knew *who, what, where,* or even *when* she was captured. Not until she began to understand the language and talk with Otter did I finally place her in history. I knew I wanted only three things: that she be captured by a tribe that was *matrilineal* (all family heritage is traced through the woman rather than *patrilineal* as we are in our society), that she be somewhere on the east coast of the United States - an area I was most familiar with, and that the story have a happy ending. Little did I know how difficult that would prove to be.

The history of the Native American Indians is about as bleak a story as you'd care to read. Starting with DeSoto's arrival in 1540 and following up through the arrival of the English, Spanish, and French by the early 1700's, it is estimated that nearly half the Native American population had died from small pox and other "white men" diseases and vices (slavery, greed, alcoholism…). Whole tribes simply ceased to exist. Add in the French and Indian War (1754-1761), the Revolutionary War (1776-1783), the War of 1812 (1812-1816), *including* the fierce battle between the Upper Creeks also known as the Red Sticks and the Lower Creeks, who joined with the Cherokees, *and* then General Andrew Jackson and the Civil War (1861-1865), *what's an author to do?*

The Cherokees called themselves *The Principal People* and from the moment I read Chief Ostenaco's documented quote, "*Where are your women?*" spoken to British representatives who had come to negotiate with him back in the early 1700's, I knew I'd found my tribe.[14] By the early 1800's, the Cherokee Nation was a stellar example of success, with a population of approximately 17,000 men, women, and children and land boundaries encompassing the north eastern corner of Alabama, north western corner of Georgia, a small western tip of North Carolina, and a small eastern tip of Tennessee. In 1820, the Old Nation Cherokees reorganized the tribal system and adopted a republican form of government that was modeled after the United States Government: they had a national council consisting of an upper and lower house, a council president, thirty two representatives who were elected by the people, laws, a judicial system, a superior court, a Cherokee Light Horse militia, and an established capital: New Echota, Georgia. They even collected taxes.[15] They had developed a written language by 1821 invented by an Indian man who went by the name of Sequoyah ("Pig's Foot") or George Gist, wrote their own constitution, and even published their own bilingual newspaper called *The Cherokee Phoenix*, with the first issue dated February, 1828, with Elias Boudinot as the original editor. The Cherokees became successful in business, politics and life in general, and it was reported that a vast majority of the Cherokee people were literate as well.

The story of the Cherokee Nation versus the United States of America is one no author could make up. It has murder, deception, intrigue, betrayal, infighting, and assassinations. And it is a tragic example of a people who began to fight amongst themselves and in some cases became their own worst enemies. During the 1820's, as the Cherokee nation shifted from the Old Way matrilineal structure of family to the newly adopted patrilineal structure of the whites, a number of significant figures were produced that would greatly influence the fate of the Cherokee Nation: John Ross, Major Ridge, his schooled son, John Ridge, and Elias Boudinot, among others. These men "were men of intellect and ability who could see into and debate issues on a level with the best of minds."[16] The unfortunate part of the story is that they did not agree with each other on the best course for the Cherokee Nation, causing it to eventually crumble in on itself.

As I researched through all of this sorry history, I felt truly discouraged and seriously doubted whether my goal of a "happy ending" could be accomplished. At one point in my frustration to find a safe place in history for Bear and those I planned to have her love and care about, my husband said, "*Just make it all up, why don't you?!*" But in the end, it was my decision that a *good* historical fiction novel could not twist the truth of things so much that the reader comes out misinformed. And then I found the name *William Holland Thomas*, and I knew I had found a place for Bear to be.

William Holland Thomas *was* adopted by a chief named Drowning Bear or *Yonaguska* if you're more inclined toward the Cherokee. This small band of Cherokees that William Holland Thomas was adopted into did take the option for citizenship. The Treaty of 1819 lists the names of those Cherokees who made what must have been a most difficult decision to sever their connections with the Cherokee Nation and choose the frightening path of citizenship with the United States. I think of the confidence they had to have had in Thomas to make such a decision and the weight of the responsibility he carried on his shoulders as the result of it. This area became known as the *Qualla Boundary*, named after an old woman named "Polly" ("Qualla" was the best they could pronounce "Polly") who was well thought of in the village.

The Cherokee who embraced the Old Way did not focus on time, wealth, or power. In fact, their language makes no reference to the future or the past, but just focused on the present, today.[17] As you read the history of the Eastern Cherokee, it is a stunning example of a people who were committed to surviving *at all costs*. They bent when the wind was too strong, but they never broke. They looked carefully into the future and recognized their strengths and their weaknesses, and consequently made wise choices for survival that others could or would not see. I see no conflict between the Old Way of the Cherokee and choices that were made back in the early 1800's by the Qualla Indians. Those Qualla Indians, who became the Eastern Band of the Cherokees, made these difficult decisions so that their Old Way of life could be preserved.

A wonderful book I stumbled on, *Footsteps of the Cherokees, A Guide To The Eastern Homelands of the Cherokee Nation*, helped me - as I sat at my computer - feel what it must have felt like for Bear as she tromped through the woods and experienced the beauty of the North Carolina forest wilderness. At last I found a safe place to put her that could have a happy ending.

They are The Cherokee, The Principal People, the Ani-Yun-wiya.

You can't judge a man by his color
you can't see the savage within
but the deeds that he may do to his brothers
will reveal the true hearts of men[18].

Acknowledgements

Personally, the entire process of this book, from the initial idea (a very vivid image of a frightened white girl being very gently touched on the cheek by a fierce Indian brave) to the final, *real* possibility that this could be published has been nothing short of a miracle. I could write pages about all the wonderful coincidences (some that gave me chills) that occurred during the writing, but the book is too long already. Suffice it to say that I could *not* have done this on my own.

There is a strong Christian message in this story, and that is not by chance. Had the book arrived, packaged with a nice neat bow on my front step, God could not have shown me more clearly what He wanted to do. While I did not want to cram any of this "God stuff" down reluctant throats, I could not escape the very essence of what I strive to be; "a woman after God's own heart". No one's life is perfect; there is great sorrow we must face, things rarely work out just as we'd hoped they would, and disappointments are not difficult to find. But I don't believe you go through this life alone, and so my story *must* reflect that.

From the very first time I hesitantly said, "I think I'm writing a book…" (said with great wonder and trepidation) family and friends have encouraged and championed me. To Mom, Marylynn, who read it and said, "Best Seller" (in her best Mom's voice), to Dad, Herb, who gets teary when he talks about his girls (and the good things they get up to), to Wendy who carried the 500 pound binder with her on her two week vacation to Cape Cod *and read it*, to Aunt Evie and Debbie Francis who, between the two of them sent me close to *fifty pages* of corrections and will remain forever as the world's best proofreaders, to my sister, Amy, who after reading all 700 plus pages was furious because the last chapter was "so short", to my wonderful husband, David, who dealt with no dinners, unfolded laundry, and a general lack of care and attention and kept saying, "just tell me when I can retire", to my son, Ian, who said, "If you get famous, do you think I could get to meet J.K. Rowling?", to my daughter, Gracie, who upon opening and reading yet another rejection letter said, "Well … at least she said she liked it before she sent it back to you. She didn't have to do that, you know", to my youngest son, Luke, who when I said I was going to miss him when he went off to kindergarten said, "Don't worry, you'll just have more time to work at your computer", to my friend, Linda who has been so patient – and yet *so certain*, waiting for me to get famous so that she can get on television (Hi, Regis!), to Pam Frueh the world's best editor who seems to be able to get inside my head and make changes and suggestions that still match my style and goal (I really appreciate you even if I groan when I get the hundreds of changes…!) and to my Bible Study ladies who are all powerful women each in their own right and wonderful role models for me to follow: Patti, Beth, Melony, Kate, Jen, Jenn, Maria, Judy, and Kim, and to Laury Vaden, artist extraordinaire who brought the face of Bear to life with her talent and has tirelessly and patiently designed for me The Best Book Covers In The World … For want of better words: THANK YOU.

Sue McG

Cast of Characters: Book I

The People of The Maple Forest

- ❖ **Bear** – Elle Grave's Indian name
- ❖ **Deer** – adopted son of War Woman, also known as William Holland Thomas
- ❖ **One Who Is Always Alone** – Indian brave
- ❖ **Raccoon** – Indian brave, mate of Otter
- ❖ **Otter** – Indian woman, daughter of War Woman, mate of Raccoon
- ❖ **Little Bird** – Raccoon and Otter's son
- ❖ **Great Elk** – Chief of the Indians of The Maple Forest
- ❖ **War Woman** – Mate of Great Elk
- ❖ **Cloud** – Indian brave
- ❖ **Red Fox** – Indian brave
- ❖ **Beaver** – Indian brave
- ❖ **One Who Knows** – Indian woman, village healer
- ❖ **Turtle** – Indian woman who lives with One Who Knows

The People of New Echota, Georgia

- ❖ **Dark Cloud** – Chief, known in the white world as Major Ridge
- ❖ **Weasel** – Indian brave
- ❖ **Reverend James Wilder** – Missionary to The Real People, based in New Echota, Georgia, called The Messenger by the Indians
- ❖ **Rebecca Wilder** – James Wilder's wife
- ❖ **Martin DuBois** – French trader

The People of Ward's Mill, Virginia

- ❖ **Elle Graves** – daughter of Andrew and Elizabeth Graves
- ❖ **Andrew Graves** – Elle's Father
- ❖ **Elizabeth Graves** – Elle's Mother
- ❖ **Henry Graves** – Elle's brother, four years older
- ❖ **Eli Graves** – Elle's younger brother, eight years younger
- ❖ **Cornelius Cooper** – Proprietor of Cooper's General Store

❖ **Naomi Cooper** – Cornelius Cooper's wife

❖ **Johnny Cooper** – Cornelius and Naomi Cooper's son

The People of Forest City, North Carolina

❖ **William Holland Thomas** – Proprietor of Trading Post in Forest City, North Carolina, also known as Deer of The Maple Forest

❖ **Possum** – Deer's mate, also known as Mary Thomas

❖ **James, Red Bird** – Deer and Possum's eldest son

❖ **Eliza, Sleeping Rabbit** – Deer and Possum's daughter

❖ **Richard, Small Turtle** – Deer and Possum's youngest son

Book Timeline: Book I

Black type = actual facts

BOLD CAPITAL TYPE = NOVEL STORYLINE

🔲 *BOOK CHAPTER*

Date	Event
1540	DeSoto explores.
1684	England makes treaty with Cherokees.
1738	Smallpox arrives in South Carolina and ½ of nation dies in one year from small pox.
1754-1761	French and Indian War (Cherokees side with British.)
1763	Proclamation of 1763 a royal decree of George III of Britain, which prohibits colonists from settling west of the Appalachian Mountains and reserves this area for Indians.
1775	Cherokees sell what will become Kentucky to English.
1776-1783	Revolutionary War (Cherokees side with British.)
6/25/1788	Virginia becomes the 10th state of the USA.
4/30/1789	George Washington elected as President.
3/4/1801	Thomas Jefferson elected as President.
1802	**BIRTH OF BRIGHT FEATHER.**
1802	William Holland Thomas born.
1807	**MARRIAGE OF ELLE'S PARENTS: ANDREW AND ELIZABETH GRAVES.**
3/4/1809	James Madison elected as President.
1809	Sequoyah begins work on a Cherokee alphabet.
1809	Cherokees set up a central government that acts for the whole tribe and models the white style of government.
1810	**HENRY GRAVES' BIRTH.**
1810	**WILLIAM HOLLAND THOMAS IS FOUND AND ADOPTED BY GREAT ELK'S VILLAGE.**
6/1812-12/1814	War of 1812
3/27/1814	The Battle of Horseshoe Bend
10/1814	**ELLE GRAVE'S BIRTH**
1817	**WILLIAM THOMAS, KNOWN AS DEER, RETURNS TO THE WHITES IN SEARCH OF HIS WHITE FAMILY.**
1817	**ELLE'S FAMILY MOVES TO HOMESTEAD IN FAR WESTERN VIRGINIA; WARD'S MILL.**
7/8/ 1817	Treaty of 1817, ratified Dec. 26, 1817.
Spring 1818	**WEASEL OF DARK CLOUD'S VILLAGE MARRIES ONE**

	WHO KNOWS' OLDER DAUGHTER; RAVEN, OF GREAT ELK'S VILLAGE.
6/6/1818	Census taken of all Cherokee.
2/27/1819	Treaty, Proclaimed Mar 10, 1819, tribal lands given up, offer of citizenship made, small number of Indians in North Carolina near the Oconaluftee River take the option for citizenship.
1820	**BRIGHT FEATHER MARRIES ONE WHO KNOWS YOUNGER DAUGHTER, BLACK FOX.**
1821	Cherokee Written Language, Sequoyah develops a system of 86 symbols that stand for Cherokee syllables.
1821	William Holland Thomas establishes trading post near Indian Territory.
1822	**DISAPPEARANCE OF ONE WHO KNOWS OLDEST DAUGHTER, RAVEN.**
1822	**DEATH OF BRIGHT FEATHER'S MATE, BLACK FOX, AND UNBORN SON.**
1822	**ELLE'S MOTHER'S DEATH, ELI GRAVES' BIRTH.**
3/22/1828	✂ *CAPTIVE*
Late summer 1828	✂ *BEAR*
2/1828	Cherokees print a bilingual newspaper, *The Cherokee Phoenix* with Elias Boudinot as editor.
5/6/1828	Treaty, proclaimed May 28, 1828.
Early spring 1829	✂ *POWERFUL WOMAN*
Late summer - Early fall, 1829	✂ *MATE* ✂ *LISTENER*
Today	✂ *ACTUAL FACTS*

Family Tree

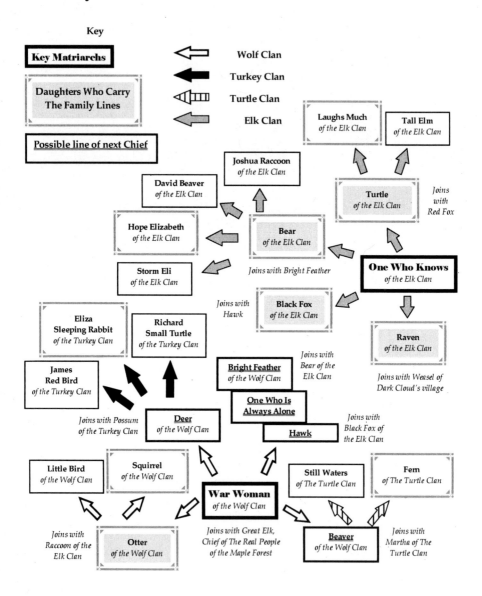

Key

Key Matriarchs ⟸ Wolf Clan

Daughters Who Carry The Family Lines ⬅ Turkey Clan

⟸ Turtle Clan

Elk Clan

Possible line of next Chief

Laughs Much
of the Elk Clan

Tall Elm
of the Elk Clan

Joshua Raccoon
of the Elk Clan

Turtle
of the Elk Clan

Joins with Red Fox

David Beaver
of the Elk Clan

Hope Elizabeth
of the Elk Clan

Bear
of the Elk Clan

One Who Knows
of the Elk Clan

Storm Eli
of the Elk Clan

Joins with Bright Feather

Raven
of the Elk Clan

Black Fox
of the Elk Clan

Joins with Weasel of Dark Cloud's village

Joins with Hawk

**Eliza
Sleeping Rabbit**
of the Turkey Clan

**Richard
Small Turtle**
of the Turkey Clan

Joins with Bear of the Elk Clan

Bright Feather
of the Wolf Clan

**James
Red Bird**
of the Turkey Clan

**One Who Is
Always Alone**

Deer
of the Wolf Clan

Hawk

Joins with Possum of the Turkey Clan

Joins with Black Fox of the Elk Clan

Little Bird
of the Wolf Clan

Squirrel
of the Wolf Clan

Still Waters
of The Turtle Clan

Fern
of The Turtle Clan

War Woman
of the Wolf Clan

Joins with Raccoon of the Elk Clan

Otter
of the Wolf Clan

Joins with Great Elk, Chief of The Real People of the Maple Forest

Beaver
of the Wolf Clan

Joins with Martha of The Turtle Clan

Cherokee Lands in 1791 and in 1838, Before Removal[19]

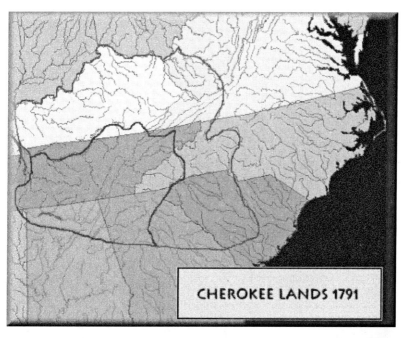

CHEROKEE LANDS 1791

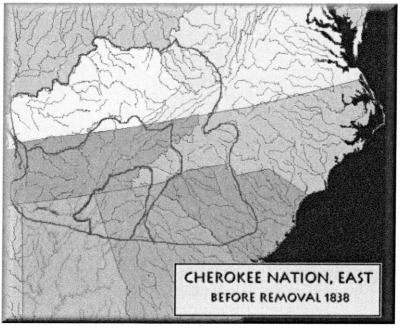

CHEROKEE NATION, EAST
BEFORE REMOVAL 1838

1820 Map of the Five Civilized Tribes[20]

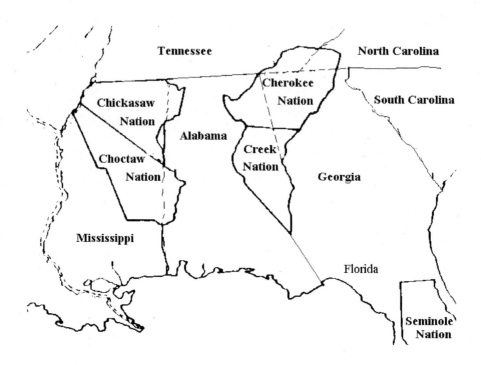

North Carolina Today

The stared counties are all part of the Qualla Boundary, the Eastern Tribe of The Cherokee Nation.

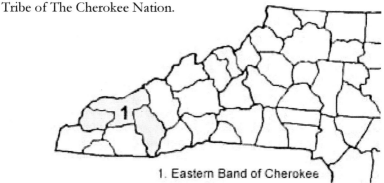

1. Eastern Band of Cherokee

Counties: Swain, Graham, Jackson
Population: 13,400
State Recognition: 1889
Federal Recognition: 1868

"The Eastern Band of Cherokee descended from the Cherokee who in the late 1830s remained in the mountains of North Carolina rather than be forced into Oklahoma along the infamous Trail of Tears. These thousand or so tribal members lived along the Oconaluftee River, some hiding out. The Cherokee eventually gained the Qualla Boundary reservation, the 56,572-acre site where the tribe resides today. The Cherokee are the only indigenous people in America to have their own written language, developed by Sequoyah.

The Eastern Band of Cherokee is the only federally recognized tribe in North Carolina and the only tribe living on land held in trust. The tribe actively promotes tourism on the boundary, with cultural activities, events, and an outdoor drama. In addition, the Cherokee sell traditional arts and crafts such as baskets, pottery, beadwork, stone carvings, and wood carvings. The tribe's involvement in many business ventures helps ensure its livelihood."[21]

About The Author

Susan McGeown is a wife, mother, daughter, sister, friend, aunt, uncle (don't ask), teacher, author … but, most importantly, a "woman after God's own heart." Living in Bridgewater, New Jersey, with her husband of over fifteen years and their three children, writing stories is just about the best way she can imagine spending her free time. Each of Sue's stories champions those emotions nearest and dearest to her: faith, joy, hope and love.

Philippians 1:20-21

For I fully expect and hope that I will never be ashamed, but that I will continue to be bold for Christ, as I have been in the past. And I trust that my life will bring honor to Christ, whether I live or die. For to me, living means living for Christ, and dying is even better.

Footnotes

Portions in the book that tell of stories from the Cherokee: Beaver's story of the Ceremony of Life, One Who Knows story of The Beginning of Time, Bright Feather's story of the Four Sacred Directions, and War Woman's story of Grandmother Corn and the song that she sings are based on the descriptions of these stories given in the book Meditations with The Cherokee, Prayers, Songs, and Stories of Healing and Harmony, by J.T. Garret, Ed.D., Bear and Company Publishers, Rochester, Vermont, 2001.

---

[1] *The Cherokees, A First Americans Book*, By Virginia Driving Hawk Sneve, Holiday House, New York, 1996, p. 4

[2] Sir Thomas Overby, *The Wife*, December, 1613, Stationers' Register

[3] *The Cherokees, A First Americans Book*, By Virginia Driving Hawk Sneve, Holiday House, New York, 1996, p. 28

[4] *Women in American Indian Society*, By Rayna Green, Chelsea House Publishers, New York, 1992, p. 32-33

[5] Psalm 23:4, King James Version

[6] Jeremiah 29:11-14, King James Version

[7] Lloyd Carl Owle, Cherokee Poet, http://www.homestead.com/spirithorse/mp.html

[8] Psalm 23:5-6, King James Version

[9] Cherokee Expression

[10] "Teach Me The Measure Of My Days", Isaac Watts, 1674-1748

[11] Lamentations 3:22-25, King James Version

[12] "We Are A Garden Walled Around", Isaac Watts, 1674-1748

[13] Henry David Thoreau, http://www.quotationspage.com/quotes/Henry_David_Thoreau

[14] *The Cherokees*, By Virginia Driving Hawk Sneve, Holiday House, New York, 1996, p. 22

[15] The Cherokees and Their Chiefs, by Stanley W. Hoig, University of Arkansas Press, Fayetteville, Arkansas, 1998, p. 121

[16] The Cherokees and Their Chiefs, by Stanley W. Hoig, University of Arkansas Press, Fayetteville, Arkansas, 1998, p. 124

[17] <u>Meditations with The Cherokee, Prayers, Songs, and Stories of Healing and Harmony</u>, by J.T. Garret, Ed.D., Bear and Company Publishers, Rochester, Vermont, 2001, p. xiii-xiv

[18] Written by Carl Towns(©1998) Abiel Publishing, BMI)

[19] http://www.cherokeehistory.com

[20] http://www.arkansaspreservation.org/preservation-services/trail-of-tears/images/ahpp_map_area_southeast.gif

[21] http://ncmuseumofhistory.org/workshops/ai/Session1.htm